Praise for Edne

'Journalist Edney Silvestre's debut novel tells its story in deceptively simple prose, bringing home the full shock and horror of the subject matter by filtering it through the eyes of children. Most effectively of all, he evokes the special nature of friendships and the lifelong vacuum left by their passing, something subsequent adult relationships can never hope to match' *Daily Mail*

'Silvestre has fun with a murder mystery, but his real subject is Brazil, "a country capable of advancing fifty years in only five of full democracy", as it lurches out of the developing world' *Guardian*

'On the day that Russia launches its first cosmonaut, two children find a woman's body. What follows is a whodunnit and coming-of-age set in small-town Brazil. A remarkable debut' *Financial Times*

'Affirms that crime fiction is to the twenty-first century what the grand social novel was to the nineteenth. Sadistic sexual politics, investigated by an unlikely trio of sleuths (two schoolboys and an elderly man); misogynistic murder, syncretic Christianity; municipal shenanigans, all fester beneath the raging Rio sun' *The Tablet*

'Edney Silvestre makes innocence and reality collide . . . in a look at the history of Brazil as a scene of a crime and perversion' *Folha de S. Paulo*

'A minutely detailed examination of the political, social and psychological connotations of a murder' *Veja*

'Edney Silvestre's plot is agile and engrossing, replete with references to Brazil and a particular cultural and political moment in the world' *Estado de Minas*

IF I CLOSE MY EYES NOW

Edney Silvestre

Translated from the Brazilian Portuguese
by Nick Caistor

BLACK SWAN

TRANSWORLD PUBLISHERS
61–63 Uxbridge Road, London W5 5SA
A Random House Group Company
www.transworldbooks.co.uk

IF I CLOSE MY EYES NOW
A BLACK SWAN BOOK: 9780552778855

Se eu fechar os olhos agora first published in Brazil by Record, 2009

First published in Great Britain
in 2013 by Doubleday
an imprint of Transworld Publishers
Black Swan edition published 2014

Obra publicada com o apoio do Ministério da Cultura
do Brasil/Fundação Biblioteca Nacional

MINISTÉRIO DA CULTURA
Fundação BIBLIOTECA NACIONAL

Edney Silvestre has asserted his right under the Copyright, Designs
and Patents Act 1988 to be identified as the author of this work.

This book is a work of fiction and, except in the case of historical fact, any resemblance
to actual persons, living or dead, is purely coincidental.

A CIP catalogue record for this book
is available from the British Library.

Addresses for Random House Group Ltd companies outside the UK
can be found at: www.randomhouse.co.uk
The Random House Group Ltd Reg. No. 954009

The Random House Group Limited supports the Forest Stewardship Council® (FSC®),
the leading international forest-certification organisation. Our books carrying the FSC
label are printed on FSC®-certified paper. FSC is the only forest-certification scheme
supported by the leading environmental organisations, including Greenpeace. Our paper
procurement policy can be found at www.randomhouse.co.uk/environment

Typeset in 11.75/15pt Minion by Falcon Oast Graphic Art Ltd.
Printed and bound by CPI Group (UK) Ltd, Croydon, CR0 4YY.

2 4 6 8 10 9 7 5 3 1

'The dead don't stay where they're buried.'

John Berger, *Here Is Where We Meet*

IF I CLOSE MY eyes now, I can still feel her sticky blood on my fingers. Stuck to my fingers as it was in her blonde hair, and high on her forehead, on her arched eyebrows and black eyelashes, on her face, neck and arms, on the torn white blouse and the remaining buttons, on the bra ripped in two, on the nipple of her right breast.

I had never smelt that pungent smell before. Ever afterwards I associated it with the odour of other women, the ones I knew intimately, the odour overpowering theirs, always taking me back to her. That mixture of sweet perfume, gouged flesh, sweat, blood and – as far as I could tell – salt. The smell you find close to the sea. When it sticks to your hair, for example. Not grains of salt, but the invisible, strong tang of salt you get on damp days by the sea.

But back then I did not know the sea either; I had never smelt or seen it, so the smell of that woman in the mud, naked . . . I had never seen a naked woman, nor smelt the smell of a naked woman so close up. Well, she was not completely naked, but that breast with its big nipple, and . . . her thighs were splayed open, her skirt lifted, and I saw the tangled black hairs at the top of them, of her thighs, the point where her long legs met, and from there came – no, not from there, from all over her – came the smell of woman mingled with blood. I think she must also have shat herself, soiled herself the way I now know we all do at the moment when life leaves our body and it completely relaxes, the sphincter opens and . . . that's another word I had never heard then. Or read. Sphincter. I was twelve years old and words like that were never spoken in my house. We didn't even know such words existed.

She was there, dead. Naked. Almost naked.

I knew she was dead. Both of us knew it. Her skin was cold. The skin on her arm, which was the first thing we touched. The skin of her face, so . . . pallid. Was that the word, pallid? It was. With her mouth open. Half open. As if she were starting to smile. Big, dazzlingly white teeth, only partly visible, glinting between her soft lips. Had she been beaten? Were there other marks on her face? There were. But it was on her lips that the blood . . . I think I touched her lips. I don't know. Yes I do, I did touch them. Smooth lips. Red lips. Blood-red lips. Red with blood or lipstick? With blood and lipstick. And mud. She must have twisted round when she fell. Or did she hit her face on the grass and mud? When the heel of her shoe got stuck, it snapped off and she almost flew over the grass and wet mud. Was that her last flight, filled with horror and sadness? Flying. A silent flight. Interminable. And, either struggling or surrendering, she registered the blue sky and the fresh autumn breeze, the cry of a bird and the killer's breath, as the blade repeatedly punctured her flesh.

Later, neither he nor I were able to say how many times she had been stabbed. Lacerated in so many places, her skin reminded me of the wounds of the Christ in the cathedral's central nave, his arms spread wide just like hers in the mud, beneath the cloudless sky that April morning.

Even here, now, in this foreign city where I live off and on, even now occasionally when I'm not concentrating, when I leave the metro, or turn a corner of harmonious buildings that make the world seem organized and logical, or leave a café where I've casually bought cigarettes, put the change in my coat pocket and fumbled for the lighter, I feel on my face the same cold wind that suddenly arose on that April morning: sometimes, not always, sometimes, the same fresh breeze that began to stir that warm day, making the tall grass sway gently from side to side round the lake where we had gone to hide, far away from adults, as we had done all that summer.

From the top of the hill it was hard to make out the lake's irregular outline, hidden behind tall bamboo canes where dozens of noisy macaws had made their nests. The macaws and bamboo groves that he recalled so often later on in the long, melancholy letters he wrote me.

I don't know what the lake was really like. After that day in April I never went back there. All I have is the image in my memory: its bright blue, transparent water, sparkling in the rays of a sun that always seemed to shine in those days.

I think it was a Tuesday. I could look at the calendar to make sure. I don't want to. I prefer the certainty of my memory, which tells me it was a Tuesday.

Tuesday, 12 April 1961.

On the radio early that morning a presenter announced: a man has travelled into space. The first man in space. A Russian.

His name was Yuri Gagarin.

He said the Earth was blue, and I thought – we both thought, him and me – we talked about it as we rode along lazily on our bikes, escaping punishment at school because we had been caught looking at a dirty magazine – talking about Gagarin the way we did about everything: that's what we could be, we could also be a man flying through outer space.

At twelve years old, when any fantasy can seem real, Yuri Alekseevich Gagarin's flight on board *Vostok*, a metal sphere two and a half metres in diameter, with windows scarcely larger than a book, literally opened up the skies for us.

Astronaut: another word I did not yet know.

Astronaut as well. I could be an astronaut. Everything was possible for someone still hesitating between becoming an engineer or a cowboy, a football player or a bandit in the Sertão, a pilot, test driver, a businessman, deep-sea diver, an archaeologist, or Tarzan.

Until that April day, Tarzan had been my favourite. I was good at swinging from creepers, and yet without my knowing why, both Lord Greystoke's African jungle and Oklahoma, which is where I thought the Wild West of good guys and bandits was to be found, were starting to pall. I was also toying with the idea of being a scientific genius and inventing remedies that could cure the most dreadful illnesses, possibly a vaccine so powerful it would eliminate all pain. Or perhaps he was the one who wanted to be a scientist. One of us thought we might be president of Brazil and put an end to the century-old drought and hunger in the north-east. I think that was him. Among the ambitions that seemed to us perfectly possible, we both wanted to go and live in Rio de Janeiro one day. Brasilia had been inaugurated less than a year earlier, but whichever of us got to be president was going to transfer the capital back to Rio. We were twelve. It was another country. Another world.

1

The High Mountains and Areas in Shadow

THE LAKE, AT LAST.

They turned off the paved road and took the winding gravel path. They stopped pedalling. The bikes rattled down to the barbed wire fence at the foot of the hill, where they dismounted. They removed their books from the baskets and hid them under some tree roots, then took turns lifting the wire to help each other through.

The dark-skinned boy's bike was rusty and battered, with only one mudguard at the front. It had belonged to his father, when he still worked at the textile factory, and then his brother, before he bought a new one. On the frame of the other boy's bike the name of its English maker was still visible, twelve years after it had crossed the Atlantic, imported after the war along with thousands of other goods from Europe, when the Brazilian currency was strong. This boy was taller, lighter-skinned and skinnier.

They pushed their bikes through the mango plantation,

their tyres leaving tracks on ground still damp from overnight rain. To avoid getting any mud on his trousers, the lanky boy pulled them up to his knees. His dark-skinned companion didn't bother. No one would notice. The school badge was coming off the pocket of his grubby shirt. Both of them had taken off their black clip-on ties – the part of the uniform they most detested. Only the tall boy folded his carefully before stowing it in his trouser pocket.

As they walked along the narrow path through the bamboo grove, the macaws rose into the air above them, squawking loudly.

They talked about the kind of things twelve-year-old boys discussed in those days: terribly important things about themselves and a world they didn't yet understand, but about which they had very precise ideas; ideas soon forgotten and replaced by others, as fabulous as the dreams that lulled them to sleep. To them, adult life seemed distant, pleasant and luminous – nothing like the brutal world they were plunged into that morning.

They dropped their bikes on to the turf by the lake's edge: one of them carefully, the other just letting it fall to the ground.

The darker-haired boy tore off his clothes, threw them on to the bike and kicked off his shoes, while the pale-faced youngster undid his shirt buttons and took it off, unbuckled his belt and pulled his trousers down. He carefully folded all his clothes. He was still tucking his rolled-up socks into his shoes when his friend raced towards the water in his underpants, shouting to his companion to catch him, calling him a slowcoach, hey slowcoach, and then diving in, clumsily but powerfully.

The lighter-skinned boy went over to the bushes where they kept the inner tube they used as a buoy. He squeezed it: still hard. He carried it to the water's edge, threw it in. He joined his hands in front of his body, lowered his head, and waded into the lake, almost without a sound.

The water was as warm as the day, so the two boys swam for a good while.

Then the thin boy lay back on the inner tube, arms and legs dangling, and floated around. He could hear the noises his friend made as he dived, came up, went under once more, then came back to the surface, swam a few strokes and dipped down, popping up again quickly, talking all the time, shouting phrases or asking questions that at first the other boy answered. Then, cradled by the warm waters, he became immersed in his own thoughts. His friend's voice and all the other sounds faded away.

He floated along in silence. All he could see was the blue sky above.

But hadn't the Russian astronaut said the opposite?

'*I can see the Earth. It's wonderful. It's blue.*'

How could it be blue? the thin boy wondered. The Earth, not the sky? Was that because of the oceans, or the seas? The continents aren't blue. Aren't mountains black, jungles green and deserts white? That's how they appear to us down here. And on the maps. How could the Russian astronaut have seen a blue planet, when the concrete buildings, the bridges, the viaducts, are all as grey as ashes? What about the tracks of red and brown earth? And the tarmac roads? He must have seen them all from above. Railway lines, ports, avenues, landing strips, cities, Amazonia, Siberia, the North Pole, Australia, Mongolia, the Himalayas and the Sahara; everything. He saw it. The Russian, the astronaut, saw it all down here, this morning, as no man had ever seen it before. And he said: blue. The Earth is blue. So what we've been learning until now in our geography classes is wrong. Just like the maps made before Columbus were wrong. In those days they said the world was flat and ended in an abyss, didn't they? What else that we learn today is going to make people laugh at us five hundred years from now? Will all the planets and places we know now seem insignificant, as happened with the world after Pedro Alvares Cabral reached Brazil? He used maps made by the Phoenicians, who were here long before 1500. What if the same thing is happening today?

What if there are secrets the scientists know but we cannot even suspect? That the governments hide from us the way the Portuguese sailors hid their maps from their enemies? Perhaps the Russians have the real maps of the heavens. What about the Americans? Do they have real maps of the heavens too?

'*I can clearly see tall mountains and areas in shadow . . .*'

If as they said on the radio the Russian astronaut circled the Earth in an hour and forty-eight minutes, thought the boy, he must have seen day and night at the same time.

'*. . . the forests, islands, and ocean shores. I can see the sun, the clouds . . .*'

If Japan is twenty-four hours ahead of us, on the far side of the Earth, that means it's already tomorrow there. So the Russian travelled from the future back into the past. But that's impossible. He can't do that. Or can he? How can he? If I go into the future, can I meet myself as I am today, the light-skinned boy wondered. Or as I was today? Me, today, now, as I am at this moment, will I be able to see how I will be? What I will be?

'. . . *and the shadows the light casts on my beloved, distant Earth.*'

So says the Russian. The Russian astronaut. Major Yuri Gagarin, aged twenty-seven. That was what they said he said on the radio. It could be a lie. Father Thomas is always telling us that the Russians lie in order to conquer the world. That's what he says in every Latin class: the Communists lie. But the other teacher, Lamarca, says it's the Americans who lie, the boy remembered. Because they want the riches from our soil, our gold, oil, our monazite sands . . .

Paulo swam underwater as quietly as he could towards Eduardo. He could see his body from underneath the buoy, and played the joke on him he knew he hated: tipping over the inner tube, he pulled his friend's underpants down.

Eduardo went under, swallowed a mouthful of water, and came up spluttering.

Paulo swam quickly towards the shore, laughing and making whooping sounds like the Red Indians after they had defeated the invading palefaces in the Westerns they saw in the Sunday matinees at the Cine Theatro Universo. Eduardo recovered, muttered something and swam a powerful crawl to try to catch his friend.

Paulo ran a few metres out of the water, still laughing, and then came to a halt.

He waited.

His furious friend was getting close.

Very close.

Paulo laughed again, enjoying himself. This was his favourite trick. He knew he was quicker and more nimble than Eduardo, he knew how to dodge much better – being shorter was an advantage, so that when he swerved to left or right he could bend and slip through Eduardo's open arms.

Disconcerted, unable to dart in and out like his friend, Eduardo still kept up the chase, his feet slipping now and then on the wet grass and mud, while Paulo raced on, never once losing his balance.

All of a sudden, Paulo tripped over something and fell head first.

It was a body.

A blonde woman, her arms and legs splayed out, filthy with blood and mud.

Her left breast had been chopped off.

All Eduardo could see in the rough wall the policeman had pushed him up against was a chink in the stones and the black ants emerging from it in a busy, orderly line. The ants climbed up towards the grille high above his head, through which the afternoon heat and occasional distant street sounds seeped: the wheels of a cart and the iron shoes of a mule on the paving blocks, the voices of two women walking past on the far pavement, the long, muffled wail of a crying child, or perhaps of someone being held in the police station basement.

The three cops stank. Eduardo was sweating. He wanted to believe it wasn't out of fear.

'I saw first,' he repeated.

'But I was the one who tripped over the body,' Paulo explained, yet again.

They were standing with their backs to each other. Paulo was facing the opposite wall. The police took turns to ask the same questions.

'Why were you with her?'

'How come she went there with you?'

'Who called her?'

'I already told you, we don't know her!'

'Sir, neither Paulo nor I know who she is.'

'Of course you do.'

'Whose penknife is it?'

'How many times did you stab her?'

'How did you get her down there?'

One of the cops laughed. Eduardo thought he heard them whispering together.

'I already told you, and so did Eduardo, we don't know her.'

'We didn't know who she was. I never saw her. We never saw her.'

'Never.'

'How many stabs?'

'What d'you mean, you didn't know her?'

'How many times did you stab her with your penknife?'

'It's not Eduardo's penknife, it's mine.'

'How many times?'

'It's my penknife, but we never did anything to her, we don't know her; never, nothing.'

'Everybody knows her, you monkey.'

'I'm not a monkey.'

'Shut your mouth! Only speak when I ask a question, monkey.'

'I'm not a monkey! And there's no reason I should answer any questions!'

'D'you want to feel my fist, monkey?'

'Please, sir, stay calm! Calm down, Paulo! We went to the lake to swim. That's all, sir.'

'How many stab wounds? Talk, monkey!'

'I don't know. We didn't want to look.'

'We didn't count. Neither Paulo nor I counted.'

'A penknife doesn't make wounds like that. It was a dagger.'

'How d'you know, monkey? Have you already sunk a dagger in someone?'

'I'm not a monkey! And I haven't done anything. I simply tripped over the dead body.'

'How did you know she was dead?'

'You two killed her.'

'Why did you stab her so often?'

'When I tripped she was already dead!'

'We didn't touch her, sir. We found her, and I told Paulo we had better come here to the station to tell you what we had found. The body.'

'And I told you it would be better not to have anything to do with the police!'

'We went back there with you, didn't we? To show you. We only found her. That's all.'

'I told you the police wouldn't believe us, Eduardo!'

'We don't believe you because you're lying. What did you do to her?'

'Nothing! She was already cold when I tripped over her.'

'You're lying, little monkey.'

'Paulo and I went to the lake because our geography teacher threw us out of his class.'

'He sent us to talk to the headmaster.'

'Which of you pulled up her skirt?'

'You, or you?'

Paulo realized he was hungry. I'm hungry, I'm thirsty, I want a pee, I haven't had lunch, I haven't eaten anything apart from that bit of bread with coffee, why did they push me and Eduardo into this stifling room, why do they keep on asking us about killing that woman, why, what for? Can't they see we didn't have anything to kill her with? We couldn't have done it with my penknife. I didn't pull her skirt up, it was already pulled up to her waist, or perhaps it was torn, who knows? No, it wasn't torn, and if it was, I didn't do it. Eduardo didn't pull it up either. The guy shouting in my ear spits whenever he speaks, filthy bastard, it must be the one who talked to us first, the one with a rotten front tooth, the one who pushed us into this room at the back of the police station, when we came to tell them about the body we'd found. His breath is so bad you can smell it from yards away. Or it was the other one. My stomach's rumbling: what time is it?

'Was it you, monkey?'

'We didn't touch her. I only tripped. When I was running.'

'We went to the lake because our teacher threw us out. And we couldn't go home.'

'We couldn't go home until the end of the school day.'

'Did he throw both of you out?'

'Yes.'

'What were you doing?'

'Nothing bad, sir.'

'We were looking at a magazine.'

'In the class.'

'What magazine?'

'The teacher took it. He sent us to see the headmaster.'

'What kind of magazine was it?'

'A dirty magazine; I bet these little monkeys had a dirty magazine.'

'Were you doing dirty things? Together? With each other?'

'No! We were swimming!'

'The headmaster wasn't in his office, so we thought it was better to get out of there.'

'We thought it was better to run away.'

'You wanted to do dirty things to her!'

'We didn't see her! We don't know her!'

'I've never seen her, I swear. Nor has Paulo.'

'You're lying, monkey.'

'Everybody knows that woman.'

'We don't.'

'I've already told you, we never saw her before!'

'Everybody knows that woman. Or knew her.'

'But I don't, sir.'

'Of course you do. That woman was a whore.'

'A whore?'

'The dead woman was a whore?'

'A whore. A tramp. You knew that.'

'But we didn't, sir. I've never been to one of those places. Nor has Paulo. His father goes, and so does his brother. He never does. We never do.'

'Was she a whore from the red-light district?'

'I'm the one asking the questions, monkey. What did you want with her?'

'You wanted to force her to do dirty things, didn't you?'

'She refused, so you attacked her.'

'With the penknife.'

'You even took a dirty magazine with you.'

'Where is it?'

'The geography teacher took it. Mr Lemos took it. You can ask him.'

'You cleaned the knife on her tights. The blade is clean, and the stockings are covered in blood.'

'No, sir. We took our bikes to the lake, that's all.'

'To swim.'

'Until Paulo tipped over the inner tube and pulled my pants down, and I started running after him, and—'

'So both of you were naked? In the midst of the bushes?'

'You were doing dirty things to each other.'

'No, no! It was a joke!'

'A dirty joke.'

'No!'

'We've sent for your father. And yours.'

'No, not my father!'

'Calm down, Paulo. I'll explain we haven't done anything wrong. That we came to tell the police. That the blonde woman was already dead when you fell over her.'

'How did you know she was dead?'

'She was already stiff!'

'The blood was already stiff!'

'You mean congealed, Paulo.'

'So you touched her body.'

'You played with her body.'

'No! We only touched it lightly.'

'To see if she was still alive.'

'But she wasn't.'

'How could she be? Stabbed to death like that!'

'Stabbed by a penknife. Your penknife.'

'It wasn't my penknife! Those wounds were made by a dagger! I know they're dagger wounds.'

'And how do you know that?'

'My father's a butcher. There was no need to send for him.'

'Are you scared?'

'What did you do? You can tell us.'

'I'm not scared.'

'You're a minor, nothing will happen to you.'

'You didn't need to send for him . . .'

'Is my mother coming as well? Did you call my mother too?'

'Do you often go there, to the lake?'

'What do you do when you're together?'

'Do you swim naked? Do you go around naked?'

'Where did you hide the dirty magazine?'

'We didn't do anything wrong. All we did was bunk off school.'

'Aren't you ashamed, monkey? Your mother's outside, in tears.'

'She's my mother. Paulo's mother died.'

'Worse still. All that sacrifice to give children an education, and you two spend your time running around naked.'

'But Mr Lemos threw us out of his class!'

'Because you had a dirty magazine.'

'Let me speak to my mother, sir. So that she won't worry.'

'Afterwards.'

'In a little while.'

'After you've given a proper explanation of why you pulled his pants down and what you were doing by the lake, why you pulled her knickers down, and about the penknife – everything.'

'But we already told you. All three of you.'

'So tell us again. From the beginning.'

'Why are you so scared of your father?'

'Not mine – he's Paulo's father.'

'If you were my son, I'd show you how to educate a good-for-nothing.'

'I'm not a good-for-nothing.'

A fourth adult voice interrupted them, opening the door and announcing:

'The little mulatto's father is here.'

∾

The first blow, with the back of the hand, caught Paulo on his right ear. He stumbled, a wave of pain flashing across his skull, and the only reason he didn't fall was because another slap, this time with the palm of the hand, hit him on the left side of his head, knocking him against the dining table. He just had time to save himself from crashing into it, and watched in a daze as his father came closer, knowing he wanted to give him another one, two, as many blows as possible until he calmed down again. Tainted blood, shouted the fair-haired man looming over him, tainted blood, he repeated, narrowing his blue eyes between lashes that were so light-coloured they sometimes looked almost white, you've got tainted blood just like your mother and all her family, you monkey son of a bitch.

Paulo said nothing. It wouldn't help to say anything. His father wouldn't hear – he never heard anything when he was in a rage like this. In a rage against him, usually. Or always. Paulo could try to wriggle his way out, squeeze under the table and then rush into the street, run to . . . where exactly? He had nowhere to go. And no one to take him in. And it would only make his father all the more furious. It would be worse. When he beat him, and sooner or later he would beat him, the thrashing would leave marks and pain for days, as it always used to until he learned that the best thing was to stay and face the punishment. Better to stay now, it would hurt less.

Paulo saw the huge hand aiming for his face. He anticipated the stinging pain, knowing he would sleep and wake up with that throbbing ache, which was also the ache of shame and sadness he felt towards this man who could only call him a monkey.

He felt his father's vast paw strike him between his nose and ear. He stumbled again.

He let himself fall on his side between the chairs, curling up under the table, instinctively pulling his legs up to his chest and lowering his head, hoping against hope the beating would end there and then, but prepared to take more blows on his neck, then lashes from the leather belt his father was busy removing from his trousers. But his father did not drag him out from under the table. He lashed out once, twice, three and four times between the chairs, but only struck glancing blows to Paulo's head. He stopped, striking the furniture with the belt buckle several times, then tossed the belt down on to his son, ordering him: come out of there, you son of a bitch, come out of there.

Paulo raised himself on all fours and crawled out. He stood with his back to his father and waited. Would the next blow be to his head? Another slap across the ears?

He could hear his father's heavy breathing, mixed with the curses he kept repeating, but he did not come any nearer. A good sign. When he didn't move, his father usually stopped hitting him. Instead he almost always let loose another string of abuse, so perhaps the thrashing would end there. Paulo desperately hoped it would.

His father simply said: 'Pick up that crappy belt.'

Paulo bent down and picked it up.

'Give me that piece of crap.'

Paulo gave it him.

'You're no good for anything, you little monkey, you've got their tainted blood in you, you brat, you've got their blood all right, you're a good-for-nothing like all your mother's family.'

Paulo lowered his head. Yet again he felt a deep-seated pain, the same pain he was to feel so often in the future whenever he recalled those moments with his father, a pain he knew did not come from the blows he received, but which as yet he didn't know where to situate or how to understand.

His father slammed the door and left the room.

Paulo was on his own. The pain was increasing, coursing through his legs, arms, his chest, until it reached his eyes and turned into tears. He bit his bottom lip harder and harder, trying to transform one pain into another. The tears fell anyway from the corners of his eyes, running down his face, which was already starting to swell. Paulo ran to the bathroom, shut the door as best he could, hoping that neither his father nor his brother would come in, took the face cloth and stuffed it in his mouth. Hidden in the bathroom, he secretly sobbed and moaned while from a nearby house a radio once again trumpeted the first flight of a man in space.

When he went into the bedroom he shared with his brother, Antonio was doing exercises with dumb-bells in front of the wardrobe mirror. He was wearing a pair of shorts. Even though he was only sixteen, his large frame and hairy body made him look adult. Like his father and many descendants of people who came to Brazil from the north of Portugal, he had inherited the physique and pale skin of the Visigoths. His thick hair was slicked back with brilliantine apart from one quiff that fell artfully over his forehead. Beneath thick eyebrows, eyes as dark as his mother's peered with pleasure at his own body. He was counting the repetitions out loud as he raised and lowered the iron weights.

'What's all this about a dead woman, golliwog?' he asked, deliberately using the nickname that emphasized the difference in their skin colour, without pausing in his exercises or taking his eyes off his own body.

Paulo didn't reply. Making sure his brother did not see his still-red eyes, he went over to his bed, lined up beside the wardrobe. Keeping his back to his brother, he lifted the pillow in search of something. He didn't find it.

'And they kept you in, golliwog? All afternoon?'

He pushed back the bedcover, the blanket; it wasn't there either.

'Talk, golliwog! What did you do this time?'

Paulo lifted the mattress. Not there either.

'They say she was naked. Nude. Is that true, golliwog?'

Bending down, Paulo searched on the wooden floor. He straightened up, stood on the bed. He glanced at the top of the wardrobe, saw nothing, ran his hand over it. Nothing but dust.

'That dentist's wife was hot stuff. She looked like Brigitte Bardot. A cross between her and Sophia Loren.'

Paulo had no idea who either of them were, and didn't care. But something his brother had said took him by surprise.

'The dentist's wife? Wasn't she a whore?'

'The dentist's wife.'

'But at the station they said she was a whore.'

'She went with everybody. She was a whore. A slut. A hot bitch who couldn't get enough of it. But she was married to the dentist.'

Paulo got down from the bed.

'Did you see her in the nude, golliwog? She was really hot, wasn't she?'

'She was covered in blood. Filthy, full of mud . . .'

'Bouncy tits. Bouncy arse. Big thighs. Really hot. I'd like to have had her. If I'd stuck my prick in her, she'd have been crazy for me.'

As with his biceps and pectorals, Antonio was proud of the control he believed he exercised over any woman he penetrated. After his first visit to a prostitute three years earlier, he and their father went regularly to a brothel a Polish madam ran in a city centre street. Occasionally, they slept there. Paulo would sometimes run into them coming out of the Hotel Wizorek on his way to school.

'Did they really cut her breasts off? And did she have no knickers on?'

Paulo lifted the horsehair mattress again, looked carefully underneath, then pushed it up against the wall.

'Did she have blonde hairs? A pink pussy?'

'I don't want to talk about it. I don't know. I didn't see.'

'A real blonde has a pink pussy and blonde pubic hairs. I've seen lots of them. I've eaten lots of blonde pussy.'

Paulo let the mattress drop back. There was only one dentist in the town, a frail-looking man with thinning hair whom Paulo had seen a few times, all on his own, always wearing a coat and tie. It couldn't be him.

'The dentist is old. She was young. She looked young.'

'She was about twenty-four or -five. The dentist must be twice that. Or more. She only liked old men. She only gave out to old men. She never looked at me.'

Laying the weights on the floor, Antonio puffed out his cheeks and posed sideways on to the wardrobe. He breathed out, put his hands on his flat abdomen, and caressed the blond fuzz there. He turned to the other side, took a deep breath once more, flexed his arms. The pose confirmed it: his biceps were growing bigger and bigger. Picking up the dumb-bells, he bent each arm in turn behind his head, breathing noisily in and out, now working on his triceps.

Annoyed, Paulo pushed the blanket and cover to the bottom of the bed, but still found nothing.

'Where's the book I left here?'

'How should I know? Did you see the husband arrested?'

Paulo turned to his brother, surprised again.

'The police arrested the husband? Why?'

'He turned himself in. He confessed to killing her. How come you didn't see the dentist at the police station, if you were there?'

Paulo did the calculations: he had left the station more than two hours earlier, dragged away by his father. Together with Eduardo and his mother, they stopped off at the school, where the headmaster wanted to see them. They had to wait for twenty minutes or half an hour before he saw them, and then were given a long lecture. Night was falling by the time they came out. The street lamps were lit when they finally reached home. Paulo concluded that the dead woman's husband must have given himself up during this interval. He went over to Antonio's bed, almost certain he was hiding the book Eduardo had lent him there. He only needed to reach under the mattress for his fingers to close round it.

He carefully pulled out the book. On its brightly coloured cover, his favourite hero was gazing from a clifftop into a deep valley through which ran a broad, powerful river, lined with the palaces of a civilization lost for centuries in the jungle.

Paulo went back to his own bed, lay down, kicked off his shoes without looking where they fell, and opened the dog-eared copy of *Tarzan and the City of Gold* at the page marked with a piece of string. He began to read.

'What are you reading, golliwog? A dirty book? I don't like reading. Not even dirty books. It's a waste of time. My thing is fucking. What I really like is sticking it in. Into cunts, arses, mouths: my thing is to fuck, to shove it in and enjoy myself. A lot. I've got lots of sperm, so . . .'

But Paulo was a long way away. The pain had vanished. He didn't feel ashamed or sad any more. He was roaming the streets of a fabulous city hidden in the depths of the African jungle, lined with sophisticated architecture, the walls made of precious materials that aroused all kinds of envy, centres of empire built thanks to highly advanced scientific knowledge, and inhabited by a race unlike any other in the world, and protected by proud warriors clothed in skins and armour studded with emeralds and rubies, brave soldiers who in the end would yield to the courage, nobility and fearlessness of the king of the jungle.

'How many times was she stabbed?'

Antonio's voice brought Paulo back unwillingly to the room. He concentrated on a paragraph and flew back to the land of Onthar, where stood the ivory and gold towers of the lost cities of Cathne and Athne.

'How many wounds did she have? Seven? Eight? People say there were more than twenty. How many were there?'

Paulo tried to return to the city in which Tarzan had been thrown into an arena where, when the trumpets sounded, he would have to face the fearful giant Phobeg, in a combat in which the loser would have his throat cut, to the delight of the beautiful and perverse queen, Nemone.

'How many stab wounds?'

Tarzan freed himself from the ropes binding him and—

Antonio snatched the book out of Paulo's hands.

'How many wounds?'

'Give it me! Give me the book!'

'How many? How many stab wounds?'

Paulo tried in vain to reach the book his brother was holding in one hand above his head, while he fended him off with the other.

'Give me the book! Give it to me!'

'How many? First you have to tell me how many stab wounds she had.'

'I didn't count. Give me the book, Antonio!'

'Tell me: how many? How many?'

'I don't know; I don't remember, I don't know.'

'You were there; you saw. How many?'

'The book, Antonio . . .'

'How many? Tell me!'

'Give—'

The memory of the chopped-off breast and the sight of the raw red flesh smeared with mud and blood suddenly flashed through Paulo's mind. He felt very weak. He collapsed on to the bed, and fell quiet. Dropped his head.

Thinking it might be a trick, Antonio kept his eye on him for a few seconds, ready to react if he jumped up at him, keeping the book high above his head in his right hand. But Paulo just sat on the edge of the bed, head down, hiding his face. He didn't move. His brother threw the book at him, and went to dress to go out.

2

Out on the Prowl

Moonlight breaking
On the shadows
Of my solitude
. . . Where are you going?

Where was the voice coming from?

Tell me if tonight
You're going out on the prowl
The way she once did . . .

Where did I first hear that song? he was to ask himself
many years later. Was it a distant sound like it was now, and a
man's voice? Or was it a woman?

Who can she be with . . . ?

He remembered that the voice had sounded hesitant,

quavering. Coming from a radio, or from a nearby record player. Someone listening to a disc. Or a cassette. Did cassettes exist in those days, in 1961? In that town? Who could own them? Not a workman. No one in that street could own a cassette player. Nor could his butcher father. Nobody in his street, that was for sure. Or perhaps it was possible. Perhaps there was easy credit and anyone with social security, or even without it, could buy a device with a radio and cassette player on the never-never. An engine driver, a metalworker or even a seamstress could possess whatever they wanted: the days of the illusion of easily reached abundance had begun. Or a tape recorder. Did they exist at the start of the 1960s? Someone I knew must have had a tape recorder with those two brown tapes turning, reproducing the words of that song: otherwise, how could I remember them now?

> *Tell her that I love her,*
> *Tell her that I'm dying*
> *from waiting so long,*
> *Tell her to come home . . .*

Years later, he thought it must have been a gramophone. A radiogram. One of those that played heavy black records with round labels in the centre, and were kept in cardboard sleeves. Like the records Hanna Wizorek had. Perhaps it was a radiogram that was playing the song sung in Spanish. But back then we didn't know Hanna Wizorek. And in my house there was no gramophone and no records. Nor in his. Would I even have recognized a song sung in Spanish?

Night-time prowling
isn't good for her . . .

All these years later, he began to doubt whether he had even heard the voice that now permeated his memories. Or did I add the music in memory of that night? Did I simply imagine that the woman whom we had only seen dead liked that Agustín Lara bolero? That I heard 'Noche de Ronda' on a phonograph, a radio-phonograph, or on a cassette player. Or did I learn later on that she sought consolation in sentimental songs like this one, laments for lost loves, nostalgic pleas?

No.

No.

That night I had no idea what her life was like. I must have dreamed up the song later on. I heard the song later on. The song in Spanish, the voice in the night, it was all in my imagination, and . . . No. No. No. I'm sure of it: I heard it that night. A man's voice, I think. It makes sense: a male voice. *She left me*, he sang. He was the one who regretted being abandoned. A male voice. I think. No, I'm certain. A deep male voice. The same day that we discovered her body.

It can destroy you,
It causes sorrow . . .

The whistle echoed round the dimly lit street. Followed by an imitation of the call of the tinamou bird, repeated four times close to the row of silent, dark, identical houses. The employees of the Brazilian Central Railway went to bed early.

A few hours later, noisy alarm clocks or still-drowsy wives would awaken them, and they would leave beneath a sky as dark as the one they had left the evening before, their stomachs lined with the coffee and bread and margarine they had eaten standing up in the kitchen, taking with them their thermos and tin lunch boxes prepared the night before, walking along paved streets damp from the morning mist that formed bright haloes round the still-lit iron street lamps, even before the night-workers in the textile factory had finished their shift.

Paulo waited, leaning on his bike handlebars, next to the low wall outside one of these houses, shifting his weight from foot to foot. He was growing impatient, staring at the window of Eduardo's bedroom. Minutes went by without any indication that he had managed to wake his friend.

He repeated their secret sign, louder this time. A long whistle, then four calls. No luck again.

The thin mist of April dawns drifted down from the dark mountains encircling the town. The wispy veil shifted above his head, occasionally clearing to show patches of starry sky.

He propped his bike up and climbed over the wall, avoiding the gate that might creak and wake the adults. He crossed the garden in a few strides. The flowerbeds, planted in between narrow paths decorated with fragments of coloured tiles, were enclosed by cement borders whitewashed to keep off ants. The only tall plant, a rose bush that twined its way round an iron support like the spokes of a parasol, was probably left behind by the railway-worker's family who had lived here before. In the two years she had been in the house,

Eduardo's mother had planted only small plants with feminine names that Paulo did not recognize, each one in a bed of similar colours and shapes, creating delicate clusters.

The same careful organizing hand was obvious inside the house. Shiny furniture smelling of peroba oil, decorated with crocheted squares she herself had made. In the oven there was always something for Eduardo to eat, whenever he felt a pang of hunger. Curtains on the windows. Doors with proper latches. Lengths of cloth, paper patterns striped with chalk and unfinished outfits for clients folded and stacked on the Formica table beside the always oiled sewing machine. The smell of sweet sedge in the bedlinen. Floors waxed and polished every Saturday. A feeling of solidity and order that Paulo could sense but not properly define, as happened with so much all around him.

He often thought he would like to live in a place like this: somewhere that was always clean, where someone would be waiting when he came home from school with a freshly cooked, still-hot meal, that he would eat sitting at the table while his mother or someone else asked him about what he had been taught that morning. In the afternoon, between attending to her customers, his mother would bring a piece of freshly baked cake to his bedroom, with a glass of milk. What would the smell of cake baked at home be like? What would warm cake baked at home taste like?

Rubbish. He didn't even like cake. He was free to eat or not to eat whatever food the cook left in the pans on their stove. He did his schoolwork and homework out of interest, and to learn new things. He had a bath whenever he felt like it: often in hot weather, rarely when it was cold. He changed or kept clothes on as he wished. If his mother were alive like Eduardo's, he wouldn't have the same freedom. Still less to come and go as he pleased. At any time. Or almost any time: he was not allowed to stay out late at night. But when his father and Antonio were sleeping at the brothel, he didn't have to worry. Like tonight.

Standing directly beneath the window he whistled and imitated the bird call once more. Once. Twice. As he was repeating the call for a third time, Eduardo appeared, in his blue-and-grey-striped pyjamas, done up to the neck.

'What's going on, Paulo? What time is it?'

'After midnight.'

'What's the matter with your face?'

'Nothing.'

'It's all puffy.'

'I want to talk to you about something else.'

'Did your father beat you again?'

They whispered together. Paulo could not stay still. Ever since his talk with Antonio he had been on edge.

'The dead woman's husband confessed.'

He said it again, as Eduardo looked on, unimpressed.

'The husband. The dentist. He confessed.'

'I know.'

'He's been arrested.'

'I know.'

'He says it was him.'

'I know that too. I heard my father talking about it with my mother.'

'It's not true.'

'Who says so?'

'It can't be.'

'Why not?'

'The dentist is old and weak.'

'But he killed her.'

'How could he kill a big woman like her, Eduardo? You saw how big she was.'

'He confessed.'

'It wasn't him.'

'First he drugged her with something, then stabbed her.'

'I doubt it.'

'More than twelve times, my father said.'

'Why did he take the body so far away?'

A brief silence.

'To the lake,' Eduardo suggested, 'because it was harder to find?'

'If he was going to confess, why didn't he leave it in the house?'

'He only confessed later on. He felt remorse. He was nervous, so he carried the body away—'

Paulo interrupted him:

'How did he load such a heavy body into his car?'

'Perhaps he dragged it? That's it, he dragged it.'

'Why didn't he throw the body out before he reached the lake? Why didn't he throw it down a bank? Or in a river? Why didn't he throw it in the lake with a heavy weight attached so that it would sink and be eaten by the fish, and no one would ever find it, and he could have said that his wife vanished, that she ran away from home?'

Eduardo's replies were also questions:

'Perhaps he didn't have time? Perhaps she was too heavy to drag through the mud? Perhaps he had nothing he could tie to her?' And he added, dismissively: 'If he didn't kill her, why did he confess?'

Paulo, who had been going over the same question for hours alone in his bedroom, voiced his own doubts: didn't she scream when she was being stabbed? Didn't any neighbours hear the screams? Why didn't she try to escape or call for help?

Eduardo yawned. He could see the mist curling around the street behind Paulo, thought he was beginning to feel cold, and that he would like to get back into his warm bed as soon as possible. Paulo insisted.

'Her hands were slashed, don't you remember?'

Eduardo wasn't sure if he remembered that.

'She must have been trying to grab the knife, Eduardo. She must have struggled not to die. She must have struggled. Everybody struggles to avoid being killed. And the dentist wasn't strong enough to overpower her.'

'What difference does it make? It's past midnight, Paulo. We've got school early tomorrow morning. No, not tomorrow – today.'

'It wasn't the dentist who killed her. It wasn't!'

'But he confessed. That's it. It's over.'

'Oh, it is, is it? Then tell me one thing: why did he cut her breast off, Eduardo? Why, Eduardo? Why did he cut it off, Eduardo?'

They both fell silent. In the distance they heard the intermittent, scratchy sound of a radio, or phonograph. A deep baritone voice.

Night-time prowling
isn't good for her . . .
It can destroy you,
It causes sorrow . . .

The beam from Eduardo's torch shone on the metal semicircle surrounding the head of the wooden statue of the saint. She was clutching a crucifix and two roses, one white, the other red. Carved with great care in the eighteenth century, painted in delicate and already faded colours, the image contrasted strongly with the gaudy tones and doll-like face of the statuette behind her, made in the second half of the twentieth century. To the right, the plaster figure of a young woman with long tresses was holding a bunch of lilies in her arms. Several other small statues stood on the oval jacaranda-wood table, flanked by two silver candlesticks holding tall candles.

Paulo's eyes strayed to the paintings of different sizes and shapes ranged above the table. They portrayed women and men with pious expressions on their faces. Some had wounds to their hands and feet. Others had haloes round their heads. Paulo recognized one of them: a bearded old man leaning on a staff who was crossing a river carrying on his shoulder a smiling young baby with golden curls and blue eyes. It was the same saint a driver friend of his father's had hanging from his taxi's rear-view mirror.

'It's St Christopher,' he explained. 'Carrying the infant Jesus.'

'Not so loud,' Eduardo warned him. 'If anyone catches us here, we're done for!'

Paulo thought this was a bit unnecessary. He was sure nobody had seen them climb the wall behind the house, or get in through the bathroom shutters. There was no one in the streets at that late hour. Even if somebody did pass by the dentist's house, they would not hear anything said behind its thick walls. In any case, he could not really control his voice, which was beginning to mix the gruffer tones of adolescence with the higher ones of childhood. He clicked his tongue in protest, but Eduardo ignored him, still gazing at the statues in amazement.

'I've never seen so many.'

'So many what?'

'Male and female saints. And they're so old. Look at that one. See how well made it is. Look at the nose, the hands, the detail of the fingernails. The crucifix signifies devotion to Jesus Christ.'

Paulo did not know what the word 'devotion' meant.

'It's like love, only more so.'

His reply meant nothing to Paulo.

'Who's this?'

'It's St Teresa. Her devotees are greeted with a shower of roses when they enter paradise.'

44

This didn't make sense either, but Paulo said nothing.

'And the one with all that hair?'

'St Maria Goretti. The lilies are to show that she was pure.'

'How do you know it means that?'

'Everybody does.'

'I don't.'

'All Catholics do.'

'My mother was a Catholic. My father isn't interested in religion. Nobody makes me go to mass.'

'Nor me. I go because I want to.'

'You mean that when your mother and father go to church on Sunday they allow you not to go?'

'I go because I want to.'

'And I don't go because I don't want to.'

Eduardo closed the discussion by pointing to the female saint with long hair.

'That one had a film made about her.'

'Which one?'

'The one with the lilies. St Maria Goretti. Somebody tried to behave indecently towards her, she wouldn't let him, and he stabbed her to death.'

'That's what must have happened to the dentist's wife.'

'But wasn't she a whore?'

'Oh yes, she was.'

'And the dentist had the right to enjoy her. He was her husband.'

'Yes.'

'So let's continue with our investigation. Let's look further. What's that up there?'

The beam of light picked out a tall piece of furniture against the back wall. It had two doors in the top half, with a drawer underneath. They opened the doors: one of them creaked. The light showed some charcoal-grey jackets, a couple of black coats and matching trousers, white formal shirts, black and navy-blue ties, white coats with the dentist's initials embroidered on the pockets. In the drawer they found piles of underpants, vests and handkerchiefs, all of them white. Rolled up in one corner were several pairs of black socks.

'It's all men's things,' said Eduardo.

'An old man's things.'

'And dentist's clothes.'

'This must be his bedroom.'

'Their bedroom, Paulo. A husband and wife sleep together.'

'Look over there: it's a single bed.'

'It must be the guest room,' said Eduardo, glancing at the image of a crucified Christ over the bed. 'Rich people have a spare room. The couple's bedroom must be somewhere else.'

They went out. The torchlight guided them down the corridor and past the bathroom where they had climbed in. Up ahead was a small room lined with tiles. It contained only a dining table, two chairs, a stove and a gas canister.

In the opposite direction, the corridor led to the front of the house, where the dentist's consulting-room was. It was separated from the rest of the house by aluminium screens and recently installed milky-coloured plastic tiles. A few feet before this, two closed doors stood opposite each other.

They tiptoed towards them.

The left-hand door was ajar. They pushed it and went in. It was filled with X-ray plates and photographic negatives hanging from strings. To one side, on a sink, stood two rectangular metal box trays, half filled with liquid. A sheet of dark plastic was floating in one of them. Eduardo picked it up, examined it in the torchlight, then held it out to Paulo: images of a tooth with a long root. Paulo dropped it back into the liquid.

At first the door to the room opposite seemed locked, but it yielded when Eduardo turned the porcelain doorknob and pushed hard. The torchlight fell on a dressing-table mirror, and they saw their own reflections: two young boys in a darkened house, searching for they had no idea what.

Most of the room was taken up with a wide double bed, covered with a green woven bedspread. Against the wall next to it stood an inlaid wooden chiffonier with rounded edges and several drawers. There was nothing on its marble top. No pictures of saints on the walls. Or crucifix above the bed. No pillows either.

Eduardo went over to the dressing table. He saw cosmetics, boxes of powder, sponges, bottles of nail polish. They were no different from the ones he knew from his mother's dressing table, except for the colours: all the murdered woman's lipsticks and polish were as bright red as a rotten guava.

He opened the four drawers carefully, one by one. He found a comb here, hairpins there, a hairbrush in another one, a manicure set, a couple of buttons, a pincushion with needles and pins sticking in it, a pair of scissors, a few coins. No revealing note, letter or message.

'Shine the light over here, Eduardo.'

He turned, and pointed the torch. Paulo was holding several identical pieces of clothing he had just taken out of the bottom wardrobe drawer. He put one on his head. It looked like a double bonnet. He smiled, delighted with himself.

'It's a brassiere, Eduardo!'

'Put it back.'

'Why?'

'They're a dead woman's clothes.'

'Have you ever seen so many of them?'

'Don't go messing around.'

'But aren't we looking for clues?'

'A brassiere isn't a—'

He stopped. He raised his finger to his lips, urging Paulo to be quiet.

'What?'

Eduardo repeated his signal. He pointed towards the corridor. There was a new, irregular-shaped patch of brightness.

The beam of light crossed the corridor ceiling, then the floor. Another torch. Someone else was in the house. He must be wearing rubber-soled shoes, because all they could hear was a creaking sound as the old floorboards were pressed down at regular intervals. Short, cautious steps.

'Who—?'

Eduardo clasped his hand round Paulo's mouth. The sound of footsteps continued along the corridor. The light from the other torch turned towards the room they had left earlier. The corridor was plunged back into darkness.

They heard the creak of the double wardrobe door, then the sound of coat-hangers being moved. Eduardo pointed his chin to indicate they should get out of there. He took the brassiere from Paulo and put it back in the drawer. As he was doing so, he spotted a rectangular box. He lifted it out, hesitating whether to open it or take it with them. Straightening up, Paulo knocked against it. The contents spilled on to the floor.

'Condoms!' exclaimed Paulo, recognizing the rubber sheaths his brother used. 'Look how many there are!'

He bent down to pick some up, but Eduardo tugged on his sleeve and dragged him out of the room. In the bathroom, Paulo helped Eduardo through the shutters. Then he stood on the edge of the lavatory bowl, put one foot on the window-sill, leaned out and pushed his left shoulder between one strip of glass and the next, then his left leg: he squeezed out and was soon standing next to Eduardo in the garden.

They ran across the road and hid behind a rubbish bin.

They heard the cathedral bell. It pealed once. A silence. A second time. Silence.

'Two in the morning! If my mother finds I'm not in bed she's going to be worried.'

Paulo was hoping that the party with prostitutes, rum and laughter that he imagined his father and brother were enjoying would be even livelier than usual.

'If my father gets back and finds I'm not at home, he'll kill me.'

'Why does he always beat you?'

'It's not always.'

'But I've seen you so often with a swollen face . . .'

'It's my fault.'

'Why's that?'

'I'm no good.'

'What d'you mean, Paulo?'

'I'm no good.'

'I've never seen you do anything that—'

'I think lots of bad things,' Paulo interrupted him.

'What things?'

'Things. Ugly thoughts.'

'Like what?'

Paulo fell silent.

'You can tell me.'

'There are times when I . . .'

He fell silent again.

'Go on, Paulo.'

'No, it's nothing.'

'You can tell me.'

Paulo wanted to say there were times when he longed to plunge a dagger into his father's heart. To stab him. And twist the knife. To cut his throat and send all the blood spurting everywhere, like a pig. To stab him in the eye, to smash him on the head with a stone until everything was so destroyed that no one would know whose face it was; to sprinkle his bed with petrol and light a match, to set fire to the house and watch him and Antonio burn until they were no more than two chunks of blackened meat; to shoot him in the mouth, to shoot him in both hands and feet, to cut off each finger, one by one, to cut off his nose, ears, lips, tongue, to cut off his penis and his balls. I think all the things my father knows I think, and he knows I have these thoughts because I've got tainted blood, I was born with it. It's not like his or Antonio's blood, I've got tainted blood like my mother's family and he knows, because I'm no good and if I can't drive those thoughts out of my head I'm capable of doing all that because I . . . because I have . . .

Perverse desires, he would have said if he had been able to understand the meaning of what he felt and what remained with him each time his father thrashed him. All he said was:

'Things. Bad things. Angry thoughts.'

Eduardo couldn't understand.

'Why does your father treat you like that?'

'I don't know.'

'Doesn't he like you?'

'I don't know.'

'But if you solve this crime, he will like you.'

'Yes.'

'He'll be proud of you.'

'Yes.'

'If you prove it wasn't the dentist who killed his wife, he'll treat you differently, won't he?'

Paulo said nothing. He was staring across the road, his attention focused on a figure who was opening the gate to leave the dentist's house and walking off in the opposite direction to them.

They followed.

Possibly because the surface was uneven, or because of the upward slope, the man was walking slowly along the middle of the road. Each time he came to the circle of light beneath a street lamp, they could make him out more clearly. Short. Thin. Wearing a loose jacket. White or greying hair.

If he looked back he would see two boys, one taller than the other, creeping along as close as possible to the walls of the century-old houses, trying to hide as much as possible in the shadows, like the detectives in the films they had seen. But the thin, short man in the jacket with white or greying hair kept on going, unconcerned. Was he out for a stroll? At that time of the morning?

He turned to the left, disappearing down an alley.

Eduardo and Paulo ran so as not to lose sight of him. They had no need to: he was still walking slowly, steadily.

He came out into the next paved street, which was also lined with solid houses from the mid-nineteenth century, built for the region's coffee growers when they visited or came shopping in the city. When most of them were ruined by the freeing of the slaves, they had to sell their town houses, or their impoverished descendants turned them into their permanent homes, driven from their parents' and grand-parents' estates by debts they owed to banks, or by newly arrived immigrants from Europe. Only a few of the original houses were still preserved. Most of them were disfigured by additions or changes: modern façades, rounded stones replaced by the straight lines of bricks and cement, Portuguese tiles giving way to mortar and paint, pinewood window frames supplanted by aluminium, bevelled French glass panes by corrugated plastic newly made in the factories now multiplying in São Paulo. Two of the houses had caved in. A third one next to them had been demolished, and a two-storey, vaguely art-deco cinema had been built on the land.

The man came to a halt outside the cinema. He seemed to be reading the title written in capitals on the black wooden billboard that was hanging from a thick wire grille: *Shoot the Pianist*. The film shown the previous evening. As with many other cinemas in cities of the Brazilian interior in those days, the programming at the Cine Theatro Universo was changed daily, except at weekends. The films could be French, Italian, Mexican, Argentine, German, Japanese, American or locally made. The film to be shown the next night was advertised on a poster standing on an easel in the foyer behind the iron gates. It was a Brazilian film: *Um Candango na Belacap*, starring Ankito and Grande Otelo. Paulo thought the actors were really funny, though Eduardo preferred Oscarito. In the external showcases was a poster in red, with its title in English: *West Side Story*, and another one in black and white, in which the photo of a blonde woman in a fountain appeared beneath the name of Federico Fellini and three words: *La Dolce Vita*.

Paulo was behind Eduardo, and could not make out the features of the man they were following. That did not stop him announcing:

'He's a suspect.'

'Why?'

'Isn't that what you say when somebody could be the killer?'

'Yes, suspect is the word.'

'Well, that's what he is. Just look at him.'

'He's standing with his hands in his pockets, reading the film posters.'

'If he's not a suspect, what was he doing in the dentist's house?'

'What do you think?'

'Hiding evidence of the crime! I bet he's the real murderer.'

'He's as short as the dentist. And as thin.'

'What if the two of them got together to murder her? While she was struggling with one, the other stabbed her.'

'We didn't see anything broken in the house. There was no sign of a struggle. We didn't find any kind of evidence.'

'Because the suspect turned up. We had to run off.'

'If he's a suspect, why is he so calm?'

'So who is he then? And what was he doing in the dentist's house?'

Paulo's suspect turned, walked a few steps, and entered the square bearing the name of a local hero who was killed at the battle of Monte Cassino in Italy during the Second World War, but which the local inhabitants still insisted on calling simply the Top Garden Square. In the centre stood a bandstand built like a Chinese pagoda. The man with white or greying hair climbed the four steps up to it and leaned on the wrought-iron balustrade which imitated bamboo. He looked all round the garden, came down the steps again and sat on a bench.

'Did you see his face?' asked Paulo.

'More or less.'

'Who is he?'

'I don't think I know him.'

'You've never seen him?'

'I don't think so.'

Protected by the shadows under the cinema awning, they saw the man take something out of the inside pocket of his jacket, but couldn't see what it was. They thought he was writing. He stopped, looked down, and seemed to write a few more words. Then he put it back in his pocket. He crossed his legs and sat there for a while. He stood up, looking around him as if to make sure which direction to go in. Then he left.

He walked down the slope where signs above unlit shop windows and iron shutters advertised the shops in the city's main street. At the far end, another incline led up to the highest part of the city, occupied by the cathedral and its twin towers. Far too grandiose for its surroundings, it had been inaugurated in 1835 by a representative of the young emperor Pedro II in recognition of the religious feelings, prestige and economic power of the coffee barons.

The man passed by the cathedral, walked round it, and then set off along a road that descended sharply to the right. When it levelled off, he was still in the road, and crossed opposite a long red-brick building with slit windows. A concrete white-painted eagle on a globe holding in its mouth a bronze plaque declaring *Founded in 1890* and with cotton stems in its claws stood above the words: *Union & Progress Textile Factory.*

Paulo's mother had once worked there as a weaver. That was where she had met her future husband, a worker in the dyeing section before he became a butcher.

'Where do you think he's going?'

'I don't know, Paulo. Home?'

'He's walking further and further away from the centre.'

The two boys were not familiar with the part of the city the man was venturing into now. There were fewer houses and more waste lots, some of them surrounded by brick walls or bamboo canes, many covered in tall grass and castor-oil bushes. Beyond one of these ran a long, high, moss-covered stone wall, dotted with clumps of ferns and weeds. Above it, beyond the streetlights, the wall was overhung by the thick branches of one of the trees growing on the other side.

The man came to a halt beneath the tree. Going as close as he could to the wall, he stretched out his arms, feeling for something. He found it: a rope. As he began laboriously to pull on it, the tips of two wooden posts appeared, joined by parallel bars. The rope was tied to one of them. A painter's stepladder.

The man with grey or white hair lowered the ladder to the ground, then stood it against the stones. He carefully climbed each step, and sat on top of the wall. Precariously balanced, he tugged on the rope, pulling up the ladder. He let it down on the other side. Clinging to a branch, he put one foot on one of the steps, then the other. He let go of the branch, put both hands on the ladder support and disappeared among the foliage.

The boys ran to the wall. The rope was still swinging in

between the leaves. A glance at each other was enough for them to decide:

'We're going in there!'

Paulo cupped his hands and Eduardo stood on them and pulled, expecting to be able to climb the rope. To his surprise, he fell to the ground, with the rope between his legs. It wasn't tied to the stepladder any more.

After a moment's disappointment, they recovered their spirits. Paulo wound the rope round his chest, while Eduardo looked for another way in. He walked along the wall until he came to a big double gate, almost as high as the stone wall. It was locked. There was a plaque nailed to it, which read: *St Simon Old People's Home.*

In the distance, the cathedral clock struck one, two, three times.

3

Cowboys and Indians

THE OLD MAN lay sprawled in a canvas deck chair, fast asleep, protected from the afternoon sun by the foliage of a tree spreading its branches over the courtyard wall. A thin trail of saliva dribbled down from his open mouth to his chin and the collar of the old people's home uniform he was wearing. Dark patches were visible on his scalp beneath thin strands of hair. Another old man, still in pyjamas, gave the two boys a toothless smile. Opposite him, two others were playing cards, and a third sat motionless at a chessboard, while a fourth was leafing through a magazine. On a bench by the wall, a red-headed old man with freckles was rocking back and forth, mumbling an inaudible song. Further on, a fat man on crutches sat down in the sun, pushing his one bandaged leg out in front of him. His face was a mass of purple bruises. Near him, in a wheelchair, a figure wrapped in blankets was moaning softly. There were more old men in other hammocks, deck chairs, on benches. Dozens of them.

Surrounded by all this human misery and bodies maimed

in ways they had never even imagined, Eduardo and Paulo did not know which way to turn. The fate of these old people was completely different to anything they knew, had seen, or heard of: in their experience, men lived out their final days protected by their families, breathing their last in their own beds, comforted by wives, children, grandchildren, or at the very least a friend.

'He's not here. None of them is the man who climbed the wall last night.'

'He has to be here. We saw him come in,' insisted Paulo, the rope still wrapped round his chest.

'Just look at these old men, Paulo!'

They had never seen such decrepitude. The abandoned, the crazy, the sick and the frail, the wounded, the mutilated, the senile, the alcoholics, the weak, the poor, the illiterate, the beggars, the crippled, all abandoned to their fate. The nephews, grandfathers, fathers, uncles forgotten in sanatoriums or hospitals, turfed out of their houses or picked up from doorways, under bridges, from alleyways, rubbish dumps, squares, gardens or pavements, from roadsides in a country that was busy industrializing, growing at a gigantic pace, modernizing. The nation that, in a South America of banana republics, was steering a course out of the Third World by manufacturing lathes and cars, trucks, tractors, refrigerators, lamps, liquidizers, televisions, sound systems, shoes, soft drinks and washing machines. A country capable of advancing fifty years in only five of full democracy, a country that had no room for any of these men.

'Nobody here would be able to get into the dentist's house. Or to do that rope trick,' said Eduardo.

'Perhaps he's hiding inside?'

'They're all out here. It's the time of day for sunbathing. Only the very sick must still be inside.'

'So . . .?'

'He can't be from here. He came in here, but he lives somewhere else,' Eduardo concluded, turning on his heel and heading for the exit. Paulo started to follow him.

'What now?'

'We're leaving.'

'But that means we let the suspect escape.'

'What suspect, Paulo? Look at all these old wrecks.'

'I'm looking.'

'Can you see anyone who looks like the man we saw early this morning?'

'No. No one. Wait . . .'

They came to a halt. Paulo pointed to a pair close by them: one seemed to be staring in their direction, while the other's face was hidden behind a newspaper, as if he were reading it.

'Those two.'

'One of them's bald. The other is tall. Our suspect is short, and has white hair or—'

He was interrupted by a voice behind him:

'Do you play chess?'

It was the man sitting at the chessboard. He pointed to the empty chair opposite him:

'Do you want to play?'

'No, thanks, we're just leaving.'

'We doesn't know how to play,' added Paulo.

'We *don't* know, and we're just leaving,' Eduardo said rapidly, trying to cover his friend's slip.

'Neither of you plays chess?'

'My father plays draughts with my brother. Is it the same?'

'Do you know the game?'

'I've seen it on television,' said Eduardo.

'So you've got a Tele-Vision set?' the old man said wonderingly, pronouncing the two words separately. 'I've never seen Tele-Vision. Is it as good as the cinema, like they say?'

'No, it's all in black and white. But in my house, we don't—'

'Your Tele-Vision isn't in Technicolor?'

'There is only black and white TV. And the image comes and goes. As if it were waves, if you follow me?'

'Fluctuating?'

'That's right, fluctuating! The people on it look twisted. It has a small screen, inside a box. The box contains lots of wires and valves, which are like lamps, d'you understand? Only different.'

'Your family must be well off. A Tele-Vision set costs a lot.'

'We're not at all rich. And we don't have—'

'Eduardo's father is a mechanic on the Brazilian Central Railway,' explained Paulo.

'I watched television at my uncle's house.'

'In Rio de Janeiro,' Paulo added.

'Your uncle must be a man of means.'

'I think so. Yes, he is.'

'His uncle lives in a district called Tijuca. Everybody there has a car.'

'My uncle has a Willys Aero, do you know them? It's a big car: it can fit six people.'

'His uncle is an aeronautical engineer.'

'He works for Brazilian Panair.'

'His uncle has been to Europe and the United States.'

'Brazilian Panair is an airline. One of the biggest in the world. He's my uncle because he's married to my aunt. My mother's sister.'

'His uncle has been to Europe twice.'

'And once to the United States. They both went. Him and my aunt. She says they're going again, next year.'

'That's the uncle who has television at home. In Tijuca.'

'My father said he's going to buy one. As soon as he has the money.'

'And when they've put up a mast here, for the reception.'

'For the reception of the images. They're transmitted through the air, just like radio.'

'They don't let us listen to the radio in here. It's forbidden. The nuns don't like it.'

'They don't like music?'

'They don't like noise. Loud music. A lot of the old men here are deaf, and can only hear the radio when it's turned up loud. That's why the nuns forbade it. But they don't like anything. They even banned the news. We can't even listen to the *Repórter Esso* programme. All the magazines here are out of date, the newspapers are from days ago. We're isolated: we don't know what is going on in the world. Is that my rope?'

Startled, Paulo didn't know what to reply.

'That rope round your shoulder, boy: is it mine?' persisted the white-haired, slightly wall-eyed old man. His voice had a soft north-eastern twang.

'What d'you mean, yours?'

'Mine. Bought with my money. It was tied to the ladder.'

'Ladder?'

'What ladder?' echoed Paulo.

'The wooden ladder that was over there, leaning against the wall.'

'I don't know anything about a ladder.'

'Yes, you do. Both of you do. That's why you came here.'

'I came to deliver an order from my father's butcher's shop.'

'That's a lie. You and your friend were nosing around the yard.'

'His father sent him to deliver a package of meat, and I came with him.'

'You didn't have any package with you when you came in.'

'I handed it in at the door.'

'Give me that rope. It's mine.'

'It's ours,' Paulo insisted.

'You were the ones who followed me.'

'Us?' Eduardo's surprise was genuine.

'You two. I saw you.'

'You saw?'

'No way. We never . . .'

'You broke into the dentist's house. Then you followed me here.'

'We . . . did what?' Eduardo tried to sound offended.

'You followed me and took my rope.'

'I didn't leave home last night. And Paulo isn't allowed out.'

'If I went out at night, my father would kill me.'

'My mother has a heart murmur. I can't be roaming the streets in the early hours.'

'You broke into a house that had been sealed by the police. You disturbed a crime scene.'

'No we didn't!' protested Eduardo, without conviction.

'We only looked from outside.'

'Yes, that's what we did. We kept an eye on the house from outside. To see if anything happened.'

'You searched through everything. You rummaged through Dona Anita's underwear.'

'We stayed outside the whole time.'

'You disturbed a crime scene. You got in through the kitchen or bathroom window. You went into the bedrooms and the darkroom; you opened the wardrobes and drawers. You took some evidence from the house. You may have hidden it.'

'We're not thieves!'

'You stole my rope.'

'We didn't steal it.'

'It fell when I pulled it.'

'So give it back to me.'

'How do we know it's really yours?'

'What were you doing in the dentist's house?'

'Nothing.'

'My brother Antonio said that the dentist's wife . . .'

'What were you looking for?'

'His brother said things about the dentist's wife, so Paulo came to my house . . .'

'We thought that he, the dentist . . . that he was small and old – no offence meant – but we were wondering how an old man like him could have killed such a—'

'Give me that rope.'

'We didn't take anything from the dentist's house, you must believe us,' said Eduardo.

'Tell your friend to give me the rope.'

'Finders keepers.'

'Do your parents know you spend the early hours out roaming the city streets?'

'It was only that once!'

'Please don't tell my father.'

'The game of chess is very interesting, you know. I'd say, and I don't think it's an exaggeration, I'd say that playing chess – metaphorically speaking – prepares us for life's misfortunes. Do you follow?'

'Yes, sir,' Eduardo lied, ready to concede anything to get out of this embarrassing situation.

'What do "misfortunes" and "metaphorically" mean?'

'I'll explain later, Paulo.'

'What were *you* doing in the dentist's house anyway?'

'Living in an old people's home is very boring. I'm not here out of charity, you see: I pay to be here out of my retirement income.'

'In-coming what?' Paulo was confused again by the big words.

'Income,' Eduardo corrected him. 'Money. Pay.'

'My pay, my money,' the old man stressed. 'My retirement pension. I don't owe anyone any favours.'

'But you broke into the crime scene too!'

'I did no such thing. The old people in here only talk about the past. When they manage to talk about anything. The nuns are concerned about the kingdom of heaven, and nothing else. They lock the doors after supper. Everyone in bed by eight o'clock! I only discovered that a man had gone into space because I slipped out last night. The first in the history of mankind, and not a word from the nuns or this lot of gaga old men!'

'Yuri Gagarin,' Paulo remembered.

'The Earth is blue!' Eduardo quoted the astronaut.

'A Russian,' added Paulo.

'I can't stay a prisoner in here. Give me my rope.'

Paulo glanced at Eduardo, who nodded his head slightly, and then held the rope out to the old man.

He didn't take it.

'Put it behind that bush over there.'

Paulo and Eduardo walked over to the shrubbery next to the wall, searched for the thickest bush, and hid the rope behind it.

By the time they turned round, the old man was walking back inside the home, carrying the chessboard under his arm.

Sitting on the pavement outside the wall to the old people's home, Eduardo was whistling a tune. He was doing so under his breath, without thinking, waiting for Paulo. He was staring up at the sky, hoping to see a shooting star.

At first the sounds had no rhythm. A boy whistling in the middle of the night to keep himself amused. After a while, almost without him realizing it, the notes fell into place, each one harmonizing with the next, starting to form a melody. Softly, like footsteps on a smooth, cold floor. The notes flowed together until they became a tune he often heard before the films started at the Cine Theatro Universo, and when his mother hummed it as she bent over her sewing machine, the foot pedal marking the beat. A voice that was little more than a whisper, singing a sweet, melancholy song:

> *Poppy flower,*
> *Lovely poppy flower,*
> *My heart is yours, for ever.*
> *I love you,*
> *Little child of mine,*
> *The way a flower is loved*
> *by the sunshine.*

Everything around him – the wall opposite, the stars above his head, the stones in the road beneath his feet – became blurred. It was exactly the same feeling that had occasionally come over him in the past. He'd never been able to understand it, or why his eyes filled with tears. Here it is again, he thought, again that . . . that what? It felt like something pressing on his whole body, something beating at him, burning. There it was again. Inside. A twinge. Not a pain: a twinge. A slight, slight twinge. It hurt a little. And took time to go away. Or at least, to ease off. When it finally disappeared, it left him wanting to stay still, not to laugh or talk to anyone, not to play or go out.

> *Poppy flower,*
> *Lovely poppy flower,*
> *Don't be so ungrateful*
> *And love me,*
> *Poppy flower,*
> *Poppy flower,*
> *How can you bear*
> *To live so alone . . .*

If Eduardo had been at home, he would have closed his bedroom door, lain down on his bed, and tried to recover from this uneasy feeling by mentally conjugating irregular verbs; reciting the names of every country in South, Central and North America, and their capitals; repeating declensions in Latin; then going over in turn – as he was doing now – first the tributaries on the right bank of the River Amazon: Javari, Juruá, Purus, Madeira, Tapajós and Xingu, then on the left-hand side: Iça, Japurá, Negro, Trombetas, Paru and Jari. If the images of these powerful rivers zigzagging through the jungle were not enough to calm him, he would try the names of the presidents of the republic, starting with the most recent: Jânio Quadros, Juscelino Kubitschek, Getúlio Vargas, Eurico Gaspar Dutra . . .

'What are you doing?'

Paulo had just arrived, and was standing over him.

'Reciting the presidents of Brazil. You're late.'

'My father and Antonio took their time leaving. Has the old man appeared yet?'

'No. Where's your bike?'

'I left it at home. That way they'll think I'm there.'

Eduardo held out two pieces of folded paper with something written on them. Even before he unfolded them, Paulo knew what they were: the meaning of the words the old man had said that afternoon: 'misfortune' and 'metaphorically'. Eduardo had a dictionary. At school he was the only one who did, apart from the children of rich families. But they didn't count: the volumes belonged to their parents.

Explaining words was part of a tacit pact of mutual assistance. In a fight or in class, a friend should always be ready to lend a helping hand. Paulo kept all the many scraps of paper hidden under his underpants and socks to one side of the wardrobe, so that Antonio wouldn't find them. He would only laugh, make fun of him for it. Words! Synonyms! Hidden away like treasure . . . What nonsense, golliwog!

Paulo took a deep, pleasurable breath. The air was filled with the scent of ladies of the night. It felt as though the ardent smell was caressing him inside. It was a shame that the flowers were coming to an end. Winter was drawing near. When it grew cold, the flowers with their delicate, mother-of-pearl sepals would wilt and lose their perfume in the daytime, and fade from his life. The disappearance of their intense fragrance marked the end of summer.

'What time is it?' he asked.

Eduardo stood up, stretched his neck upwards, but couldn't see the clock on the right-hand cathedral tower.

'Some time after ten, I think.'

Paulo kicked an imaginary stone. Then an imaginary football. Then an imaginary football in front of a stand full of open-mouthed spectators in a foreign stadium. He was wearing the Brazilian team shirt, alongside Zito, Didi, Pelé, Garrincha, Nilton Santos, Bellini, Orlando, Mazzola, De Sordi, Zagallo and Gilmar. On radios and loudspeakers, in the biggest cities and the most remote villages, the presenters shouted above the roar of crowds gathered in all the streets and avenues. The gre–aatest fooootba–ller of aa–ll time, dear listeners, a herooo for all the cou–ntries in the wooorld! Ladies and gentlemen, the gre–aatest gooooooal scooorer ever!!!

Before his imaginary ball, propelled by the most powerful kick in the whole history of sport, could flash past the blond goalkeeper's head into the opposition net, Paulo saw something moving among the foliage of the big tree inside the wall. He saw the rope, then the ladder, and then the white-haired man climbing down to the pavement.

'What are you two doing here?' he grumbled when he saw them.

The rope and the ladder had disappeared from sight. Paulo couldn't contain himself:

'How do you manage it?'

'Physics, logic, and the desire for freedom,' replied the old man, wiping his hands on a handkerchief.

Paulo smiled. The old man scowled.

'It's late. Time for kids to be in bed.'

'I'm not a kid! Nor is Eduardo! We'll soon be thirteen!'

Eduardo launched into the series of questions he had pre-pared and rehearsed with Paulo.

'Did you find anything in the dentist's house that—'

'Go away!' the man interrupted him.

'We only wanted to—' Paulo insisted.

'Shoo! Shoo!' The man waved his hands as if he were driving off chickens. 'Get out of here!'

'We think that whoever killed the blonde woman, it wasn't—' Eduardo tried again.

The man's hands windmilled:

'Shoo! Get out of here now!'

'The dentist confessed, but we think that—'

'Out! Go home! Shoo!'

'But we think—'

'Go away, go away!'

'We—'

'Be off with you!'

The boys glanced at each other.

'Go away! Didn't you hear me? Away! Shoo! Go home, go to bed! Go on, get moving!'

Eduardo and Paulo turned their backs on him and walked away. The old man waited until they had vanished from sight, then headed in the opposite direction.

As soon as he turned a corner, Paulo came out of the shadows. Eduardo soon followed suit.

It was not hard to follow the old man. As on the previous night, he walked down the middle of the empty streets. He

71

went unhurriedly past the textile factory. He slowly climbed the hill behind the cathedral. Walked round it. Stopped, turned and peered up at the big clock. He set off again. Small, frail-looking, he shuffled along the deserted, silent main street. To Eduardo he made a desolate sight.

'I don't want to grow old,' he whispered.

Paulo didn't seem to hear.

'Old. It's sad.'

'Why?'

'When I see an old man like that ... it makes me feel ... I can't explain. There's nothing more for him, is there?'

'I don't get it.'

'Finished, isn't it?'

'What's finished?'

'Everything. For him.'

'I don't get it.'

'Let's drop it.'

When he reached the main square, the white-haired man went towards the only place that was still open. A small bar. The two last customers were talking to the owner behind the counter. The old man joined them.

'They're his accomplices,' said Paulo, fascinated by the word.

Eduardo didn't agree. He didn't think accomplices would dare to meet so openly. But he couldn't explain the old man's strange behaviour either. Paulo suggested a theory that had just occurred to him.

'He's the murderer. He went to the dentist's house to

conceal the evidence. Criminals always return to the scene of the crime.'

'But the crime took place near the lake.'

'Didn't the dentist tell the police he killed her in their house?'

'But we know it can't have been there.'

'Isn't it strange that the old man went there?'

'Yes, it is.'

'If he's not the dentist's accomplice, then he's off his head.'

'He could be. My granddad was like that.'

'The one you used to call *Nonno*?'

'No, *Nonno* was the Italian, my father's father. The crazy one was Portuguese, my mother's father. He ran away from home, vanished for days on end, went on benders, sang in the street. My mother was ashamed of him.'

One of the customers staggered out of the bar. Shortly afterwards, so did the other one. The white-haired old man stayed at the counter. He was drinking a clear liquid that the bar owner served him in a small glass. Paulo thought it must be *cachaça*, white rum.

'Did the crazy grandfather visit your house a lot?'

'The Portuguese? He lived with us in São Paulo. When my father was transferred to the interior, my mother sent him to her sister's house in Rio. He died there. I can't recall exactly what of. I can't remember his name either. I think it was Vicente, but I always called him Granddad. He took me to the district once.'

'The red-light district?'

'Yes. My mother was furious when she found out.'

'Were they naked?'

'The whores? I don't remember. I was still a kid.'

'You don't remember whether the women were naked or not?'

'No, I don't think they were.'

'Yeah,' said Paulo with a sigh. 'They can't have been. If you'd seen a naked woman, you wouldn't have forgotten it.'

The bar owner began closing the long wooden shutters. The old man came out. The boys got ready to follow him, but he simply walked over to one of the benches and sat down. He took a small notebook out of his inside jacket pocket. He read through a few pages, then wrote something down. He put the notebook away, and from another pocket took out a rolled-up cigarette and a box of matches. He lit it, inhaled deeply, blew out the smoke, drew on it again.

Paulo yawned. He felt very sleepy.

The tip of the pen closed the semicircle of the last letter, a consonant, descended slightly to the left, underlined part of the surname. Lifted from the paper, it crossed the letter 't'. Moving to the end of the signature, the pen made two dots on the right, one above the other. Finished.

'The reason for you being absent from school, signed by your father,' said Eduardo, holding out the school notebook to his friend. 'You can go to class again tomorrow with no worries.'

Paulo examined the text and the signature. Perfect.

'It's exactly the same. It's no different to the one above.'

Eduardo smiled.

'I did the one above as well.'

He might be hopeless at football, skinny, clumsy, ugly, a weirdo, a swot – the boys who always chased after him in every new town his father was transferred to could say what they liked about him, but none of them could forge anyone's handwriting and signature as well as he could.

It was a skill he had acquired on boring, lonely afternoons, copying his mother's florid signature, then the small dots above and below his father's writing, and later the circles and slants he discovered on the envelopes of the letters his relatives wrote. It was a slow, unintentional process that had no real goal or time limit. He only realized how good he was at it when he'd forged the notary public's signature on his own birth certificate, flourish for flourish, when he presented it in order to enrol at school in the previous town.

His talent, kept secret from everyone apart from his one real friend, had yet again proved useful. It made no sense for them to be cooped up in school on such a fine morning, listening to each teacher's blah-blah, one lesson after another. They both understood this the moment they met outside the school gate. They simply looked at each other, and didn't even bother to get off their bikes. They headed straight for the lake. Time enough the next day to present the reasons for their absence, with their parents' signatures.

Eduardo stretched his arms. He was tired. Another late night, thanks to the old man. The worst of it was they hadn't achieved anything. Nothing new. They were no further forward than on the night they had gone out to investigate for the first time.

He looked round for a clean, dry spot in the grass, and lay down. His uniform was folded up neatly beside him. In the nearby bushes, birds were celebrating the morning. Clouds were gathering overhead, reflected on the surface of the lake.

'When?' Paulo's voice came from some way off. He had to be close to the water.

'When what?'

'When did you do the signature above?'

'The last time you were suspended.'

'Oh, right. When I punched Sávio Januzzi.'

'No. When you put that little mirror under Suzana Scheienfeber's desk to see her knickers.'

The sound of someone plunging in, then noisy swimming strokes. Silence. Paulo must be floating. A squawking macaw. Silence. The call of a fly-catcher. A gentle breeze in his ear. Silence. The sound of bamboo rustling against bamboo. A slight rubbing sound. The bamboo swaying. A distant whine – a mosquito, or a dragonfly? Silence. Drowsiness . . . feeling sleepy. Closing his eyes. The clouds building up. Black.

'She wasn't wearing knickers.'

Paulo's voice woke him with a start.

'She what?'

'No knickers.'

Paulo was standing in front of him. Sprinkling him with water.

'What d'you mean, no knickers? Suzana had a pair on, I remember.'

'The dead woman, Eduardo. That Anita. She had no knickers on.'

Eduardo raised himself up on his elbows.

'The murderer must have torn them off.'

'Torn them off?'

'To have his way with her. To rape her.'

Paulo leaned over him.

'But there weren't any in the dentist's house either.'

'Any what?'

'Any knickers. Not a single pair.'

'There must have been – we simply didn't see them. We didn't have time to find them.'

'We opened everything.'

'There must have been some. All women wear knickers. Knickers, bra, slip, petticoat, suspender belt and stockings. They wear all that under their dresses.'

'How do you know?'

'I just know.'

'Does your mother wear all those?'

'Don't bring my mother into this.'

Paulo sat down. Mothers were something neither of them discussed. Paulo's because she was dead. Eduardo's because she was still pretty. Another tacit understanding between the two of them.

'Do you remember yours?' Eduardo suddenly asked, afraid of breaking their pact, but genuinely interested.

'My what?'

'Mother.'

'Hmm.'

It wasn't a reply: it was meant to close a topic Eduardo imagined must be painful for his friend.

'I'm sorry. I shouldn't have asked.'

'Hmm.'

'The thing is, I sometimes wonder . . . I wonder . . . if you don't . . .'

'Hmm.'

'Miss her . . . If you don't feel . . .'

'Hmm.'

'Don't you feel . . . ?'

'Hmm.'

'Don't you remember her?'

'My father.'

'Your father what?'

'My father.'

'Your father?'

'My father has.'

'Your father has what?'

'One.'

'Your father has one what?'

'Photo.'

'Photo?'

'A small one. One of those three-by-fours.'

'Your father?'

'He has one.'

'A photo of what?'

'Of her. A small photo. Hidden in his wallet.'

'A photo of your mother?'

'Just one. That's the only one I've seen.'

'Your mother.'

'I took his wallet to pinch some money.'

'Does he never give you any?'

'I saw it. A tiny one: a three-by-four.'

'He keeps it in—'

'She was dark. Thin. Teeth sticking out a bit. An identity photo. The only one I've ever seen of her.'

'You don't have any others?'

'I don't remember her.'

'Didn't you manage to—'

'When I think of her—'

'Yes?'

'I think of that photo. Hidden in my father's wallet. It's not the same as remembering.'

He fell silent. Eduardo didn't know what to say next either.

'If that crazy old man hadn't appeared,' Paulo went on, 'we would have find—'

'Found,' Eduardo corrected him, glad to be back on safer ground.

'*Found* something.'

'We found the condoms.'

'We've got piles of them at home.'

'Your father and brother are always going with prostitutes. They have to use condoms with them, or they'll catch a disease.'

'Was it your grandfather who told you that? The crazy grandfather?'

Eduardo couldn't remember. He thought he had read about it. But where would it have been possible for him to read about prostitutes and diseases? He couldn't recall any book talking about things like that. Or newspaper. Or magazine. Not even in Carlos Zéfiro's dirty mags that he sometimes snitched from the kiosk when he was paying for the German fashion and dressmaking publications his mother ordered. It probably was his grandfather.

'The day he took you to the red-light district?'

'Possibly. Didn't you know that prostitutes give you diseases?'

'Yes, I did. Antonio told me.'

'Well, then?'

'Yes, you need condoms if you go with prostitutes. You have to wear one. But the dentist . . . why do you think he needed so many?'

'So as not to have children. So that his wife wouldn't get pregnant.'

'How do you know that?'

'We have them at home.'

'You never said.'

'We have them.'

'Where did you find them?'

'I saw them.'

'Where?'

'In the same bedside table where my father keeps his revolver.'

'What revolver?'

'He has a revolver. From the days when he had to guard the railway.'

'You never told me.'

'I didn't think of it.'

'Does he leave the drawer open?'

'No, locked.'

'So how come you saw it?'

'I opened it, didn't I?'

'How?'

'With a bit of wire.'

'You know how to open a lock without a key?'

'Yes.'

'How did you learn that?'

'I just did.'

'And the rubbers were there? In the locked drawer?'

'That's right.'

'Your mother and father use them? So as not to have kids?
They're still . . .'

'I don't want to talk about it.'

'You were the one who said you had condoms at home.'

'I don't like to talk about it.'

'All right. But we could have find . . . found . . . more things
if that crazy old man hadn't appeared.'

'Yes.'

'Yes.'

Silence again. Paulo sat with his back to him. Eduardo
heard a sharp cry, but couldn't tell which bird made the
sound. He thought it might have been a flycatcher. He was
suddenly overwhelmed by the memory of the woman with
dark thighs, fleshy lips parted over dazzling white teeth, her
arms flung wide. He couldn't help crying out:

'She was pretty. Really pretty.'

His face felt hot. He thought he must be blushing, and was embarrassed. Paulo said nothing: perhaps he hadn't heard.

The image of the tall, blonde woman filled his mind. Wrapped him in an unwelcome embrace. He could see the streaks of mud on her face. And on her body. Blood. Cuts. On her hands, her breast, her neck. Stab wounds. Stains. Slime. A breast. Only one.

'Why did he chop her breast off?'

His question seemed to hang in mid-air. Paulo still said nothing.

'I don't understand. I can understand stabbing someone. I can understand killing them. I don't know why he killed, but I understand. But to cut her breast off? Why? What for?'

Paulo didn't reply. Eduardo stared straight in front of him. He thought about getting up and going for a swim. But he didn't move. He heard the same sharp cries. Like shrieks. Even without seeing them he was sure this time: they were fly-catchers. They sounded ominous.

'Eduardo . . .'

He had never heard Paulo's voice at such a low pitch.

'What is it?'

'Do you remember the cowboy films we saw?'

Paulo's big, black eyes were fixed on him.

'Which film?'

'Any of them. The ones where the Red Indians attack the palefaces' wagons.'

'What about them?'

'When they kill the whites.'

'In the end, it's the whites who kill all of them.'

'Yes, they do. But when they surround the wagons and kill the white people, before the hero appears ... what do they take back to their tribe?'

'Weapons. Ammunition. Food. Anything they can find in the settlers' wagons.'

'No, Eduardo! They kill the whites and scalp them!'

'Yes, I know.'

'They tear off a piece of the enemy's body!'

'So what?'

'It's a trophy, Eduardo!'

'A what ...?'

'The breast, Eduardo!'

'The breast ...?'

'The dead woman's breast. It's a trophy!'

4

Anita's Birth

HE HAD ONLY just reached the lowest rung when the boys rushed over. The skinny one apologized, but said they needed to talk to him urgently. His darker-skinned friend, the one with the curly ringlets and flap ears, was staring at the rope. The old man protested, annoyed at their intrusion.

'You have to help us,' said the tall one.

Wiping his hands on his handkerchief, then putting it back in his pocket, the man did not even deign to look at Eduardo.

'Please,' Eduardo added. 'We really need you.'

'We've discovered an important lead. The most important!'

'Not a lead, Paulo. A trophy.'

'That's right! The murderer wanted a trophy.'

'Like the redskins!' explained Eduardo, sure that the reference to the Indians of the Wild West would make sense, but unsure if it was the darkness under the trees or the old man's squint that made it impossible to tell which direction he was looking in.

He realized that neither of the old man's eyes stayed fixed

on one spot. Each of them seemed to move independently. If his right eye was looking slightly upwards, then the left one pointed to one side. And vice versa. The one that pointed towards the side, whether it was the left or the right, gave the impression of being stable. Or almost. All of a sudden, it would start to move again, uncoordinated with the other one. For a brief moment it seemed as though they were parallel to one another. Only for them to drift apart again.

The old man didn't even seem to be listening as he hid the end of the rope, with the ladder perched among the tree branches. Paulo thought he should explain further.

'When the Red Indians defeat the palefaces who've invaded their lands, they scalp them.'

'As a proof of victory.'

'Did you hear?'

'With the dentist's wife, the proof of victory was . . .'

Eduardo didn't manage to finish the sentence. The old man turned his back on them and walked off. Not knowing what to do, Eduardo didn't move.

'Whoever killed her . . .' he tried again.

He couldn't go on. He felt like an idiot. The invisible boy. The invisible boy who was no use to adults. The useless, invisible, idiotic boy to this particular adult. The idiotic, invisible, useless boy to all adults. His heart was pounding. He was gasping for breath.

Paulo ran alongside the old man for a few steps. He started and stopped a few phrases about cowboys and Indians, settlers and ambushes, victories and scalps, then gave up. He fell silent, and turned back to his friend. Spreading his arms wide, he shrugged: what now? This wasn't the reaction they had imagined, or counted on, to continue their search for the real murderer. They weren't expecting this indifference. What now? What now? What do we do now?

All at once, unconsciously, Eduardo could feel a hot wave spreading over first his face and then his whole body. It was followed by a loud shout that took him by surprise and made Paulo stare at him wide-eyed.

'Catch him! Catch the old man running away!'

Eduardo's greatest surprise came when he realized the shouts were coming from inside him. From his throat. It was his voice he could hear, loud and piercing in a way he had never heard before, roaring in the silent night.

'Look! An old man escaping!'

After a minute's astonishment, Paulo joined in, as enthusiastic as a child with a new toy:

'Stop him! Catch the fugitive!'

The man came to a halt. Both the boys were shouting at the top of their voices. He turned round. They carried on shouting. He stared at them. They were still shouting. He stood with hands on hips, in the attitude adults adopt to get children to obey without having to say anything. He was demanding they be quiet.

Normally Eduardo would have obeyed, because he was a reasonable sort, and because that was how he had been brought up. Paulo would probably have done the same, not because it was in his nature, but because this was how he had learned to behave, like a wary creature that had the memory of his father's brutality imprinted on his mind. But together, treated with what they saw as disdainful arrogance, the anger of one complemented the other's bitterness. This gave them the strength to openly defy an adult for the first time in their lives. They continued shouting.

A light went on in a nearby house. A dog started to bark in the distance.

'Sshh! Be quiet!' the man ordered them.

They shouted louder and louder, calling him a decrepit old man, a lunatic, a crazy fugitive, an idiotic escapee, anything and everything they could think of to insult him.

'Shut up! That's enough!'

His imperious tone only made Eduardo and Paulo the more indignant. The words they were shouting no longer made any sense. They were nothing more than abusive roars.

'Silence! Shut your mouths! You'll wake everyone up!'

The barking intensified. Now there were at least two dogs, then a third joined in. A veranda light came on at the end of the street. The old man came towards them with surprising agility, fists clenched. When he was close, Paulo took a step towards him, still shouting defiantly.

'Old maaan! Escaped from the home!'

'Be quiet now! Both of you!'

Before Eduardo and Paulo could redouble their efforts, he added in a low voice:

'Please.'

The kids glanced at each other.

'Please,' the old man repeated. 'Don't shout.'

Their gesture of revolt had been justified. It had made them feel good, and they weren't ready to make peace yet. They started shrieking again. But not for long. The old man's next words and the sincerity behind them made them pause.

'The nuns mustn't know I climb out every night,' he begged them.

He spread his hands and arms, in a clear sign of surrender.

'Please. They'd throw me out.'

Eduardo had never known an adult plead with him in this way. Paulo, who was more practical, asked the old man defiantly:

'What do we get if we stop?'

'What do you want?'

'Help,' Eduardo was quick to say.

'To solve the crime,' added Paulo.

'To prove the dentist isn't the killer.'

'The dentist. It wasn't him.'

The old man gestured for them to be quiet. He pointed all round him.

'I mustn't be seen. Let's get out of the middle of the street.'

They went back close to the wall.

'You're just a couple of kids.'

'We isn't . . .' Paulo corrected himself. 'We're not kids.'

'We'll soon be thirteen.'

'I'm a retired teacher, not a detective.'

'But you went to the dentist's house to investigate.'

'We saw you.'

'I only want to get out of this home occasionally. To have a quiet drink and a chat. I'm not sleepy. We old folk don't sleep a lot.'

'Paulo and I found the body. By the lake.'

'It was covered in blood! Filthy! Stab wounds all over!'

'It can't have been the dentist.'

'He scalped her breast!'

'He scalped what?'

'Don't you watch cowboy films?'

'I never go to Hollywood films,' said the old man, pronouncing 'Oliwud' with a strong north-eastern accent. 'They're Manichaeist.'

'What does a "Manichaeist" mean?'

'I'll look it up in the dictionary, Paulo. We want to prove the dentist is innocent.'

'But the husband confessed to the murder, boys.'

'He couldn't have done it! He's old! You can't imagine how big she was!'

'Appearances are deceptive. You'll learn that sooner or later. Nothing in this country is what it seems. And this city is a microcosm of Brazil.'

Paulo made a mental note: 'microcosm'. Yet another word to look up in Eduardo's dictionary.

'Old men are capable of great atrocities,' the man added.

Another word to look up the next day: 'atrocities'.

'Have you ever heard of Getúlio Vargas? Josef Stalin?'

'Of Getúlio, yes.'

'Vargas, the man who created the labour laws.'

'Getúlio Vargas's henchmen tore out my fingernails. One by one. In cold blood. They tortured me. Killed my friends. That same heroic Vargas you study at school. The martyr of the republic. It was thanks to us that Getúlio came to power. We believed in him. The father of the poor. Vargas betrayed us. Like Stalin.'

Then he went on talking about deaths, persecutions and massacres in the Soviet Union. Eduardo was curious, because history had always interested him, but Paulo was not so pleased: to him this was an unnecessary digression. He interrupted the old man.

'Are you going to help us or not?'

'Under duress.'

'What's that?'

'I'm being blackmailed. Either I collaborate or you give me away, is that right?'

'But you yourself started an investigation,' Eduardo argued.

'Possibly.'

'We know we're not children. Neither Paulo nor me.'

'We're not.'

'But you adults still think we are.'

'You think that.'

'Just now you called us kids.'

'You did.'

'It's because you think Paulo and me are only kids that we can investigate lots of things about the dentist's wife's death, without attracting anyone's attention.'

'Because nobody is going to pay us any attention.'

'That's why I said we can go unnoticed, because of our age.'

'But there are other things we can't do, if you know what I mean.'

The white-haired man waited for Paulo to go on. The two

boys were waiting for an answer. After a few moments' silence, it was the old man who spoke.

'So, what then . . . ?'

'Well, then . . . you're older, and have more experience . . . There are things you can do that we can't.'

'Such as?'

'For the moment, I don't know. When they crop up, we'll see.'

'One for all and all for one?' Paulo urged.

'You and us. The three of us, you, Paulo and me, if we work together, we could find things out and—'

'What exactly do you intend to do?' the old man cut in.

His question implied precise intentions the boys did not have. Instead, they were acting on a suspicion, nourished by countless films and melodramas they would soon not even remember the titles of, that the accepted version of who had killed the blonde woman was wrong. How could they admit this was all they suspected, and still manage to convince the old man to join them? Eduardo tried to find a good reason for him to do so, but couldn't. Neither of them could. So Eduardo would have to think up a lie. Right now. On the spot. A convincing one. But to invent a lie that would convince someone to reject a series of lies backed up by the whole city left him nonplussed. He said nothing. He couldn't find the words. Paulo stared at him anxiously. Once again, it was the old man who broke the silence.

'Well . . . ?'

'Just a minute,' Eduardo pleaded, trying to gain time.

'You two . . .'

'He's going to explain – aren't you, Eduardo?'

'We . . .' Eduardo began, but could not go on. He flushed.

'You want to go on investigating, just like you think you've been doing since the first night after the murder, when you broke into the dentist's house.'

Paulo tried to deny they had broken in, but the old man wouldn't let him. Then he said in a single breath, as though reciting a lesson learned by heart:

'You thought you could do everything on your own, but you've discovered that you can only make progress with my help, because you think you've found a lead, a clue that may or may not be important, which could be crucial in solving the murder, but which so far has not got you anywhere, because you don't know what to do with it. Is that what you're trying to tell me?'

'Yes . . .' Eduardo said grudgingly.

'You came to me, even though you think I'm a crazy old man, because you don't know who else to turn to.'

Neither of the boys knew what to say.

'Is that right, then? You two want to carry on investigating?'

'Yes, we want to!' said Eduardo, emboldened.

'We want to!' Paulo echoed him.

'Even if no one else is interested in finding out who the real murderer is?'

'So you don't think it was the dentist either?' asked Eduardo, almost shouting.

The old man stuffed his hands in his coat pockets, stared first at one of them, then the other, and asked:

'Do you know where birth certificates are kept?'

'In the city hall,' Paulo quickly replied.

'Inside the city hall, in the municipal archive,' Eduardo specified.

'Can you two get in there?'

'Of course,' said Paulo.

'Could you do it now?'

'At this time of night?' Eduardo said doubtfully. 'The archive is shut.'

'That's why I asked if you can get in.'

'Of course we can,' said Paulo.

'We can try.'

'We can get in anywhere! At any time of the day or night!'

The old man drew closer to them and whispered:

'OK, so let's get organized and share out the tasks.'

Paulo was the first to climb down. With the rope wrapped round his left foot, he let himself down bit by bit, steadying himself with his hands. His body swayed slightly from side to side, like a pendulum. He reached the floor with his right foot, and released the other one. When he was firmly on the ground, he looked around him.

The light from a streetlamp came in through two high sash windows and dusty blinds. Apart from a tall table and a roll-top desk, the entire room was taken up with metal shelves that ran round the walls, and stood in two rows in the centre. They were filled with big bound volumes. Numbers and dates were written in Roman numerals on their spines.

Paulo opened the nearest one. A quick glance was enough. He gave a thumbs-up in the direction of the wooden roof, where an open rectangle gave access to the basement. This was the room they were looking for.

Eduardo grasped the rope, wrapped it round one foot, and began his descent. He felt himself swaying more than he had expected. He carried on down. He reached the top of the shelves. The soft skin on the palms of his hands was stinging. He lost his balance: his foot came out of the rope, and his body started to turn. He saw the room spin and ended up head first. He fell to the floor, groaning. Paulo ran over to him.

'Are you hurt?'

'No, no,' replied Eduardo, more annoyed than injured.

'Did you break anything?'

'It was nothing. I slipped, that's all,' he insisted, beating the dust off his clothes. 'We're in the right place, aren't we?'

'I think so.'

Eduardo got hold of one of the volumes. He opened it.

'Yes, this is it. This is a register of births. Wedding and obituary certificates must be here too.'

'Obituary?'

'Death.'

'Ah . . . and what's this writing with the letter "m" then an "x", another "m" and . . .'

'It's a date. In Latin. We learned them in class.'

'Oh, yes. I didn't think they wrote things in Latin in Brazil.'

By examining the spines and the labels stuck on the shelves, it didn't take long for Eduardo to realize they would have to look elsewhere.

'These books are all from the last century.'

'Which one are we looking for?'

'The one for 1937. If Dona Anita was twenty-four when she died, she must have been born in 1937.'

'The old man said she got married very young.'

'At fifteen. If that's the case, it must be in the 1952 register. We need that too.'

They found the row for the 1930s, then the book with the birth registers for 1937. Between them, they took it over to one of the windows, laid it on the floor, and started to go through it. They reached the last page without finding any certificate in the name of Anita. They went back, page by page. Paulo thought they should have brought a torch. Eduardo ran his finger over the handwritten entries, shaking his head.

'No, no ... no. No. There's no Anita. There's Angela, Antonia, Aparecida, Apolonia, Almerinda ...'

Paulo suggested they look at the wedding certificates for 1952. Eduardo agreed, but did not take his eyes from the yellowing pages he had in front of him. He read out, in a low voice:

'Adelina, Adriana, Alfredina, Amarílis, Ana Beatriz, Ana Cristina, Ana Elisa, Ana Helena, Ana Isabel, Ana Lúcia, Ana Maria, Ana Olívia, Ana Paula, Ana Rita, Andralina ... Ane ... Anemona ...'

Paulo soon returned.

'So?'

'There's no register of the birth of any Anita in 1937.'

'Let me see,' said Paulo, pushing the 1952 volume towards Eduardo.

The room smelt of dust and mildew. It couldn't have been cleaned in a long time. The damp was beginning to upset Eduardo. He could feel a sneeze coming on. He covered his nose with both hands, held his breath, stared at the streetlamp outside. None of these tricks worked: he sneezed anyway. Dazzled by the bright light outside, for a few moments he couldn't read anything at all. He asked Paulo:

'Take a look here. See if you can find the dentist's name among the wedding certificates.'

'But I don't know his name. I only ever heard him called the dentist.'

'He's Dr Henrique something.'

'There's an Eriberto – without the "h".'

'No. If that dentist isn't Henrique, it's Ernesto. Or . . . Hélio?'

Paulo went on looking, but with no luck. Page after page.

'I can't find any Hélio. Or Ernesto. Or Henrique. There's an Umberto. Umberto Moreira.'

'No, not Umberto.'

'Heleno Costa?'

'No.'

'Amancio?'

'Possibly. Who did he marry?'

'Nanci Andrade.'

'No. Is there nobody married to an Anita?'

'Nobody. There's an Ana Viana who married Waldir Haddad. A Djalma Carvalho who married an Alice Felix. Luis Perrone married someone called Antonina Giuseppe. A Francisco Andrade who married Aparecida dos Santos.

Emanuel Gottschalk who married an Amélia Lobo. Ari Passos, who married Aurea Sanchez. And a Vanderlei Mendes who married someone called Ana Rita Mendonça. There's—'

'Wait!' said Eduardo. 'What name did you say?'

'Vanderlei.'

'Before that! What name did you read before him?'

'Ari Passos.'

'No! Before that!'

'Emanuel Gottschalk? Francisco Andrade? Luis Perrone?'

'Andrade! That's the dentist's name!'

'The dentist's surname?'

'I'm sure of it! Andrade!'

'His full name here is Francisco Clementino de Andrade Gomes.'

'Dr Andrade! That's the dentist.'

'That's impossible,' said Paulo, showing Eduardo the page. 'Look here: this Dr Andrade didn't marry an Anita, but an—'

They ran back to the square, where the old man was dozing on a bench near the bandstand. They were in such a rush to tell him their discoveries and not to lose the thread of their reasoning that they stumbled over the words. They were panting for breath.

'You were right,' Paulo began. The rope was wrapped round his shoulder.

'She didn't have a father.'

'Or a mother.'

'It was written there: girl without known parents.'

'The birth was registered by the nuns at the orphanage.'

'The girls' orphanage. There's another one in the city for boys. Nuns are in charge of them both. But I think they're from a different order to the ones at your home. They don't dress the same. The colour of their habits is—'

'She wasn't called Anita!' Paulo burst in.

'He means, the woman who Dr Andrade—'

'Doctor Andrade is the dentist's name. Francisco Clementino de Andrade Gomes.'

'. . . married.'

'Her name was Aparecida dos Santos!'

'Maria Aparecida dos Santos!'

'Aparecida is the one registered in 1937 by the nuns at the orphanage as the daughter of unknown parents,' explained Paulo.

'And Aparecida is the one who married Francisco Clementino de Andrade Gomes on 6 June 1952. Maria Aparecida dos Santos.'

'When she was fifteen.'

The old man reached for half a hand-rolled cigarette in his pocket, put it in his mouth. He took a box of matches out of his other pocket. He lit the cigarette, puffed on it. Blew the smoke up into the night air. He didn't once look at the boys.

'Fifteen,' Eduardo repeated. 'That was how old Aparecida was when she married the dentist. Just like they told you.'

'The dentist never married anyone called Anita.'

'He married Aparecida.'

'Anita doesn't exist!'

'We mean: she did exist . . .'

'Because that's what Aparecida came to be called.'

'They called her Anita.'

'Dona Anita.'

'Dr Andrade's wife.'

Eduardo was becoming worried by the old man's silence.

'Do you understand?'

'Did you hear?'

'Did you hear what we're saying?'

'The murdered woman had another name!'

'Aparecida!' Eduardo shouted. 'Aparecida!'

Another puff on the cigarette. The smoke rising slowly. His eyes pointing nowhere. Eduardo was exasperated.

'I almost broke a leg going down the rope! I could have broken it! Both of them! I could be crippled!'

'What about me?' said Paulo, not wanting to be left out when it came to describing the perils they had faced. 'I had to face rats, you know. Enormous great rats! Huge ones!'

He fell silent when he realized the old man was muttering something under his breath. Eduardo kept quiet too.

'In 1952,' they heard him say in almost a whisper, still not looking in their direction, 'the dentist must have been in his forties, well into them.'

The lighted tip of the cigarette was close to his fingers. Eduardo was going to warn the old man, when he heard him say, in a slightly louder voice:

'Anita . . . or Aparecida, was fifteen . . .'

He stubbed the cigarette out with his shoe.

'How old are you two?'

'Twelve,' Paulo said quickly.

'I'm going to be thirteen,' Eduardo boasted. 'In ten months' time.'

'My birthday's earlier. In January.'

'Only a month earlier.'

'Forty-eight days!'

The old man stared at them. Or perhaps only in their general direction.

'It doesn't make sense.'

'I'm not as tall, but I'm older,' Paulo insisted. 'And I'm going to grow. My brother's almost one metre eighty tall. So is my father.'

'However mercenary, however venal those nuns were ...' The white-haired old man went on muttering, as though talking to himself. 'Even so, it doesn't make sense.'

'What are you talking about?' asked Eduardo.

The matchbox came out of the pocket again. The stub of the cigarette was placed inside it, and then the box went back into the jacket pocket.

'How did the nuns at the orphanage allow a ... a girl who was only fifteen to marry a man of almost fifty? I've never heard of anything so ridiculous, even in a Mexican melodrama.'

'Perhaps the dentist was her father?' Paulo suggested.

'And he told the nuns the secret!' Eduardo elaborated on his friend's fantasy. 'And they got married so that she could inherit his fortune.'

The old man stood up and walked off towards the bandstand.

'A man who's a bachelor until well into his forties,' he murmured, 'suddenly marries a girl of fifteen . . .'

The two boys followed him. They embarked on a whirl of extravagant theories.

'Dr Andrade was in love with her mother, but she died . . .' said Eduardo.

'. . . he lived with her for ten years, she betrayed him constantly, but that didn't bother him . . .'

'The dentist killed her mother.'

Now it was Paulo's turn. 'No! He killed her father! Then, out of remorse, he married the daughter!'

'. . . and he paid no attention to the gossip going all round the city . . .'

Paulo had a new hypothesis:

'Her father was a Nazi!'

Eduardo joined in:

'And her mother died in a concentration camp!'

'. . . ignoring the malicious comments whispered by the sanctimonious faithful when they went arm in arm to mass on Sundays . . .'

'She was the daughter of a nun and a priest!' Paulo fantasized.

'. . . pretending not to see the lascivious looks when he crossed this square with her, out for their Sunday promenade . . .'

'She was his youngest sister!' suggested Eduardo.

'. . . sleeping alone at night in his single bed . . .'

'The nuns! It was the nuns who killed her!' Paulo crowed.

'... while she was out with other men. Always much older men.'

'She was the lover of the priest who was the nuns' lover too!' said Eduardo.

By now they were inside the bandstand. The boys were walking round in circles with the old man. He came to a halt, and they looked at him expectantly.

'I don't know about the priest. But my friends in the bar told me she went with the mayor. And with the textile factory owner. With the estate owners. With all the city's powerful men. And always, always, with men much older than she was. As if they were passing her from hand to hand. Did you see everything there was in the drawers at the dentist's house?'

Eduardo wasn't sure, but he thought they had.

'Did you go to the maid's room?'

Paulo said there wasn't one, and that the couple didn't have any domestic help.

'Did you take anything? Any jewellery?'

'We're not thieves!'

'I didn't find any,' the old man went on, ignoring Paulo's protest. 'Nothing. No rings, bracelets, not even a medallion. I've been told she never wore any. Only her wedding ring. How is it that the wife of an important man doesn't wear jewellery? A necklace, earrings, even a brooch. And they didn't have a maid?'

'Perhaps the husband was stingy?' Eduardo suggested.

'Tight-fisted!' Paulo concluded.

'A miser!'

'Possibly. Even so ...'

The old man did not finish his sentence. His eyes roamed over the empty square. The shadows engulfed the outlines of the ancient trees, framing them like a dark bell-jar, as if the world beyond did not exist. Eventually he asked:

'Did none of those rich men ever give her anything?'

Neither Paulo nor Eduardo knew what to say. Or even if the old man expected them to reply. Only adults were familiar with the world of degradation and rewards he was talking of. Then another question occurred to Paulo. He asked the white-haired man: what if she didn't want to own anything?

5

The People Out There

HE COULD SEE the outline of young breasts, some of them just starting to bud, nestling in brassieres. A glimpse of backs, a flash of arms. Bare feet pulling on white socks and canvas pumps. Navy-blue uniform skirts being taken off, white gym skirts being put on. The smooth skin of pink or tanned thighs, some of them freckled.

But it was as though he wasn't really seeing any of this. He didn't even feel the thrill of transgression. Why not, if he was enjoying a sight the other boys didn't have? Wasn't this a pleasure only he and Eduardo shared after discovering this secret place? Weren't they in the forbidden tower again? Hadn't they managed to climb on to the school roof without being seen, among all its rat droppings, dust, bits of cloth, electric cables and building debris. Wasn't the girls' changing room down below? Weren't they spying on them through the grating of the ventilation shaft? And yet. And yet. He wasn't really there. He could see girls. Young girls. But he was thinking about a woman. Her. Anita. Aparecida.

Without saying a word, he turned to his friend, who was staring downwards. He wanted to tell him what was going through his mind, but couldn't really explain. He remained quiet, until he heard Eduardo whispering to him. Eduardo was still peering at the changing room. Paulo thought he must have been mistaken, and his thoughts returned to Anita. Aparecida. Then again he heard Eduardo asking him something. Paulo wasn't sure what he had said.

'If I was what?'

'Poor.'

'But I am poor.'

'No, Paulo, I mean really poor,' said Eduardo, his eyes still on the activity down below. 'With no home. No father, no mother, nothing to eat, no—'

'But I'm going to be rich. I'm going to study, go to university and become a famous scientist. I've already told you that.'

'You told me you were going to be a writer.'

'And a scientist.'

'But if you were poor: if you were a really poor girl . . .'

'White or black?'

'What difference does it make? Poor is poor. It's the same for everyone.'

'No it isn't, Eduardo. It's much worse if the girl is black. A white girl could be adopted, live with a family, go to school and all the rest. A black girl is going to live and die in an orphanage.'

'But Anita was white, and no one adopted her.'

'Look down there. Do you see any black girls?'

'No, but . . .'

'How many black friends do you have?'

'You don't have any either!'

'My father doesn't have any black friends. Does yours? Does your mother have any black customers? None of my brother's friends are black. There's only one black girl in our class.'

'Are you a racist?'

'Why do you say that?'

'Because of the way you're talking . . .'

The last girls left the changing room. Eduardo and Paulo sneaked down from their hiding place. They soon returned to their discussion.

'It's true though, isn't it, Eduardo? The teachers are white. The inspectors are white. The headmaster is white. The mayor is white, so is the police chief. The priest is white . . .'

They went down the corridor to the sports yard. They could hear the PE teacher shouting, giving instructions. They headed for the boys' changing room: Paulo pulled off his tie and lifted his shirt out of his trousers, balancing books and notebooks in his other hand.

'If you were a woman married to a rich man, wouldn't you like to have jewels and—' said Eduardo.

'The dentist isn't rich.'

'He's not poor either. He's got that house, he has antique furniture and those statues, he's got pictures, and his consulting room . . .'

'But he doesn't have a maid.'

'And isn't that strange? A man in his position, a dentist, a friend of all the other leading figures in the city? And with that big house that must have belonged to some rich ancestor, stuffed with all the things we saw? Why no maid? To allow your own wife to cook, wash, iron . . .'

'I doubt if she did the washing.'

'I bet she did, Paulo.'

'Not washing the clothes.'

'All right then, so she had a washerwoman who went there to wash the clothes for her, and iron them. But she had to look after the house.'

'All women look after their houses.'

'All women have help. It's only if they're very poor that they don't. My mother has someone who comes twice a week.'

'And they know everything that goes on in the house.'

Eduardo paused, thinking he had made a great discovery. Paulo went into the changing room on his own. He dived into the chaos of a couple of dozen sweaty, noisy boys who had just come in from a game of football. They were too busy shouting opinions and insults to notice the arrival of a dark-haired boy with crumpled clothes, or of another skinny, pale-faced one a few moments later.

'What did they get up to that they didn't want even a maid to know?' Eduardo wondered.

'Black magic. Spells with the teeth he pulled.'

'If you were the lover of rich men . . .' Eduardo went on, ignoring Paulo's suggestion, 'wouldn't you ask them for things?'

'Money?'

'No, not money. Presents.'

'What kind of presents?'

'The old man mentioned jewels. Rich men give their lovers jewels.'

'She didn't have any. We talked about that yesterday, remember?'

A new group burst into the changing room: a volleyball team. Some were laughing, others pushing and shoving, all of them shouting. They were pleased they had just won their game. Eduardo was tying his running shoes when a big, tall boy almost knocked him over on his way to the showers. The boy didn't even notice.

Eduardo finished changing. Now he was wearing blue shorts and running shoes with a white T-shirt and stockings. He folded his other clothes and stowed them in one of the yellow Formica lockers lining the wall. He locked it, put the key band round his wrist. Paulo, who was wearing identical sports kit, threw his clothes into the bottom locker, but didn't bother to lock it. As he was heading to the exit, Eduardo took him by the arm:

'You say you're poor . . .'

'I am. You know that.'

'But you want to be rich . . .'

'Don't you? Everybody does.'

'That's right! Can't you see? That's why we can't understand Dona Anita.'

'Aparecida.'

'Dona Aparecida. Everyone wants to be rich, and yet she . . . She only went with rich people; she even changed her name – she changed it from a poor person's to a rich woman's name . . . she must have wanted to be like them. She must have wanted to have things of her own, nice things, things every woman wants. She was the lover of the factory owner, the mayor, of the . . .'

'Rich people.'

'So she ought to have wanted . . . things, shouldn't she? She ought to have . . .'

But yet again he couldn't complete his reasoning. Yet again he came up against the brick wall of the adult world, behind which operated rules beyond his comprehension. They walked on in silence.

'There are people who don't want anything,' said Paulo. 'My father's like that. He's got no ambition, no desires, nothing.'

'But he's old. He's at least forty.'

'Forty-six.'

'There's no point wanting anything by the time you're forty-six. You're not going to change anything at that age. But the dentist's wife was twenty-four. She wasn't old yet. So why . . . ?'

'Have you noticed that all we do is ask questions and more questions?'

By now they were out in the corridor again, indistinguishable from the other boys in sports outfits pushing their way along to the yard. They mixed with their classmates. The girls were lined up in an orderly fashion, in pairs, threesomes, quartets. They were giggling or whispering in each other's ears, while the boys glanced at them out of the corner of their eyes and gathered on the far side of the yard. The PE teacher's assistant soon came to organize them in groups according to how tall they were. This always annoyed

Paulo, because he was inevitably put with younger boys.

'We could go back to the scene of the crime and . . .' said Eduardo. 'And . . .'

He couldn't think how to finish his sentence.

'Again?'

'How about the dentist's house then?'

'Once more?'

'The orphanage?'

'What for?'

'To find a lead.'

'What lead?'

'That's where she was brought up.'

'That's not a lead. She was a child. She was still called Aparecida. The blonde woman the rich men knew was born later. And besides, they wouldn't let us in.'

'Perhaps we could go back to the municipal archive. Maybe there's some secret document about the dentist?'

'If it's secret, how are we going to know it exists?'

'We could look.'

'In which bit of the archive?'

'In the . . . in the . . .'

'In the what?'

No argument could outweigh Paulo's annoyance at the sight of their younger classmates lining up spontaneously like a trained flock of sheep.

A burly adult in a tracksuit came out of the corridor and trotted over to them. Everyone fell silent.

'What if our old man . . .' Eduardo started to say, when he saw the assistant coming over. He had to be quick, before he and Paulo were separated. 'Have you taken your first communion?'

Paulo didn't understand.

'First communion, catechism, religious studies? Do you know Father Basilio, the one from that little church near your house?'

Lined up with the smallest pupils, Paulo had to keep his eyes to the front, as all the boys in the line were doing. He couldn't be sure, but he thought he heard Eduardo whisper something more about that ridiculous question concerning catechism classes.

The nun took two glasses from the tray with the liqueur bottles, filled them with the golden, sticky liquid, and brought them over to the armchair where the white-haired man was seated.

'Rose liqueur,' she explained, holding out one of the glasses. 'Prepared by our sisters here in the orphanage.'

He hesitated. Do priests drink? Could he accept it?

'You'll like it,' she insisted, without being sure exactly which direction his eyes were pointing in. 'It's very smooth.'

The cassock was uncomfortable. The coarse material was itchy, and made him sweat. There was not much furniture in the director of the Santa Rita de Cássia orphanage's window-less office. Faded paint was flaking off the walls. There were four battered metal filing cabinets with patches of rust on them.

'We depend on donations,' said the nun, noticing him gazing erratically around the room. 'As you can see, there haven't been that many.'

'I wasn't . . .'

'Everything has become very expensive since they built Brasilia. The inflation in recent years has hit us badly. In hard times, charity is the first thing people cut back on.'

She brought the glass closer to him.

'It has a very delicate flavour, Father . . .'

'Basilio!' he quickly added, using the name of the priest whose cassock Paulo and Eduardo had stolen.

He took the glass, sipped the liquid.

'Father Basilio da Gama. As I was saying, I was her confessor. Dona Anita's, that is.'

The bloom of youth and health on her black skin was emphasized by the starched white bandeau round her face. She was still standing next to him.

'I never knew the lady. Anita. Or Aparecida. That's her name in our files. As you perhaps were aware. Were you? I imagine so. I never saw her. I don't know many people in the city. Not yet. I've only been director here for five months. I came from Andrelândia: do you know it? It's about three hundred kilometres from here, in the state of Minas Gerais. I know few people here. I go out very little. We go out very little. Our work is inside the orphanage.'

'So you don't know anything about her?'

The liqueur was sweet, cloying. He drank it down in one gulp: it was easier that way.

'On the contrary. I think I know a lot. Would you like a little more?'

Without waiting for a reply, she took his glass and walked over to the drinks tray. She filled it, and brought it to him. She had not touched her own.

'As her confessor, you must have heard of the . . . In confession that lady must have told you the . . . hmm . . . let's say the . . . most physical part of the life she led. The carnal aspect. I'm not judging, Father Basilio. Let's be clear. I'm not doing that. That's not for me to do. And I wouldn't do so. No, absolutely not. Besides, I never even saw her.'

'But you said that . . .' he suggested, after downing his second glass of liqueur.

'That I know a lot about her. Yes. Apart from all the inevitable gossip that has reached me since the murder. Yes. I think I do. Some more liqueur?'

She served him without waiting for his agreement. She had still not touched her own glass.

'Have you ever had to deal with orphans?'

'With orphans? Really, I . . .'

'The girl inmates learn to sew, embroider, darn, wash, iron, clean, cook . . . They also study, of course. But the aim of a girl's education in an orphanage is to make her useful. Useful. That's the word most often heard in here. Useful. A useful education. To turn her into a useful woman. So that she can survive in the outside world when she has to leave here.'

He picked up his glass, and let the liqueur roll round his tongue before swallowing it. It didn't seem so cloying any more.

'The world is a frightening thing for a girl brought up in here, Father Basilio. I imagine you've never had to cope with children from homes like this, have you?'

Not knowing what he should say, he held out the empty glass. The nun took it, but didn't move.

'To anyone brought up in a home, the world outside . . .'

She twisted the glass in her fingers, as though measuring it. Placing it on the table by his armchair, she brought the bottle over and filled his glass again.

'To a girl from an orphanage, Father Basilio, all the people out there seem rich. Well educated, well dressed. All of them. Sure of themselves. Sure of their place in the world. All of them. Better prepared for life. More deserving. More worthwhile. Prettier, healthier, happier. In short, they seem . . .'

She handed him the glass.

'Better.'

She smiled wanly at him.

'Faced with life outside, a girl has two options. One is to leave here. To go out into a world that enchants and terrifies her. Entrusted to one of those people who are better than she is. To protect her. Give her a home. Look after her. Transform her. To reveal this world full of pleasures and possibilities to her. The other . . .'

She hesitated.

'The other . . . ?'

'The other is never to leave.'

She fell silent, standing still in front of him. An awkward silence filled the room.

'Sister, you . . .'

'I was brought up in an orphanage, near Belo Horizonte.'

She raised her glass to her lips, tilted it slightly, took a little sip.

'I'm not ashamed of that. On the contrary.'

'You said before that—'

She interrupted him.

'This is a strange city. Have you been here long?'

'No, not long. I came to the St Simon home a little more than . . .' He paused, realizing the mistake he had made.

'Ah, you work with elderly people. Are they part of your parish?'

'You could put it like that,' he replied, shifting uncomfortably in his chair. 'But you were saying that . . .'

'This city. I don't know if you are aware of it. Here people are . . . Not all of them. It's simply an impression. That I had. Have. Not everyone. No. Here they are a bit . . . Some of them. A little . . . In this region, you know . . . Before the textile factory existed. Before that. When this region was one of the main coffee-producing regions in Brazil. As you know, there were big coffee estates here. In the last century. Throughout this region. During the first and second empires. The coffee barons. Huge fortunes. Large plantations. With lots of . . . slaves. They depended on them. On slaves. On slave labour. All this region. It was one of the biggest purchasers of . . . what did they call them? Specimens. That was what the estate owners called the men and women bought in Africa and shipped here. Like my grandparents. Or great-grandparents. Specimens. When slavery finished, these specimens and their owners . . .'

What was she driving at? Why was she saying all this? Why didn't she look at him? Why was she hesitating?

'Anyone who has bought specimens,' she said, transferring the glass to her other hand, 'possibly doesn't much like the idea of living alongside them. As equals. Not here. In this city. I don't think they are accustomed to it. As if it had never happened. Never happened to them . . . A chattel, a possession, isn't a person. A specimen isn't a person. Will never be seen as one. Don't you agree?'

She shifted her glass back to her right hand. Stiff, her body not moving in the slightest. Only her shoulders seemed to have lifted a little.

'You're dark-skinned, Father Basilio. That's acceptable. Please, don't be offended.'

'I don't . . .'

'A dark skin is acceptable. There are dark-skinned Portuguese. People with Moorish ancestors. Africans, as you know. But their descendants were born in Europe. They mixed with Romans, Spaniards, Goths, Visigoths, who knows what? But "specimens" are different. They're still not accustomed here to living alongside people of my colour. With people of my colour in a position such as mine. You, for example. No, don't deny it. You're obviously not comfortable in my presence. I can tell. Your reluctance to take the glass I offered you. The way you're shifting in the chair. The cassock you're constantly fidgeting with. And you're sweating.'

'It's not that, sister . . .'

'It's a normal reaction. Don't worry, I'm not offended. There are others that are much more . . . obvious. Aggressive.

More hostile. From higher-ranking people, if you follow me? The bishop himself seemed . . . Are you on good terms with the monsignor?'

'The bishop? He . . . we . . . Our relations are, let's say . . . the bishop and I . . . We hardly see each other.'

'The bishop comes from a traditional family of this region. Very intelligent. Very refined. He has a keen sense of humour. Has he never commented on your accent?'

'My accent?'

'I suspect you come from the north-east.'

'I was born in Sergipe. But I left for Pernambuco when I was little. I never realized that my accent . . .'

'Before I came here, I had never been out of the state of Minas Gerais. I've no idea if racial mixes are acceptable in the north-east. Here . . . d'you know that even some girls in the orphanage seemed rather hostile? Even the ones the same colour as me? I'm the first black woman they haven't seen working in the kitchen or cooking. They can't understand it. If that girl, or that woman, Aparecida or Anita, had been white, perhaps things would have been easier for her. But your glass is empty.'

She took the liqueur bottle over to him, and poured him another glass.

'Wasn't Anita . . . ?'

'White? No. In the orphanage's records she is described as "pale mulatto", she said, going over to one of the filing cabinets. She opened a drawer and took out a cardboard file stuffed with pieces of paper and documents.

'Pale mulatto?'

'Pale mulatto. As you know, that's a euphemism for a mixed-race person with light-coloured skin. Look at this file. It's the earliest mention of the girl, completed when the baby was brought here. As you can see, she still doesn't have a name.'

'I haven't got my glasses. What does this line say?'

'Colour of eyes. Green.'

'She was . . .'

'Pale mulatto, with green eyes.'

'A light-skinned mulatto. Who could pass for white. And with green eyes.'

'Now, her brother is registered as . . .'

'Brother?'

'Brother. Renato. They're in the same file. Renato was registered as black. Some more liqueur?'

They descended the concrete tiers of seats through the gaps among a group of fans. On the pitch, a team in blue shirts was playing against another in yellow. The old man did not recognize the game, but it looked like a more violent version of football. Paulo, who was in front of Eduardo, turned and said something about a regional semi-final of five-a-side, but the old man could not hear him in the crowd of youngsters who were shouting, waving scarves and banners.

The two boys were the first to reach the pitch, and stood watching the match while the white-haired man was still struggling down through the spectators, hindered by the height of the rows used for seats and the lack of handrails.

The three of them finally reached the blue team's substitutes' bench. Paulo and Eduardo spoke to a youngster with a military crew-cut. Leaning over to hear them, he shook his head, and pointed to the yellow team's substitutes on the far side of the pitch, under a corrugated iron shelter.

They rushed round the stand, treading on the feet of complaining spectators. By the time the old man caught up with them, they had already got the information they were after. The three of them talked together, then went to the entrance to the changing rooms. They huddled together again, and the white-haired man walked into the changing-room area on his own.

It stank of urine, damp, sweat. The lights were switched off. Thanks to the floodlights on the pitch, he could make out a corridor. His eyes grew accustomed to the darkness. The corridor led to a big room with cubicles. Tiled walls. Clothes hanging from hooks. A couple of wooden benches. A urinal. A corner with low partition walls, which he assumed must contain toilets. A row of showers. The greenish stain of damp like a map drawn on the ceiling. Drops of dirty water dripping from it, forming a large puddle he could not avoid.

The old man walked on his heels through it. He had almost reached one of the benches when he stumbled against a bucket. The hollow sound echoed off the walls, faded away in the darkness. He froze: he thought he had heard whispering. He could make out a different smell in the air: something new and fresh he couldn't identify. He stood still for a few moments, but all he could hear was water dripping into the puddle, and the muffled sounds of the game outside.

He was about to leave when he was sure he heard a human sound – possibly a gasp, or someone panting or whispering. He held his breath and waited. Once again, all he heard was the water dripping into the puddle and distant sounds from the pitch. Without knowing exactly why, he decided to go on to the far end of the changing room. He began opening the cubicle doors. First one, then the next, a third and a fourth. Before he could open the fifth, a looming figure gripped his wrist and stopped him.

'Renato?' asked the old man, when he had recovered from his fright.

The black youth did not reply. He still had hold of the old man's wrist, and was squeezing it. All he was wearing was a jockstrap.

'I'm looking for Renato.'

He was tall. The old man had to glance upwards to see his face. An adolescent. A strong jaw and prominent cheekbones that contrasted with his delicate nose and fine nostrils. His close-set eyes were staring at him hostilely.

'Are you . . . Renato?'

Instead of answering, the youngster grabbed his other wrist, and came even closer. The old man caught a whiff of the mysterious fragrance once more, this time mixed with the sweat from the young man's body.

'Are you Renato?'

'What of it?' he snapped.

'Renato dos Santos?'

'What do you want?'

The old man was certain now: his skin was impregnated with the fragrance. It came from him. He smelt of sweat and perfume.

'I need to talk to you.'

'I can't right now.'

'It'll be quick.'

'Some other time.'

'It's a rapid matter.'

'Come back in a while.'

'I won't be long.'

'Later.'

'It's about your sister.'

'I don't have a sister.'

'It's about Anita.'

The old man thought he detected a flicker in the young man's eyes, and the pressure on his wrists grew. He repeated himself.

'It's about your sister. I need some information.'

The youth didn't move.

'Information. About some things that don't fit. About Anita.'

He could feel the grip on his wrists tighten still further.

'About Aparecida.'

The youngster moved slightly away from him.

'I was at the orphanage this afternoon.'

The athletic figure's breathing seemed more agitated.

'At the orphanage.'

He could hear him breathing in and out.

'I saw the files.'

The young man looked away.

'I saw the files, Renato. Yours and hers.'

Without releasing his wrists or withdrawing, the youngster said out loud:

'You'd better go.'

The cubicle door opened. The fragrance reached the old man before he saw her. Lavender. Coming from her.

She kept her head down as she came out, adjusting her bra and buttoning up her blouse above the pleated skirt. She glanced up quickly at the old man as she scooped her fair hair into a ponytail. She could not have been more than fifteen.

The old man heard her walking off down the corridor, the noise from the pitch when she opened the door, then the water dripping into the puddle after she had gone out.

'Who are you?' asked the youth, letting go of his wrists.

'I only want to help,' the old man began, rubbing his sore arms.

'Help with what? Help whom?'

'Help to discover . . .'

'Discover what?'

'The person responsible for your sister's death.'

'I don't have a sister,' the young man snapped, moving away towards a shower. He turned the knob, and the water came gushing out.

'I was at the orphanage this afternoon, Renato.'

The youth began to soap himself.

'Where your sister was brought up.'

The old man had to shout over the noise of the shower.

'Until she became Anita.'

Renato pushed his head under the jet of water. Closed his eyes. Said something the old man did not catch.

'Your sister, Anita de Andrade Gomes,' he said, going closer.

The water splashed his shoes and trouser legs.

'Aren't you concerned about Dona Anita's death?'

The youth's lips were moving, but the old man couldn't tell what he was saying.

'Aren't you concerned about your sister's murder?'

'My sister died when I was ten years old.'

'Didn't you see each other? Didn't she ever tell you if she was afraid of someone?'

The youth turned on the next shower, and the sound of the water grew even louder.

'Didn't you stay in contact?'

Turning his back on the old man, the youngster turned on another shower. Then another, and another. He faced towards him again.

'Didn't she ever come to see you?'

The noise from the showers was so deafening the old man had to shout. His socks and shoes were soaking.

'What did you say, Renato? That your sister died when you were ten? Was that what you said?'

The youngster started to soap his penis with obscene rubbing gestures.

'So Aparecida died when she was fifteen, did she, Renato? Still a girl. Fifteen. A young girl. I must be talking about someone else. She must be . . . You're black. She was blonde. White. Are you going to carry on masturbating in front of me? Shaking your dick at me? Are you trying to embarrass me? To force me to leave? Is that what you're doing? Anita must have seen lots of men doing that. Masturbating. For her. In her. Inside her.'

The youngster moved away to the furthest shower. The old man followed him.

'The murdered woman can't have been a black boy's sister. She was blonde. A beautiful blonde. Sensual. Even blonder than that girl who just left. Tall. Pretty as a film star. She was twenty-four. She can't have been your sister. Aparecida died when she was fifteen, didn't she, Renato? The murdered woman's name was Anita. A rich woman's name. A white woman's name. She was well known in the city. Very well known. Every man in the city knew Anita. And she knew lots of them. One of those men hated her. Perhaps she had humiliated him. In bed, who knows? And he took his revenge. He killed her by stabbing her a dozen times. Or more. Fifteen perhaps, or sixteen, eighteen times. And he cut off one of her breasts. One of her beautiful breasts. As a trophy. A ghastly murder. A horrible crime. Revolting. But you're not concerned, are you, Renato? Nobody's worried. Do you know why, Renato? Because everyone thought she was a tramp. Everybody's whore. And that's the kind of end every tramp deserves. Especially a black tramp who tried to pass herself off as white, who showed herself off alongside—'

The youngster leapt at him, grabbing him by the jacket lapels. He pushed him under the showers. The old man groaned as his head hit the wall. The youth seized it and forced it up under the jet. The water blinded the old man. It filled his nostrils, so that he had to open his mouth to breathe, then gurgled down his throat. He coughed, but only swallowed more water. He tried to loosen the young man's grip, but he pushed him upwards. The old man lost his footing. His chest hurt, his cheeks felt as though they were being crushed. Every time he tried to draw breath he only took more water into his nostrils and throat; this made him cough, and swallow yet more liquid. He struggled, kicking out. One of his shoes came off. He was slipping on the tiled floor. He was blacking out. He tried to keep his eyes open, but the gushing water hurt them. His sight dimmed. He realized he was losing consciousness. He wanted to throw up. He coughed, gagged, coughed again. The water took on a bitter taste. His hands grew weak as he tried to free himself from the youngster's grip. He felt for the floor with his stockinged foot, but it no longer seemed to be there. He stopped struggling. Around him, everything went dark.

When he came to, he was lying stretched out on the wet floor. The showers had been turned off. The young man was bending over him. The old man raised his hands to ward off the blow. The youth took hold of him under the arms, and hauled him upright. He carried him over to one of the benches, sat him down. He walked off, then came back with a towel. The old man wrapped it round himself, shivering. Renato stood naked in front of him, not saying a word. Then he sat down, and said:

'What do you want to ask me?'

6

The Fragrance of Lavender

HE WAS STILL pale when he left the changing room. He searched for a cigarette, but everything in his pockets was soaking. Eduardo and Paulo were busy watching an argument between the blue team's goalkeeper and a yellow-team forward. Trainers and substitutes from both teams were trying to pull them apart, but before long they became involved in the brawl as well. The exchange of blows and insults quickly spread, and some of the fans jumped down on to the pitch to join in.

The old man walked off on his own, out of the sports ground.

Half an hour later, he found the address he was looking for. As the nun had told him, the imposing yellow two-storey mansion was surrounded by nondescript houses from a recent development, built on terrain that had been part of the mansion for more than a century.

The iron gate was not locked. He opened it, went in and began to walk up a gravel drive wide enough to accommodate the coaches and carriages of the senators and barons who came and went for evening balls and to hatch plots during the empire of Pedro II.

A black limousine stood beneath a bougainvillea-covered summerhouse. The old man had seen models like it only in magazines. It was one of those luxury European models that had just begun to be made in Brazil. The tail fins rose up from the bodywork, with big vertical rear lights. Its style was as futuristic as a science-fiction comic: the spokes of its silver hubcaps were meant as an affectionate reminder of the wheels of a cabriolet. He put his hands on the bonnet, near the silver letters spelling out the name: *Simca Chambord*. It was cold.

He reached the arched veranda. The lights were off. He walked up the five steps, went towards what he thought must be the main door, looking for the bell-pull. He couldn't find it. He clapped his hands. No one came. Clapping a second time produced no result either. He was about to try once more when a door to his left opened, throwing a rectangle of light on to the drive behind him. Even before he turned towards it, he could smell the fragrance of lavender.

The young girl trembled slightly, almost imperceptibly. She was wearing a different blouse and skirt, and her hair was loose. Even so, and despite the fact that he had caught only a momentary glimpse of her, he recognized her at once. He hadn't noticed in the changing room how much taller than him she was. Or how adult her body was.

'I'd like to talk to the mayor.'

Shaped like a bird with spread wings, her plump lips opened slightly. Her close-set dark eyes glanced quickly back inside the house, and then again at him.

'My father isn't in.'

'His car is in the drive.'

She stepped back. Grasped the doorknob.

'My father is busy.'

'I have to talk to him.'

'I don't know if he can see you.'

'Please go and call Dr Torres.'

'My father won't be able to . . .'

A light came on above the door. Dazzled, the old man blinked. Behind the girl he saw a woman with her hair done up in a bun staring sternly at him.

'What is it, daughter?'

There was an unmistakable air of authority in her voice.

'This gentleman,' said the adolescent, taking her hand from the doorknob to let her mother past, 'wants to talk to Daddy.'

Her mother stepped forward. She wore no make-up on her dainty face. She must have been around forty.

'Good evening. Can I help you?'

There were crow's feet around her eyes. When she smiled, the corners of her lips remained fixed in a firm line: the sort of condescending smile that politicians' wives practise on platforms and display at inaugurations, tributes and charity functions.

'I have to talk to the mayor.'

'I'm Isabel Marques Torres, his wife. You can talk to me. I'll pass on the message.'

She placed one hand delicately on top of the other. She was dressed in unremarkable but impeccable clothes.

'It's a personal matter.'

'My husband came home exhausted. He's already retired.'

'It's quite urgent.'

'I'm sorry. It's impossible tonight.'

'I really need to talk to him.'

'It's better if you come back tomorrow.'

'It's about . . . I'm the lawyer of the . . .' He tried to think of a name. 'I was hired in order to . . .'

'Tomorrow you can—'

'I need to talk to him about the murder of the dentist's wife.'

Her smile vanished.

'Cecilia,' she said, without taking her eyes off the old man, 'you'd better go inside.'

'Would you like me to call Daddy?'

'That's not necessary. Go to your room. It's late.'

Isabel Marques Torres waited for her daughter to withdraw.

'Cecilia was very shocked by what happened. We all were. It's an unpleasant matter, an affair—'

'A murder,' he corrected her.

'Yes, that's right. And it had to happen during my husband's term in office. He's very annoyed about it. I'm sure it would be better for you to see him some other time.'

'I need to speak to Dr Torres right now.'

'Marques Torres. Our surname is Marques Torres. Fortunately, that affair was resolved by the city police. There was no need to call in anyone from the capital. The case is closed.'

'It's not.'

'What do you mean?'

'The victim's family has hired me,' it suddenly occurred to him to say, enjoying his invention, which seemed to catch her off guard. 'Relatives in Rio de Janeiro. I arrived from there today. I need some information. The family needs it. I'd like to clarify some unclear points. They – I – want to avoid this appearing in the sensationalist press.'

He waited. She did not answer at once.

'Perhaps it would be better if you came in,' she said eventually.

'I prefer to wait out here.'

'As you wish.'

She turned her back on him. He saw her disappear inside the house. A few minutes later, he heard the sound of heavy footsteps descending stairs.

The man who appeared almost filled the door-frame.

'You wanted to speak to me?'

White stubble was sprouting on his reddish face. The tight-fitting shirt, possibly bought when he wasn't so stocky, emphasized a broad chest that seemed out of proportion to his short, bowed legs. He was wearing boots.

'Dr Torres?'

'Marques Torres. You want to speak to me?'

'I need to. I'm the lawyer for—'

'You can talk. But that murder is a matter for the police chief.'

'It's not about Dona Anita's death that I want to talk to you. It's about before. About Aparecida.'

The mayor stepped forward, pulling the door closed behind him. The old man could see how big and clumsy-looking his hands were. His nails were manicured.

'What Aparecida?'

The old man realized he was talking to someone who ever since childhood was used to being obeyed. His fleshy mouth and full lips reminded him of Cecilia. His daughter had also inherited his small, close-set eyes.

'The director of the orphanage suggested I came to see you.'

'Ah yes, that black woman. She suggested you see me? What on earth for?'

'It appears that your father . . .'

'My father?'

'Your father, Senator Marques Torres . . . he was a member of Congress in 1952, wasn't he?'

'He was. Why do you ask?'

'It seems that around that time the senator wanted to adopt a girl.'

'Adopt?'

'A girl. By the name of Aparecida. The daughter of an estate worker.'

'I couldn't say. By that time I was already married; I had my own life, my own family. My father spent more time in the capital, in the Chamber of Deputies, than here.'

'Do you have adopted brothers or sisters?'

'No.'

'Yet in the case of that girl, that Aparecida . . .'

'In 1952? That was the year my father founded the high school. What I remember from back then is my father being involved in providing free secondary education for the city. I remember the struggle he had to obtain funds from the federal government.'

'That was the year Aparecida was married. Her mother, Elza—'

'Four hundred and twenty pupils, studying for free. From the first year of high school to university entrance. That was when the road to the capital was asphalted too. Thanks to his efforts. Thanks to the funding he obtained.'

'In 1952—'

'Dr Getúlio was very fond of him.'

'Your father was friends with the dictator?'

'In 1952, Dr Getúlio was an elected president. My father talked of him more as a friend than as Dr Vargas, the president of Brazil.'

'Didn't your father ever mention anything? About adopting a girl? Or about her mother, Elza?'

'We didn't see much of each other; I was on the estate, he was in the capital. I mean Rio de Janeiro. That was before Brasilia existed. Before Dr Getúlio committed suicide.'

'Aparecida was born on your estate, wasn't she?'

'We don't own the estate any more.'

'But you did when she was born?'

'Now it belongs to Dr Geraldo.'

'Elza, her mother, was a worker on the estate, wasn't she?'

'Dr Geraldo Bastos. The textile factory owner. After my father died, we sold him the estate. In 1955. A year after Vargas's death.'

'Like Vargas, your father—'

'My father was very upset at Dr Getúlio's death.'

'Was he aware that you knew Dona Anita? Aparecida?'

'Dona Anita's husband and I have known each other a long time. We studied together.'

'Are you a dentist too?'

'No, an engineer. An agronomist. We met at the Valença seminary in the state of Rio.'

He turned back towards the door, grasped the knob, cleared his throat. His back was astonishingly broad.

'If you want to know anything more, I suggest you consult the police. And tell that black woman . . . that nun, to do the same.'

With that, he closed the door. The veranda light snapped off.

'My granny came from a place like this,' said Paulo, getting off his bike at the roadside.

In front of them, the valley stretched for kilometres to a line of black, gleaming mountains. Pastureland, scrub, a coffee plantation: wide strips of different shades of green shone in the afternoon sun. A hawk took off from the top of a glory bush, flapping its wings hard until it found a rising current of air. Then it relaxed, gliding high above the bends of the wide stream below. A goat was wandering along its sandy banks, followed by her kids.

Eduardo watched the flight of the hawk until it disappeared between two hills dotted with trees that had survived being cleared by burning. He looked in the opposite direction: an arched stone bridge crossed a narrower part of the river. On

the far side was a gravel path lined with imperial palms. The
path led to an ivy-covered wall. Beyond the wall, a garden
extended to the summit of a hill, on which stood a big, three-
storey whitewashed house. The ground floor was an open
area, where two carts, saddles, bridles and piles of sacks were
stored. A woman was sweeping the steps that led up to the
first floor. Above that, all the blue-and-green-framed
windows were shuttered. There were a lot of them: Eduardo
began to count: two, three, five, eight . . .

'I've never seen so many windows,' he said, losing count.
'How many bedrooms can there be? Who lives there? Is that
where your granny was born?'

'Nobody lives there any more. It used to belong to the
Marques Torres family.'

'But you said that your granny . . .'

'She was a tenant farmer.'

'A tenant farmer?'

'A sharecropper. Isn't that what they call them in São
Paulo?'

'I don't know. I don't remember.'

'She was a tenant farmer. Before she left the countryside
and got a job in the textile factory.'

'I thought it was your mother who worked in the
factory.'

'Yes, my mother did too. Before she got married. Before my
granny died.'

'And her family? Where do they live?'

'I don't know. My father never talks about them.'

'But your brother must tell you.'

'I don't know if any of them are still alive. I only know about my granny.'

'Everybody has relatives. A cousin, an uncle . . . Someone.'

'I've never met any. Let's go!'

Paulo climbed on to his bike, pedalled hard, then free-wheeled down the dirt track to the bridge. Eduardo took off in pursuit.

When they reached the big estate house, the woman stopped sweeping to listen to their questions. She pointed across the river, beyond the coffee plantation.

They walked through two rows of coffee bushes. Eduardo, who had seen coffee plants only in photographs, was surprised at how tall they were.

They came out on to a beaten earth track, with deep parallel ruts made by ox-carts. There were no tyre tracks. In the rainy season, which began in June, eased off in July and returned more strongly in August, no jeep would be able to pass here.

They followed the track, pushing their bikes up each incline, bouncing over the potholes on downward slopes. They went through grassland where the cattle did not seem to move at all. Nowhere was there any sign of human life. The setting sun lent everything a melancholy orange glow. Used to cities, Eduardo found it hard to believe anybody could live in the midst of such quiet tranquillity. He spoke, less out of any real interest but more to break the silence.

'Was she from the estate?'

'Who?'

'Your granny.'

'No.'

'Where was she from?'

'Somewhere near here.'

'Where?'

'I don't know.'

'Was she the only one who left? Did her brothers and sisters stay? What about her parents?'

'I don't know if she had any brothers or sisters.'

'What about your granddad?'

'I don't know where he was from. He died before my grand-mother. I never knew him.'

'So your mother was brought up without a father?'

'It must be that house there,' said Paulo, pointing to a dot in the distance surrounded by uncultivated land.

They cycled more quickly. It took them longer than they had expected to reach the adobe hut. A black boy, younger than them, was poking a bamboo stick at a line of ants in the red earth.

'Is this where Dona Madalena lives?' asked Paulo.

The boy nodded.

'Is she here? We want to talk to her.'

The boy left the ants and, still clasping the stick, went to the door of the hut and waved for them to go in.

It was a single, tiny, dark room. The walls were grimy with soot. No chair or table. Or wardrobe. A clay pot stood on a wood stove that had gone out. What could be in it, what could these people eat, what did they have to eat, wondered Eduardo, who had never been in such a poor place.

The fading evening light streamed in through the only

window, half blocked by the end of a crate. They could just make out a skinny woman lying on a canvas camp bed in one corner of the room.

'Dona Madalena?'

When she heard Paulo's voice, she opened her eyes. It took her a few moments to focus on the two boys. Even so, it was as if she didn't see them. She made no sound, and lay there motionless. They were quiet too. The silence lasted only for a few seconds, but it made Eduardo feel uncomfortable. Without knowing why, he wanted to leave at once. Then he recalled a similar silence and someone staring at him in the same way, many years earlier: his grandfather, the *nonno*, on his hospital deathbed.

'Dona Madalena?' Paulo repeated, going across and squatting down beside her.

Eduardo followed him, but didn't bend down. He felt increasingly awkward.

'Dona Madalena . . .' said Paulo, in a gentle voice that Eduardo had never heard before. 'Your grandson told us to come and look for you.'

The boy playing with the ants stole out of the hut.

Paulo waited. Nothing happened. He said:

'Renato.'

'Your grandson Renato,' Eduardo explained.

Was she really looking at them? Did she see them? Did she understand what they were saying?

'Renato,' Paulo repeated. 'Your daughter Elza's son.'

The old woman moved her head feebly. Paulo took it as a confirmation.

'Renato said you might know.'

Eduardo was growing impatient. He wanted Paulo to ask the questions the old man had told them to put to her. He wanted to get out of there as quickly as possible. He butted in:

'Your daughter Elza had a daughter before she had Renato, didn't she? Five years before, wasn't it? Ask her, Paulo!'

Paulo took a deep breath.

'Your grandson. Renato. He told us to come and look for you,' Paulo began again, trying to find the right words. 'Your daughter Elza had a little girl before she had Renato.'

'In 1937,' added Eduardo.

'Do you remember, Dona Madalena? A little girl. Light-skinned. Very light-skinned.'

'On 15 May 1937. She was registered as Aparecida. Dos Santos. Tell her, Paulo!'

'Aparecida dos Santos. Do you remember?'

Eduardo thought he saw the old woman shake her head. He insisted:

'Aparecida. The daughter of your daughter.'

'The girl's mother . . . your daughter Elza . . . was twelve years old. Aparecida's mother. She was twelve years old when . . .'

Madalena's expression was indecipherable.

'Your granddaughter was born, and taken to the orphanage,' Eduardo insisted.

'Your granddaughter, Aparecida.'

'Do you remember?'

Paulo leaned over Madalena's face. He was whispering into her ear.

'Your daughter, Elza. She was twelve years old when . . . When she had . . . a little girl. She was taken away. Your grand-daughter. Aparecida. They took Aparecida away to the orphanage. Your grandson . . . Elza's other child . . . your grandson Renato said you're the only one who knows. You're the only one who can tell the story. Who knows. Who knows what happened to Aparecida. What they did to Elza's daughter. Only you can tell us all about Aparecida. Everything. Everything that . . . that . . .'

Eduardo found Madalena's silence unbearable. He burst out:

'Was Aparecida's father the estate owner? Was her father the senator Marques Torres?'

Paulo shot him a reproving glance. Madalena had still not moved. The boy who'd been playing with the ants brought a lit oil lamp from outside, set it on the stove, and went out again.

'She's not going to remember, Paulo. We're not getting any-where. Let's go.'

Paulo said nothing. He leaned closer over Madalena, and put his arm round her head. In the gloom, Eduardo could not make out his face next to the old woman's. No, alongside it. This gesture surprised him as much as the gentleness with which Paulo spoke to her. Then he realized: the old woman stretched out in front of him, without covers, her bones sticking through her clothes, could have been Paulo's grand-mother, if she hadn't fled life in the country and found a place at a loom in the city. And he, this boy leaning over an old black woman dying in poverty in a hovel in the middle of nowhere, could perhaps, who knows, have been Madalena's grandson, if one day in the past she had had the courage, the audacity or the good fortune to change her life.

Paulo was talking so quietly that even in this tiny room Eduardo found it hard to hear him. He didn't sound like the boy he knew so well. He seemed like ... almost another person. Almost ... an adult. Do you remember, Dona Madalena, he was asking, do you remember, do you? I know you do, he was saying. I don't know why you don't want to talk, but I'm sure you remember, he was saying, as if he had known her for many years. He said to her: they took Aparecida, your granddaughter, they took her away, and you had to let them do it. She was very light-skinned, too light, as light-skinned as her father, Eduardo thought he could hear Paulo whisper. You had to let them take her. She couldn't stay here. The little girl. They wouldn't allow it. They took her away, he said. When your daughter Elza was twelve. The same age as me. Later, Elza had another baby. A boy. Renato. Do you remember, he asked, do you remember? A boy. Darker-skinned than Aparecida. They took him away too. So then your daughter Elza, their mother, said Paulo, hesitating more and more, she left as well. Did Elza want to leave, Dona Madalena? Or did they send her away too? Did she run away? Did she disappear? Did you have no more news of her? What did they do to her, Dona Madalena? Do you know? Do you, Dona Madalena? What they did to Elza? Do you remember? Do you?

Eduardo saw a gleam in Madalena's eyes. It looked like a tear. But he couldn't be certain. The darkness swallowed everything. The lamp's wavering light made their shadows flicker round the walls.

Madalena struggled to raise her hand. She brought it close to Paulo's face, as if to stroke it. But she didn't touch him. Her trembling hand hung in mid-air for a moment. Then dropped again. She turned her face to the wall.

Paulo stood up, his back to Eduardo. As he passed by him, head down, on his way to the door, he said:

'Let's go.'

For a moment the sounds of the thunderclap and the factory siren mingled. In the distance, above the mountains, a lightning flash lit up the night sky, illuminating the heavy rainclouds sweeping towards the city. The thunder rolled closer and closer, while the factory whistle continued announcing the end of the shift for the workers in the Union & Progress textile factory. A wind that seemed to be coming from every direction at once started raising dust in the streets, sending the leaves it tore from the trees whirling, and shaking the *Founded in 1890* sign in the mouth of the painted cement eagle on the factory front. Beneath it, the double iron gates opened.

A man in dark-grey overalls and clogs was the first out, pushing a bicycle. When he reached the street he got on and rode off. Waves of men and women followed, all dressed in the same overalls and clogs, all with the same weary faces. They could have spent Sunday at home, but preferred to give up their weekend rest for more money, overtime, more hours at work to produce more, to produce more of the kilometres of denim needed for the uniforms worn by the millions of Brazilians leaving the countryside or the drought-stricken areas of the north-east for the industries springing up in the south-east of the country.

None of the workers with bicycles rode them out of the gates. Following the owners' instructions, they got on only when they reached the paved street, beyond their workplace. They all seemed in a hurry to pedal off, and each peal of thunder made them hasten still more. By the time the siren died away, few of them were still in sight.

The old man continued to wait.

By now the street was deserted. The wind grew colder, blowing in squally gusts. Some pieces of paper spiralled in front of him in the midst of a whirlwind of dust, and were carried away along with other rubbish, bits of twigs, dry leaves. The lowering clouds swept nearer and nearer.

Then the gates swung open again. The old man was momentarily blinded by the glare of headlights. He heard the roar of an engine. Still dazzled by the circles of light, he made out a black, sleek limousine emerging from the factory. It turned into the street.

The old man hurried across. He stumbled. The headlights blinded him once more, and a squeal of brakes told him the car was coming to a sudden halt. Even shielding his eyes with his hands he couldn't see clearly. Feeling for the mudguards, he approached the man behind the steering wheel.

'Dr Geraldo?'

He could only make out a vague shape in the driver's seat.

'Dr Geraldo Bastos?'

The shape, which now seemed to him huge, nodded in agreement.

'I'm Basilio Gomes. A lawyer. Can I talk to you for a minute?'

A big man. With glasses. Jacket and tie.

'I didn't want to disturb you in the factory.'

A white starched jacket, with initials embroidered on the pocket, over a white shirt also with a starched collar, and a tie held in place by a round gold clip from some club originally started in the United States: now he could see him clearly.

'I thought it might be inconvenient to talk about the matter in front of your employees.'

The car engine whined: the man inside was pressing his foot on and off the accelerator, but without moving off.

'It's about Anita.'

Behind the oval, metal-framed glasses, the blue eyes flicked towards the already closed factory gates, then to the empty street, and finally came to rest on the old man.

'I'm on my way home,' he snapped. 'It's late. My family's expecting me for dinner.'

'We could talk in the car. Then I'll walk back.'

'I live some distance away. We could talk on some other occasion.'

'If you prefer,' said the old man, as neutrally as possible, 'I could go to your house tomorrow and wait for you there.'

Geraldo Bastos hesitated. He glanced over in the direction

of the factory once more. He picked up the briefcase on the seat beside him, and dropped it in the back. Without looking at the white-haired man, he leaned over and opened the right-hand door. The old man walked round the car, got in and sat down. The Willys Aero pulled away.

Bastos drove slowly, staring straight ahead. They went round Tenente Valladares Square. A bony mongrel was trotting towards the bandstand. The wind and the threat of rain had emptied almost all the streets.

Inside the car, the old man admired the modern dashboard and found himself enjoying the smell of fresh leather.

'A nice car,' he said, meaning it.

'Willys Aero. A Brazilian car,' replied a disgruntled Bastos.

'The reason I was waiting for you outside the factory was—'

'A jalopy. No power, awkward to drive, poor finish.'

'Dr Geraldo, as the lawyer for the family of—'

'Uncomfortable. Like all cars made in Brazil.'

'I've never had a car. But as I was saying—'

'Old-fashioned.'

'I wanted to see you about—'

'I've got an Oldsmobile and a Mercury in the garage. Ever since that demagogue Juscelino Kubitschek banned the import of foreign cars in 1958, it's been impossible to find any spare parts.'

'The ban was intended to promote national industry. But the reason I came to see you is—'

'I was forced to buy this heap of junk. Who gains with this protectionism?'

'Manufacturing cars in Brazil has created thousands of jobs. Dr Geraldo, I want to talk to you about—'

'Could anyone seriously claim that the Renault, Volkswagen, Alfa Romeo, Mercedes-Benz or Ford factories are really Brazilian?'

'What about all the people fleeing poverty in the north-east? They found—'

'Work? Living even more wretchedly on the outskirts of our big cities? Building and crowding into shanty towns? And what for? To make models here that are already out of date abroad. They've swapped the import of good cars for the import of antiquated technology.'

'But protectionism also helps our textile industry.'

'It makes no difference. We don't need it.'

'Every industry in poor countries needs it. Otherwise we won't be able to prevent the dumping of goods made in the capitalist world . . .'

'I sell denim all over the world, even to the United States. My factory was founded in the last century. We brought the first machines over from England. With our own money. National capital. We transformed illiterate slaves who had been abandoned by their masters into trained workers, with wages and social security. We taught them skills, we paid for holidays, a dentist, a doctor. We kept people in the provinces who otherwise would have only gone to swell the numbers of those living on the margins of the big cities. That's very different from this surrender to foreign capital. But you're not from these parts.'

'What was that?'

'You have a north-eastern accent. You must be from Pernambuco or somewhere near there. If you were from here, you would know what goes on, and wouldn't need to come looking for me. Everyone here knew what that tramp was like.'

'You . . .' The old man cast his words like someone with a fishing rod. 'It seems that you . . . knew Dona Anita rather better than most.'

'The only people who didn't know that woman were those who didn't want to.'

'It seems she preferred—'

'She didn't prefer anything. She was a woman who was permanently open to the public.'

The old man felt sick.

'Is that why her husband killed her?' he asked, struggling to control his anger.

'Francisco Andrade?' he said scornfully. 'Francisco Andrade killed her? By stabbing her to death?'

'He's under arrest.'

'Does anyone really believe that Francisco Andrade is that woman's killer?'

'The police do: he's—'

'He confessed, so they had to arrest him. Any lawyer can get him out of there, whenever he likes. A first-time offender. A crime of honour. A well-respected citizen. A charitable man. Any poor person whose rotten teeth he pulled without charging a penny, or whom he gave dentures to, will testify on his behalf. A good man who was the victim of circumstance. With a wife without a shred of decency. Any jury will acquit him.'

'But the savagery with which she was—'

'No, but really! Some lunatic killed the whore and dis-appeared. Some stranger. With or without a confession, the whole city knows it wasn't Dr Andrade who killed her. He'll soon be back home. He wiped clean his honour. Using some-one else.'

At this, the old man turned his head. It was only then he noticed it had started to rain. The wipers squeaked as they smeared the fat raindrops bouncing off the windscreen. Little was visible outside the car. They were climbing a hill the old man could not identify.

'Do you think the husband hired someone?'

'I didn't say that.'

'Didn't you just say that the dentist wiped clean his honour through somebody else's work?'

'I said that Dr Andrade took advantage of the crime to pretend he had finally grown tired of being the city cuckold.'

'But why would a stranger kill her?'

'She was found dead in some bushes, like a slaughtered pig. What difference does it make whether it was a lunatic, a beggar, a travelling salesman or a psychotic who did it?'

'There's a criminal on the loose.'

'That woman was a social outcast. A whore. Cold, depraved, no background, no moral values. The life she led could only have ended that way. Tell me truthfully: what difference does the death of that woman make to our community?'

'Dona Anita—'

'None at all. No one will miss her. In fact, society will benefit from her death.'

'She was savagely murdered.'

'It's a cleansing.'

'Mutilated.'

'Are you religious?'

'Am I what?'

'Darkness or light. We have to choose. Every religion says so. Free will. We are born with it. Rich or poor, black or white, men and women. Every human being is free to choose. There are women who choose to devote themselves to their family, to being loyal to the man who protects them, gives them children, shelter and his name. Those are the women helping to build a better world. They dignify their role in society. Then there are the others. Like Anita.'

'You've known several of them.'

'Like all men. That's what her sort are for.'

A bitter, nauseous taste rose in the old man's gorge.

'Can you stop here, please?'

'What about you? Do you mean to say you've never met scum like her?'

'I have to get out. Stop, please.'

'Have you never been with women like Anita?'

'I want to get out.'

'Wouldn't you take advantage of Anita, if you still could at your age?'

'Stop here. Stop!'

The car had not come to a complete halt when he opened the door and jumped out. The stream of vomit hit the kerb, mingling with the water flowing down the gutter.

In the deserted street, with the rain pouring down, the old

man watched the black car pull away until it disappeared behind a dense curtain of water. He couldn't move. The cold drops on his head and chest seeped inside his collar, making him shiver.

A lightning bolt tore open the sky, followed by a crash that seemed to shake it. His knees were trembling from cold or rage. He tried to steady them, and finally managed to put one foot in front of the other and walk on, head down and forlorn.

He had no idea where he was.

7

How Many Madalenas Are There in the World?

ONE FOOT IN FRONT of the other, Eduardo was measuring his room, trying to recall the size of Dona Madalena's shack. He had been there only a short time, and it had been dark, but his memory of it was clear: his room was bigger than her entire hovel. Could it be? Yes. No, that was impossible.

He made a checklist of the furniture around him. Bed, bedside table, wardrobe, chest of drawers, desk, bookcase, chair. Three times as much as she had. Not counting the objects. Pencils, pen, inkwell, rubber, marker. A tumbler for the pen and pencils. A tube of glue, books, picture of his guardian angel, a first communion certificate. Crucifix. Carpet. Sheet, pillowcase, quilt, blanket. Bolster. Lampshade.

All he could remember from her hut was the pot on the stove. That was all he had seen. She must have had more things. She was bound to have. It wasn't possible for anyone to live with so few possessions. What about the young boy? Where did he sleep, if there was only one bed and Dona

Madalena was in it? Did they sleep together? Or was there a banana-leaf mat for him that they spread on the floor? On the earthen floor. How cold that must be. Perhaps there was another mattress? Could there be? And a bolster? Could there be a pillow for the boy? A blanket? Dona Madalena didn't have a blanket. Or yes, she did. It was cheap, and dirty grey, but there was one. Down at her feet. How could they live so wretchedly if her granddaughter, if Anita, or rather Aparecida, was married to a dentist? Couldn't she have done something to help her grandmother? She could have given her money. Another bed. Another mattress. A sheet, pillowcase or blanket. Something. Anything. Couldn't she have helped her grandmother? She could at least have given her a . . . a . . .

Another flash of lightning outside. Then thunder rattled the window pane. The noise of the incessant rain filled the night.

Perhaps Anita couldn't help. Aparecida. She had nothing herself. Not even a ring. Perhaps the dentist wouldn't allow Aparecida or Anita to help her grandmother. Perhaps Anita herself didn't want to. Perhaps she was angry at her grandmother or something.

No. No one could be angry at a feeble old woman like her. Suffering. Stretched out on her bed. Or could they? Because she let her be taken away to an orphanage? Because she did nothing when the senator got Elza pregnant? Or was she angry because Madalena was black, and Anita wanted to be white? Was she the one pretending, or was it the others who preferred to see the mulatto Aparecida as white Anita? Which others? Was she prevented from seeing her grandmother?

From seeing her brother? Was she ashamed of them? Or ashamed of herself? Of having become the city's tramp? Did Aparecida even know she had a grandmother and a brother? She must have known about her brother. Because if Renato knew about her, knew that Anita was his sister, no – that Aparecida was his sister – then Anita, or Aparecida, must have been aware she had a brother. And a grandmother. Mustn't she?

Blast! He lost count of his steps. He would have to start all over again. One step, two steps, three steps…

Paulo was watching his brother in front of the mirror, combing his hair for the umpteenth time. He was trying, apparently unsuccessfully, to make sure all the brilliantined locks were smoothed down. One tuft at the back of his head stuck up stubbornly from the rest.

'Are you going out, Antonio?'

'I am.'

'In this rain?'

'Not far from here. Mauro, Zé Paulo and I are going to screw Mauro's maid.'

'The maid?'

'Mauro already has. And he told her that if she doesn't put it out for us as well, he'll tell his parents she's a whore.'

'How much does she charge?'

'What do you mean, charge, golliwog? They brought her from the countryside to look after the kids. She doesn't have anywhere else to go. I want to fuck her arse. I'll stick it in her.'

'How old is she?'

'Fourteen, fifteen maybe. She's still a virgin. She only lets you do it up her arse.'

The tuft finally gave way. Antonio carefully combed a lock of hair down over his forehead, imitating James Byron Dean, to give the impression he was a rebel without a cause who couldn't give a damn about his appearance.

'What if she doesn't want to?'

Putting the comb away in the back pocket of his trousers, Antonio gazed lovingly at himself in the mirror.

'Well, Antonio? What if she doesn't want to?'

'I already told you, she's the maid.'

'But she still might not want to.'

'Then we force her to, and beat her up as well.'

He folded up the short shirtsleeves to show off his bulging biceps. Turning sideways to the mirror, he cupped his hand to adjust the bulge in his crotch. The whole world needed to see the power of what he had in there.

'I've already got a hard-on,' he said, anticipating the pleasure awaiting him.

The driving rain beating endlessly at the windows of the dormitory drowned out the snores, coughs and groans of the other old men.

He was exhausted, and yet he couldn't get to sleep. He was shivering beneath the blankets. His eyes were stinging. His joints, muscles and varicose veins all ached. His head was throbbing. He still had the bitter taste in his mouth, despite the number of times he had gone to the bathroom to rinse it out.

He wanted to sleep. He needed to sleep. He had to stop the whirligig of images that invaded his mind whenever he closed his eyes. Lips, tongues, mouths, arms, necks, breasts, thighs, arses, bellies, vulvas. His penis going in and out of them. In and out. In and out of anonymous fragments of bodies that had no faces or names, that made no sound apart from moans, sometimes protests, don't do that, no, not behind, and all the time him pushing, tearing, penetrating flesh that had no will and no individuality, only vulvas and bellies and thighs and arses and lips and breasts and holes to be penetrated by his vengeance, that and only that. The same way that Helena had been penetrated by the police, the way the torturers of Vargas's dictatorship had behaved with Helena in front of him, with their penises, their sticks, their truncheons, close to the perch he was being hung from, their enjoyment increased by raping her with him looking on, as they pleasured themselves with her breasts, her hands, her face, her mouth, while he was forced to watch, tied to the wooden perch.

He opened his eyes.

In the dormitory the other old men were sound asleep, at peace with their wheezing, their asthma, their bronchitis. For a split second a lightning flash gave their faces the ghastly, pallid look of bodies laid out in a morgue. In the sudden glare he saw his own hands, as white as the others' skin. And his own face, reflected in the nearby window. It was no different to that of Geraldo Bastos.

~

Thirteen steps long, nineteen wide. Multiplied by the length of his foot, twenty-seven centimetres: Eduardo discovered that he possessed a room measuring two metres seventy centimetres by three, almost four metres. An ordinary enough room. But one that could contain all of Dona Madalena's hovel.

He switched the light off and lay down.

Thinking over the day's events, he concluded it had been a failure. Going out to the estate had been a complete waste of time. All that way for nothing. They hadn't got any information they didn't already know or suspect. No leads. The more people they discovered linked to Anita or Aparecida's life, the less they knew about her.

He turned to the wall, ready to sleep.

The thunder rumbled in the distance as the rain eased off over the city.

What could it be like in that hovel when it rained? Did it leak? Was it cold? Were there draughts? The wind must get in through the gap between the walls and the unlined roof. How did they get warm on a night like tonight? Would that cheap blanket be enough? Was it the only one they had? They probably wouldn't have a hot soup with macaroni, meat, kale and beans before going to bed, like the one his mother gave him. Or woollen socks like the ones he was wearing. Or flannel pyjamas.

He sighed. As he was arranging the thick wool blanket over his feet, he thought he heard a groan, but paid no attention to it, his thoughts still on the miserable hut he had visited that afternoon. How horrible it was to be poor, he thought, how horrible. The groan came again. He listened more carefully. For a while he heard nothing more.

How many people could there be like Dona Madalena and the boy with the ants? Here, close to us? In the city? In the state? In the other states of Brazil? Do they go to the doctor when they feel a pain? To the dentist? Do they take medicine when they need it? Do they have money to buy medicine? If Dona Madalena died, who would look after the boy? Or did he look after her? Who is he? Why was he there? What did he tell us? Did he tell us his name? Did we even ask him what his name was?

He heard the creak of bed-springs from his parents' bedroom. Then a second time. And again. Then more, one after the other in quick succession. He recognized his father's voice, but it was too hoarse for him to make out what he was saying. Rhythmic, whispered. Short, rapid pants, increasingly rapid. And more moans.

Eduardo got out of bed.

He tiptoed over to the wall separating the two rooms and pressed his ear to it.

The groans were coming from his mother.

'. . . There are seventy million Brazilians, sixty per cent of whom live in rural areas,' the young teacher Wilson Pinto dictated to the class. He wore thick glasses and his face was pockmarked with acne. 'In spite of the gains in education since the 1940s, thanks to the creation of effective literacy programmes during the presidency of Getúlio Vargas, there are still many illiterates in Brazil, almost half the inhabitants of our country: forty-six point seven per cent, according to last year's census. Are you writing all this down? Am I going too quickly? Forty-six point seven per cent, that's right.'

Paulo was trying in vain to attract Eduardo's attention, but his friend was writing with his head down, and refused to look up. He had been silent ever since they had reached school.

'For the first time in the history of our fragile democracy,' the civic studies teacher went on, 'a civilian government, directly elected, has taken over from another civilian government, also elected by universal suffrage.'

All the pupils copied down what he was saying, word for word. They would be examined on the percentages and dates, and had to repeat exactly what they had heard. Paulo deduced that 'universal suffrage' and 'directly elected' were the same thing.

'Another unprecedented fact is that, since the proclamation of the republic in ... In what year? Exactly, Miss Maria da Conceição Pentagna: 1889. In the seventy-two years of the republic, also for the first time in our history, we directly elected an opposition candidate ...'

Interrupting a dictation to question a pupil was one of the young teacher's ruses to keep the class's attention. Paulo was interested in the topic, but the continuous string of numbers wearied and confused him. He had to make a huge effort to follow.

'Five million, six hundred and thirty-six thousand, six hundred and twenty-three voters gave victory at the polls to the Right Honourable Jânio da Silva Quadros, a teacher, born in Mato Grosso, who was the governor of which state? Which one? Who can tell me? That's right, Mr Mauro Dolinsky. Jânio Quadros was the governor of the state of São Paulo. He was elected in a massive, historic vote because . . .'

There was a knock at the classroom door. The teacher continued with the dictation as he walked over to it.

'. . . he received two million votes more than the second-place candidate, Marshal Henrique Duffles Teixeira Lott, the widest margin obtained by—'

He interrupted the dictation when he saw the headmaster's secretary in the doorway. She handed him a folded piece of paper, which he took without any great interest. She stood waiting. He unfolded the paper, and read it.

'Eduardo José Massaíni!' he called out, looking for the boy among the dozens in front of him. 'Is he here?'

'Massaranni, sir,' Eduardo corrected him, standing and holding up his hand. 'That's me. Eduardo Massaranni.'

'And who is Paulo Roberto Antunes?' asked the teacher, glancing down again at the piece of paper in his hands.

Without raising his eyes from the papers he was signing, Jaime Leonel Miranda de Macedo signalled for them to enter.

'And close the door, if you would.'

His voice reminded Eduardo of someone else's. Whose? Where? Paulo was looking at the two framed portraits on the wall above the headmaster of the Colegio Municipal Maria Beatriz Marques Torres's desk. He recognized the one of Senator Marques Torres as being the same stern-looking, retouched photograph as in the bus station and on the obelisk marking the beginning of the new highway to the capital. The wall-eyed man wearing the presidential sash in the right-hand photograph was Jânio Quadros.

'Come in. Come over.'

It wasn't the voice which sounded familiar to Eduardo. It was the tone. The way he addressed them. Warm. Polite. But distant. It reminded him of someone. Or some situation. A voice in an echoing place. Cold.

'Come closer, gentlemen.'

The headmaster talked like someone . . .

'Well now . . .' he said, his eyes puffy behind his reading glasses. 'How are your studies going?'

His voice was like . . .

'Hmmm?'

At mass! That was it, it was like the voice of the priest at mass. The voice droning on, swirling round the marble walls of the cathedral in the same way as the draughty currents of air stirring the fringes of the white linen altar cloths.

'Good,' Paulo replied curtly.

'Very well, headmaster sir,' said Eduardo.

'Please, don't call me headmaster. It's not necessary. I'm only temporarily in charge of this educational establishment.

It's a transitory thing, a title, an honour which quite frankly I don't deserve, but which I accept like a soldier going out to do battle for his ideal, the ideal from which he derives his strength: to sow culture. That is my ideal. To sow the light of knowledge. To plant the future. Headmaster? No, no. A teacher. Talk to me as if I were simply a teacher. Or Mr Macedo. It's up to you.'

He took off his glasses and laid them on the desk.

'And it's as a teacher that I called you in here.'

He shuffled the papers in front of him.

'Because a teacher's duties are not confined to the classroom.'

He screwed on the gold top of his fountain pen, imported from the United States.

'A teacher should also be a guide, a tutor, a second father. *Quod habeo tibi do.* "I give you all that I have." I want to—'

'If it's about the dirty magazine,' Paulo interrupted him, 'that was my fault.'

'No, mine!' Ediardo protested. 'I brought it into the classroom!'

Macedo swivelled his chair to the left, then right, then left again. He stopped, straightened up, peered at the two boys. He put his elbows on the desk, folded his hands, rested his chin on them. He was staring directly at Eduardo.

'The Portuguese teacher was full of praise for your compositions. Dona Odete Silveira tells me you write well . . .' Out of the corner of his eye he checked the name of the tall, skinny boy on the report. '. . . Eduardo.'

Then he turned to Paulo, as if searching for something to say.

'Yours too . . .' He glanced at the two reports once more, so

160

as not to confuse their names. 'Your compositions too, Paulo ... Paulo Roberto. Your compositions, Paulo Roberto. Dona Odete finds them surprising. They contain lots of grammatical mistakes. But the Portuguese teacher says she finds them surprising. "Original", is how Dona Odete Silveira described them to me in this very office, only a few moments ago. The maths teacher has no complaints about either of you. Nor your English teacher. Mademoiselle Célia even complimented you on your accent when you read sentences in French . . .' he checked again, 'Eduardo. Although several of the teachers spoke of a certain lack of attention, a certain rebelliousness, especially from you . . .' another glance, 'Paulo Roberto. But they agree unanimously that you . . . and you . . . have bright futures. If you study more, with more dedication. With more attention to grammar, for example. Greater care over lexical and syntactical analysis.'

'Yes, headmaster.'

'Teacher.'

'Yes, teacher,' said Paulo grudgingly.

The headmaster raised his head from his hands, and tilted his chair backwards.

'Do you see how closely I follow your progress? I'm interested in every one of my four hundred and twenty-six pupils. I share their achievements. I'm aware of their difficulties. I know their names. I know who their parents are. I know where they live and what they do. Your father, Eduardo, is called Rodolfo Mazaini, isn't he?'

'Massaranni, sir. With two "s"s and two "n"s. It's an Italian name.'

'Yes, I know – the son of immigrants. From the contingent brought over to work on the coffee plantations following the emancipation of the slaves, but who ended up moving to the city, where life was pleasanter. Your father's a railway worker, isn't he? An employee of the Brazil Central Railway.'

'That's right, sir.'

'And your mother, Dona Rosangela, is a seamstress.'

'Yes, sir.'

'And your father, Paulo Roberto, owns a butcher's shop.'

'Yes.'

'You lost your mother when you were very young: at the age of four. Her name was Maria José, wasn't it? Before she fell ill she worked in the textile factory.'

This was the first time Eduardo had heard his friend's mother given a name. Like a living person. Maria José. He added it to his fantasy of an unseen, small black-and-white image of a thin, dark-skinned woman with slightly buck teeth, kept in the wallet of a man who never called his son by his name.

'Just imagine! A butcher. A railway worker. A seamstress. And a textile factory worker . . . how proud your parents must be! How proud your mother, Dona Maria José, would have been were she alive today, Paulo Roberto! To have their children at school, seeing them learn like . . . like the children of prominent people. Back in the days when your parents were your age, that would have been unthinkable. Youngsters like you, with your backgrounds, in a school like this, getting a secondary education. What splendid progress! You two with a range of choices that your father the butcher never had, Paulo Roberto. Nor your railway worker father, Eduardo.'

'If you're saying this because I fell asleep in a Latin class . . .' Paulo suggested.

'*Quaerentibus bona vix obveniunt; mala autem etiam non quaerentibus.* "Good is granted with difficulty to those seeking it; but evil happens even to those not seeking it." To err is human, Paulo Roberto. Yet it's by recognizing our mistakes that we learn to avoid repeating them, isn't it?'

'Yes.'

'Yes, sir.'

'At your age, your parents were already working, having hardly learned to read. Now they're making huge sacrifices, saving what little money they earn, choosing not to buy clothes and shoes for themselves, doing far beyond what's reasonable and necessary just so that you two can study and, who knows, perhaps one day become part of the elite of our country. Isn't that so? And that possibility only arose because of the existence of this school you study in. Without having to pay. A state school. The only free secondary education establishment in the entire region. Conceived and built thanks to the generous vision and democratic spirit of our founder, Dr Diógenes de Almeida Marques Torres.'

He swivelled the chair again: left, right, left. Came to a halt. Leaned forward over his desk. Propped his head in his hands. A slight smile. His preacher's voice became a little more insistent.

'Do you realize what sacrifices your parents are making for you to get on in life? So that you can have a better future? A better life than them? Hmm? Well?'

'Yes, I think so, yes, headmaster,' Eduardo agreed, sincerely.

'Teacher, call me teacher. Don't you agree, Paulo Roberto?'

'Yes.'

'You are two young boys . . . young men . . . of talent. Who knows, one day you may become . . . What would you like to be, Eduardo?'

'An engineer.'

'And you, Paulo Roberto?'

'A scientist.'

Again, the slight smile. His voice announced the opening of the gates to the Garden of Eden.

'1961! We're in the second half of an extraordinary century! We've been through two great wars! And democracy triumphed in both of them! Humanist values prevailed! Science is advancing the whole time! Our country is in a frenzy of development and freedom! The second half of this century is turning out to be the best period for humanity in all history! We are enjoying an era of peace, progress and social mobility! What a marvellous time you two are living in! Fabulous! Truly fabulous. Good, good. So, a scientist and an engineer. Very good. A future Oswaldo Cruz and a future Paulo de Frontin! Wonderful. Excellent.'

He spread his arms wide.

'What an opportunity you have! One that was unthinkable even a short time ago. Impossible if it were not for a secondary school like this one, open to the children of butchers, railway workers, seamstresses, factory workers, barbers, domestic employees, children . . . from every social class, don't you agree?'

He stood up, straightened his coat and walked over to the window. He stood there stiffly, his back to the two boys.

'It would be a shame if all that were to go to waste.'

There was a long pause before he uttered the next few words.

'It would be a shame if you were expelled from this school.'

'Expelled . . . !'

'Expelled from school?' echoed a voice in which lower tones were already replacing higher, childish ones.

'Expelled? What for?'

The headmaster was silent for a few moments, before he repeated gravely:

'A shame.'

He waited for the boys' muttering to finish.

'You two were at Dr Geraldo Bastos's estate yesterday, weren't you?'

No reply. Perhaps they hadn't heard.

'The estate that used to belong to our founder. You made an unauthorized visit to the estate once belonging to Senator Marques Torres.'

'But . . .'

'We didn't skip any classes to go there!'

'It was Sunday!'

'You were with an old black woman, weren't you? By the name of Madalena.'

'Yes, but . . . expel us because we went to Dona Madalena's place?'

'It was Sunday!' repeated Paulo. 'We didn't miss classes or anything!'

'That woman died in the night.'

Even though he could not see their faces, he knew the impact this had. He could hear their sharp intake of breath.

'*Abundans cautela non nocet.* St Augustine. "No precautions are ever too much." You may return to your class.'

He moved away from the window and sat down again. Perplexed, Paulo and Eduardo headed for the door.

'Ah! One more thing.'

The boys turned towards him.

'Be careful of the company you keep. Do you know the word "paedophile"? Look it up in the dictionary. It's dangerous to go around with an old cook, on police files as a Communist, who dressed up as a priest to visit the girls' orphanage. You may go.'

The nun walked slowly across the courtyard of the old people's home, oblivious to the fact that the hem of her brown habit was getting wet in the puddles from the previous night's rain. She was looking for someone.

The air was cold. Several of the old men had brought blankets to wrap themselves in. Others had their heads covered: they would have preferred to be inside the home, but at this time of day it was compulsory to sit out in the sun.

She found the person she was looking for over to one side of the yard, sitting with eyes closed and face turned up to the sun. He hadn't shaved. His unkempt white hair fell over his face. On the table in front of him was a chessboard. He seemed to be asleep.

She stood in front of him, her shadow falling across his face. There was no reaction. She cleared her throat. He didn't move.

'So you play chess!' she said out loud.

The old man opened his eyes at once. He peered up at her, bewildered as to what she was doing there.

'Chess,' she pointed. 'I always wanted to learn how to play.'

Embarrassed, he straightened in his chair. He did up the top button of his pyjamas.

'You're . . . ?' he stammered, as he recognized the director of the Santa Rita de Cássia orphanage.

'May I?' she asked, taking a chair and sitting opposite him. She looked at him levelly. 'Do you play a lot? Do you have good opponents here?'

'No one here plays,' he managed to reply after a few seconds. 'And they don't want to learn.'

'What a shame. So you don't play?'

'I play. That is, I play on my own. But it's a bit crap and . . . I'm sorry for the expression,' he apologized. 'It slipped out.'

'Don't worry, not many people today are offended by that word. What were you saying?'

'It's rather boring. Always playing alone can be quite boring. I end up, as you can see, fast asleep with the board in front of me.'

'Yet you carry on bringing it out into the yard.'

'I do. Force of habit.'

'Did you have people to play with, where you used to live?'

'Sometimes.'

'Was that a home, too?'

'A school.'

'Were you a teacher there?'

He didn't reply.

'Games need a partner, don't they? Like so many things in life.'

The old man felt for cigarettes, but they weren't in his pyjama pocket. He remembered that the walk in the rain had ruined them, and that he hadn't set foot outside the home on Sunday.

'But partners have to be able to trust one another. Or at least to feel that the other person understands.'

'Sister, when I went to the orphanage, I didn't mean to . . .'

'There are lots of similarities between orphanages and homes like this. There are differences too, apart from the obvious one of the inmates' ages. But the basic principle is the same in both cases, don't you think?'

'What do you mean?'

'To isolate those whom society cannot absorb. Or find a use for any more. Or is unable to use yet.'

They both fell silent. The nun was sitting bolt upright in her chair. Then they said, almost in unison:

'You—'

'Sister—'

'Yes?'

'When I was in your orphanage, I—'

'Why don't you live with your family?'

Her curiosity was as open as a child's. He replied without thinking, as if he were talking to one:

'I don't have any.'

'No children?'

'None. Helena died before we could have any.'

'So you're a widower?'

'We were never married.'

'You're not from the same social class as the others in here.'

'You're mistaken.'

'Your way of speaking, your manners, your vocabulary, your education . . .'

'Sister, my name isn't—'

'Basilio, obviously. I've never read Eça de Queiroz. Of course, I know who he is. But I've never even seen a copy of any of his books. The parents and cousins in his novels are frowned on by the Holy Mother Church. The anti-clerical irony of your choice completely passed me by.'

'No irony was intended, believe me. Nor any contempt. That Basilio—'

'Am I to believe then that the name was chosen at random?'

'The cassock really did belong to a Father Basilio that the boys—'

'What part of the north-east are you from?'

'I was born in Sergipe.'

'I've never been there.'

'I moved to Recife when I was very young.'

'I don't know that city either. I've travelled very little. You must have travelled a lot, and seen many things. And many parts of Brazil. The north-east, for example: I've never been there. I may never get to visit it. I'm not likely to leave here. If I do, it will only be to see the inside of other walls, somewhere else. You seem out of sorts today.'

She was staring at him with such intensity that he lowered his head, flustered.

'You've got shadows under your eyes, you haven't shaved, you haven't . . . I was surprised to find you here in your pyjamas with the others. I thought you were more . . . how can I put it . . . ?'

'Normally I don't . . . normally I make sure I get dressed every morning. As I have done all my life. It's not because I'm in here that . . . that I no longer . . . distinguish night from morning, morning from afternoon, or afternoon from night. I'm not worried by the passage of time. It's nothing special. It's not something that worries me. I don't need any hope like that. I've nothing more to lose. It's just that today . . . I feel very . . . tired. Forgive me for being dressed like this in public.'

'Has something happened since you came to the orphanage?'

He avoided her gaze once more.

'I didn't mean to insult you. It was a ridiculous disguise, but there was no intention to . . . All I wanted was . . . I wanted some information . . . that . . . I . . . I'm sorry, but . . .'

'You really are out of sorts today, aren't you? And my questions bother you.'

'No. Yes. A little. No, it's not that. It's just that . . .'

'I haven't come here to report you, if that's what—'

'That never even occurred to me. That's not what's bothering me.'

'What is it then?'

'I find myself thinking . . . things . . . about myself.'

'Things?'

'Things I've done.'

'Things you've done?'

'In my past. Things the same as . . . other people have done. Other men. So many men. Memories. Not just hurtful ones, the kind that bring pain that never goes away. A memory of things I've done in my past. Things that made me ashamed of myself. That still do. Even today. Of how brutally I behaved. So often. And in such a cowardly way. And there's nothing I can do to change that. Because I was the one who did them, it was me who did those things. I didn't mean to. But I did. Isn't that what all criminals say?'

She replied so hastily that he was sure of something: remorse was nothing new to her.

'I believe we should only think of the past if it helps improve the present. If not, it's pure nostalgia.'

'It's not nostalgia that I feel. It's shame. I spent my life thinking I was . . . that I was, as we used to say, a tireless fighter for the causes of liberty. Of the proletariat, the wretched, the starving, women, the illiterate . . . of the oppressed. All the oppressed. But I wasn't. I played the role: even to myself. Especially to myself. But I wasn't that fighter. Ever. There's no true freedom without the recognition of the freedom and will of the other. I don't know what a woman's will is. Not even Helena's. I never respected it. It never crossed my mind that such a thing existed: a woman's will. I used them . . . Forgive me for speaking like this to you, sister, so . . . crudely, but that's

171

what I always did. I used them. Their bodies. How and when I liked. Like so many men did with . . . with that girl who . . . Anita. Aparecida. Used by so many men, and who ended up dead and mutilated without . . . without causing any . . . any . . . protests. Any indignation. Until I saw what those men had done to Anita, to Aparecida, I thought I was . . . I didn't realize that I too had been . . . I didn't think I'd also been a . . . It's depressing to discover we've spent our whole lives playing out a farce. Yesterday I discovered that. At my age. I discovered I wasn't very different from those monsters I'd always despised and fought against.'

He lowered his head again. He peered down at his feet, and saw he was wearing a pair of slippers. The same ones he had worn that morning.

'What piece is this?' asked the nun, pointing to the chessboard.

'A pawn.'

'And that one?'

'The queen.'

'And over there?'

'A bishop.'

'How interesting. Bishop, queen, pawn . . . how many plots there can be in a game of chess.'

'I wouldn't call them plots.'

'It was simply an association of ideas. I've always wanted to learn chess. Perhaps you could teach me.'

'No doubt.'

'But not now. Not here. Perhaps you could come to the orphanage this evening?'

172

'This evening?'

'Yes. That will give us time to learn and talk. About a visitor I had, for example. Who mentioned you.'

'A visitor who mentioned me?'

'You are allowed out in the evening, aren't you?'

'Yes, but at nine o'clock the nuns lock the gate.'

'That gives us more than enough time,' said the orphanage director, rising to her feet.

He also got up.

'You spoke of a visitor you had . . .'

'We'll come back to that, don't worry. So, until this evening . . . Basilio.'

'Until then.'

The nun was walking away through the other old men when he called out to her.

'Sister!'

She turned back towards him.

'I don't know your name.'

'Maria Rosa. Sister Maria Rosa.'

'A pretty name.'

'It's not the name I was baptized with, obviously. You know we have to choose one when we take our vows, don't you?'

He nodded.

'I chose Rosa, because that is St Teresa's flower. Maria because it's the name of the mother of God.'

'Of Jesus,' he replied automatically, before realizing what he had said.

'Of Jesus,' she agreed. 'In other words, of God.'

He restrained himself. Sister Maria Rosa continued on her way out.

'Wait!'

The nun halted.

'My name . . .'

She looked at him expectantly.

'My name is Ubiratan.'

'I know. See you later, Mr Ubiratan.'

'Until this evening, Sister Maria Rosa.'

'Ah!' She seemed to remember something, before she disappeared among the other inmates. 'There's no need to wear your cassock.'

8

Mater et Magistra

THE BELL RANG for the end of lessons. Mademoiselle Célia, as the French teacher demanded to be called, ignored the loud ringing and the hubbub in the classroom as the pupils gathered up their books, textbooks, pencils, rubbers and pens, stuffing them into their briefcases and bags, anxious to leave as quickly as possible. Her young audience might be indifferent to Corneille's sonorous verses, but Mademoiselle had no intention of breaking off her reading of *Le Cid*. She had reached Act Two, Scene Eight, which never failed to move her: Chimène's father has just been killed by Don Rodrigue, the man she loved. With her arm stretched out towards the class in the way she imagined Don Gómez's daughter must have done to the King of Castille, she went on:

'"*Je l'ai trouvé sans vie. Excusez ma douleur, Sire, la voix me manque à ce récit funeste.*"'

She shut the small, blue-bound book, and closed her eyes. She wiped away a tear before it ran down her cheek.

'"*Mes pleurs et mes soupirs vous diront mieux le reste.*"'

She opened her eyes, and clutched the book to her meagre chest.

'In the next lesson,' she told them, 'we'll discuss the following question: *comment Chimène et Don Diègue cherchent d'abord à émouvoir le roi avant de presenter des arguments.* And bring today's dictation properly translated.'

Those pupils who owned real leather briefcases – a rare and unmistakable symbol of the economic power of the children of a higher social class in this state school – displayed them proudly on their desktops.

'*Très bien,* class dismissed,' Mademoiselle announced, turning her back on them, gathering up her bag, books and class register from the desk, and leaving the classroom as well.

Eduardo was still sitting there, head down. The room emptied. A short while later, Paulo came running back in.

'Aren't you going home? What's the matter?'

Without raising his head, Eduardo tried to answer. He wanted to explain how confused he felt by all the things beyond their control, to ask for help to understand Dona Madalena's death, the headmaster's threat of expulsion, the risk of their futures being destroyed, his mother's moans and his father's growls the night before, the horror of discovering the existence of a poverty far worse than he had ever imagined or read about in books. All he managed to say was:

'We're in a really tight spot.'

He looked up. Paulo didn't seem any more worried than if his team had just let a goal in, and there were still thirty minutes of the game left.

'We'll find a way,' he said.

'But you don't understand, Paulo! They want to get rid of us!'

'Who are "they"?'

'Them, Paulo. Them. The headmaster, the factory owner, the mayor. The . . . Them! Them!'

'Who are they, Eduardo? It was only the headmaster who threatened to expel us. We didn't do anything wrong. All we did was go and talk to Aparecida's grandmother.'

Again, Eduardo tried to say more than he actually understood. But all he could translate into words was:

'Let's go. My mother's expecting me for lunch.'

They greeted one another with strict formality. They called each other by their first names, but said 'Mr' and 'Sister' first. They would have liked to feel more at ease, but found it impossible. Out of shyness, or from being unaccustomed to finding themselves alone with someone of the opposite sex, or because they knew this was far more important than a mere friendly visit, because they were aware that they both knew far more about the other than they admitted, yet did not know how to deal with this involuntary familiarity.

She pointed to an armchair, and he sat down. She went to the drinks tray, poured two glasses, gave him one, put hers on the side table and sat opposite him. Then she immediately stood up, went back to the drinks, took the bottle and put it beside his glass, next to a pile of papers.

'Serve yourself whenever you like, Mr Ubiratan.'

He nodded his head, thanking her.

'We were honoured with a visit from our pastor, Mr Ubiratan.'

'Please just call me Ubiratan, without the "Mr".'

She didn't even seem to be aware of his request.

'His worship the bishop paid us the honour of a visit very early this morning, Mr Ubiratan.'

'You don't need to call me—'

'We were on our way to the refectory for breakfast,' Sister Maria Rosa went on, 'with the young girls in the orphanage, when we were informed that the monsignor was waiting for us.'

'This morning?'

'Very early. Straight after the first prayers in the chapel. He was waiting for me in this very room. Dom Tadeu was accompanied by a young man. A nephew: I think he was a nephew; the fair-haired youngster who always accompanies him and acts as his chauffeur.'

There was nothing malicious about the way she said this, but Ubiratan noticed that for some reason the information about the bishop's companion was emphasized. He could not think what that might be.

'The youngster went out of the room as soon as I came in. He left without even saying hello.'

Ubiratan drank his drink and served himself another one, waiting for Sister Maria Rosa to go on.

'Above and beyond the unusual honour of a visit at that time of day, the bishop wanted to give me those papers.' She pointed to the pile of mimeographed sheets next to the drinks tray. 'Would you like to take a look at them?'

'*Mater . . .*' The old man tried to read what was written on the top sheet of paper.

'. . . *et Magistra. Mater et Magistra.* "Mother and Teacher" in Latin. Do you understand Latin?' she asked, picking up the sheets.

'No, sister. And I don't see the link between—'

'It's the new papal encyclical, *Mater et Magistra,*' she explained, leafing through the papers. 'Mother and guide is what the Catholic Church aims to be under Pope John XXIII. Welcoming, protecting and guiding. I imagine you are familiar with the ideas and changes Pope John XXIII is proposing.'

'Don't be offended, sister, but I'm not interested in anything that comes from the Vatican. I am still disgusted at Pope Pius XII's indifference to the extermination of Jews, gypsies and homosexuals under the Third Reich, which seems to me just as criminal as—'

'I'm not talking about Pius XII,' she interrupted him, 'but about his successor, John XXIII.' She searched through the papers again. 'The new pope is the son of poor agricultural workers, a very different background to his predecessor's. His ideas are also radically different from those of Pius XII. This encyclical, *Mater et Magistra*, was issued by the new pope and clearly shows the difference. That is, it will be issued by the new pope, and will show . . . because it has not yet been published outside the clergy. Ah, here it is! Can I read this passage for you?'

She went on immediately, giving him no chance to answer: 'It says as follows: "In some of these lands the enormous

179

wealth, the unbridled luxury, of the privileged few stands in violent, offensive contrast to the utter poverty of the vast majority."'

She looked directly at Ubiratan.

'Do you know our bishop? He comes from a family of wealthy landowners. One of his uncles was the state governor appointed by Getúlio Vargas, and he had a decisive influence over Dr Diógenes's career.'

'Dr who?'

'Diógenes. The father of the current city mayor.'

'So there's a link between their families . . .'

'The bishop and the mayor were in a seminary together,' she said, looking down at the bundle of papers she was now holding against her chest. 'Let me read you this other part: "Clearly, this sort of development in social relationships brings many advantages in its train. It makes it possible for the individual to exercise many of his personal rights, especially those which we call economic and social and which pertain to the necessities of life."'

She paused. 'You seem astonished.'

'So that pope of yours is preaching the benefits of socialism? He's talking about human rights? Have I understood correctly, sister? How did that passage about luxury you read earlier go?'

'"In some of these lands the enormous wealth, the unbridled luxury, of the privileged few stands in violent, offensive contrast to the utter poverty of the vast majority."'

'The Vatican recognizing the poverty of the majority?

Criticizing the luxury and wealth of the few? It's hard to believe a prince of the Church wrote that.'

'More than a prince. The pope himself. John XXIII. Angelo Roncalli. A man from a poor background. Extremely poor.'

'Why then did the bishop . . . ?'

'The bishop is part of what we might call the more conservative wing of the Holy Mother Church.'

'Yet he came to bring you . . .'

'The bishop brought us the new papal encyclical, which has not yet been published, and you are wondering what made him do that.'

'Yes, especially as he is not part of the . . .'

'Progressive wing of the Church?'

'Exactly.'

Sister Maria Rosa shrugged her shoulders, still holding the by now jumbled papers. Some of them fell to the floor. Ubiratan made to pick them up, but she stopped him with a hand gesture.

'These pages, Mr Ubiratan, serve to remind me of the goodness and charity that have always characterized our Church and, shall we say, the Catholic elite. Virtues that made possible the survival and education of abandoned children. Children like me. Like Aparecida. You know that this orphanage was founded by the mayor's grandfather, don't you? The boys' orphanage, where Renato was brought up, was also established thanks to donations made by that grandfather. A pious man, devoted to St Rita de Cássia, as the monsignor reminded me. He was a bosom friend of another good Catholic, the emperor Dom Pedro II, and of the military leaders who proclaimed the Brazilian

Republic in 1889. He was one of the first senators of the so-called "milky coffee republic", thanks to his friendship with President Afonso Pena. His son Diógenes followed in his footsteps and also became a senator. And, as you are aware, a close collaborator of Getúlio Vargas.'

'From what you're telling me, the Marques Torres family has been close to the seat of power for a very long time.'

'Ever since the Second Empire. Even before that. Yes. And more so during the New State. Of course, the secondary school is an initiative of Senator Marques Torres, when Getúlio was still alive, at the start of the 1950s. So too is the asphalt road linking us to the capital. The family has been public-spirited for many years. It began with the construction of the first electricity power plant here, thanks to the mayor's grandfather, so beloved of the emperor. A power plant that led to the arrival of the textile, lace and lathe factories, which in turn directly created hundreds of jobs and, with the passage of time, thousands more indirectly. Industries and jobs that helped promote the lengthy political career of Senator Marques Torres and his support for Getúlio Vargas.'

Ubiratan took a box of matches out of his jacket pocket, and then a rolled-up cigarette. He showed it to the nun, as if asking her permission to smoke. She went over to the table, took an ashtray out of a drawer and gave it to Ubiratan, before sitting down again.

'The history of this region's progress is intimately linked to the history of the Marques Torres family. The arrival of the first Italian settlers in Brazil is also due to them. The emperor's wife, Dona Teresa Cristina, was from Naples, and she made sure that the immigrants, many of them from her father's kingdom of Sicily, were brought here to work on the coffee plantations owned by her husband's friend and his friends.'

'The bishop told you all this,' Ubiratan concluded, blowing out smoke.

'Yes.'

'Making it very clear that . . .'

'In short, Mr Ubiratan, the Marques Torres family is responsible for so many and such a variety of benefits enjoyed by the people of this region over so many years, and in particular the most needy among them, that the monsignor believes – thinks – that where certain matters concerning important members representing the best in our community, the monsignor thinks – and so he told me – that certain matters should be left to the competent authorities.'

'Meaning?'

'Crime is a matter that should be left to the police.'

Ubiratan could not avoid a dispirited sigh.

'The monsignor also mentioned an old man who stole the priest's cassock from the São Joaquim chapel and wore it to come here to talk to me. He added that the same old man claimed he had been a teacher, whereas in fact he is a retired cook from a school in Recife, with a police record as a Communist, and has been seen in dark streets of the city in the company of two young boys. I won't repeat the word he used to describe the relationship between the old man and the boys.'

The old man almost choked on his cigarette.

'Therefore, as director of this orphanage, responsible as I am for the moral education of minors, it would not be proper, it would not be acceptable, for me to talk to you again, to pass you information, or to permit any contact with the nuns who have been here since the days when Aparecida was one of our pupils.'

'I don't understand.'

'That is what the monsignor instructed me.'

'I came here at your request.'

'As I told you, I would very much like to learn how to play chess.'

She searched again among the sheets of paper.

'Let me read you this other passage from *Mater et Magistra*, Mr Ubiratan: "Those who violate His laws not only offend the divine majesty and degrade themselves and humanity, they also sap the vitality of the political community of which they are members."'

Laying the sheets of paper down on the table, she took off her glasses and clutched them to her, trying to prevent Ubiratan from seeing how her hands were trembling.

'Aparecida was taken from here as a young girl. Aparecida was humiliated in ways . . . in ways not even animals have to suffer. They destroyed that girl. They turned her into . . .'

Standing up, she went over to the bookshelf and stood with her back to him, rummaging among the books. She wasn't really interested in any of them: she simply wanted to avoid being seen displaying an emotion as improper as anger. When she felt her rage subsiding, she turned back to Ubiratan.

'You didn't bring the chessboard. A shame. While you were teaching me, we could have talked about what I've been told by the older nuns concerning the years when Aparecida lived here. A real shame. I can learn some other time. But perhaps it would be best to give you the information now anyway.'

In times gone by, matrons and young girls used to throw rose petals from this second-floor balcony down on to the litters of the processions winding their way up to the cathedral. Now, a prostitute was drying her freshly dyed red hair in the afternoon sun. She was reading a magazine, oblivious to the activity in the steep street, ignored in her turn by the few passers-by, who avoided the pavement on her side.

A white-haired man appeared at the opposite corner, and stopped in the shadow of an acacia tree. He stood there motionless, watching.

He could not see any signs of movement inside the Hotel Wizorek. The other women must be playing cards, chatting or attending to the few early-evening clients.

He heard a squawk. He couldn't immediately make out what it was. Then a female voice. Singing. Someone had put a record on the phonograph. It sounded scratched. It came from the same mansion that in the nineteenth century had belonged to the family of a Portuguese immigrant who had made his fortune from importing and selling slaves from Angola. The music grew louder.

> 'Vissi d'arte, vissi d'amore,
> Non feci mai male ad anima viva! . . .
> Con man furtiva . . .'

The sound reached him more clearly. He recognized an aria from an opera lost in the fog of his memories. The tune was taken up by violins, a harp and other instruments he could not identify.

> *'Sempre con fè sincera,*
> *La mia preghiera*
> *Ai santi tabernacoli salì . . .'*

He crossed the street and stood a hundred metres from the building. The grimy ground-floor windows were closed, except for the two on either side of the main door, which had curtains. That was where the music was coming from.

> *'Perchè, Signore, perchè*
> *Me ne rimuneri così?'*

He knew he had heard the aria before. Perhaps on the school radio. Or on some record. Not in the theatre. He had never been to an opera. He had some opera records, but had never seen one. Helena liked the opera. She was the one who had introduced him to it. They had planned to go one day to Rio de Janeiro to hear and see the chorus of the Hebrew slaves from *Nabucco*. Helena liked Verdi, and he learned to appreciate the composer. 'Va Pensiero' became like a personal anthem for him. But they had never been to Rio de Janeiro. He had never set foot in the Theatro Municipal. They also had an album of *Il Guarany*, one with Helena's favourite Mozart arias sung by Bidú Sayão, another by Mozart with a

German soprano whose name he could never recall, and two or three more he couldn't remember very well. Like so many other possessions and mementoes, they had all been left behind when he moved to the old people's home.

He weighed up the risks of approaching the brothel. The street was almost empty. Close to the building there was only the possible occupant of a black car, parked in the street opposite.

> '*Diedì gioelli*
> *Della Madonna al manto . . .*'

It wasn't an aria from Donizetti, he thought. Nor from Verdi: it lacked the pomp and grandiloquence that always characterized Verdi's tragic heroines. It didn't sound like Rossini either. He couldn't hear the light, breezy notes typical of Rossini. This is a song of intimate suffering, he concluded. Intense and delicate. Neither Verdi nor Donizetti nor Rossini. It could be Bellini. It had the dramatic weight of Bellini's characters. But it wasn't that. Not as intense. Less sober.

> '*Nell'ora del dolor perchè,*
> *Perchè Signore,*
> *Perchè me ne rimunere così?*'

He moved towards the hotel window. Behind the curtains he could make out a salon lined with claret-coloured wallpaper. To one side, a woman with blonde curls was standing alone next to the portable phonograph. She was wearing a peignoir over her stout body. Her eyes were outlined in black like a silent movie actress. Her lips, coated with dark lipstick, moved in imitation of the voice that the needle was drawing from the big black record. She stretched her hands out in front of her. The voice on the phonograph begged:

> 'Vedi,
> Ecco, vedi,
> Le man giunte io stendo a te!'

Tosca! That's what it was, he remembered. Puccini, obviously. Floria Tosca's plea to the heavens, when she is being harassed by the villain, Scarpia. Obviously. The moment when Floria Tosca has to choose between satisfying Baron Scarpia's carnal appetites to save her beloved Cavaradossi from death by sacrificing her dignity, or keeping it and so condemning Mario to the firing squad. Vice that saves, or virtue that kills. To behave like a prostitute, although from the purest of motives.

The pale-faced woman flung her plump arms out, shaking her curls and exposing their white roots. The peignoir fell open, displaying the Polish madam's heavy body squeezed into a lace shift. But it wasn't the ageing madam who was in the room.

Instead it was the young prostitute Hanna Wizorek, disembarking at the port of Rio de Janeiro at the start of the 1920s, fleeing the war that had devastated Europe, destroyed her village and decimated her family. All alone, with a fake passport in a foreign land, unable to speak the language, and with no one to turn to. She was begging for pity and compassion.

'E merce d'un tuo ditto
Vinta, aspetto . . .'

Desperate, she let her arms drop, preparing to hear Baron Scarpia's cynical reply. At that moment, a broad-shouldered figure came into the room, went over to the phonograph and lifted the arm of the needle, interrupting the music.

The woman turned, pulling the peignoir closer. She looked at the man, said something to him, and then went over to one of the sofas and sat down. Picking up a silver cigarette box from the side table, she took out a mother-of-pearl holder and a cigarette, and lit it.

Ubiratan continued observing the room for some moments longer, while Hanna Wizorek and the mayor Marques Torres began a heated argument. Then he left, walking unhurriedly away down the street.

First it was the sound of the whistle: one-two, one-two, one-two. Then plumes of white smoke appeared over the hill, to the rhythmic beat of a steam engine. Finally, the chimney of the ancient locomotive came into view, pulling carriages blackened by years of soot. Inside, jolted on wooden benches, sat those increasingly rare passengers on the return journey from Rio de Janeiro who did not prefer the soft reclining seats of the buses that left twice a day from the modern coach terminal.

Two boys were pedalling in silence along the road beside

the railway tracks. One of them was listening absent-mindedly to the chugging locomotive, concentrating instead on the thoughts sparking in his mind: some day I'm going to take one, some day I will, some day I'll catch this early morning train, in the other direction, and I'll never come back. I'll go to wherever Uncle Nelson went. I'll find out where he lives, I'll ask him for help, he can send me money for the ticket. I'll pack my case, I've not got many things, I'll pack my suitcase and leave. I'll leave. Yes. I'll leave behind these narrow streets, these dark mountains, my father, my brother, the mist and cold. I'll go to the city where it's hot, with tall buildings and long avenues that end in the Atlantic Ocean, just like the River São Francisco or the Amazon. And me, because I'm not going to stay here. I don't want to end my days as a barber or a shopkeeper. Or a textile worker. Or a welder, petrol-pump attendant, rubber-tapper, lathe operator, typist, baker, electrician . . . or a butcher, like my father. I'm going to study something that will turn me into a . . . a chemist? Diplomat? Army officer? Astronaut? Nuclear physicist? Town planner? Archaeologist? Uncle Nelson could help me. He's never met me, but we'll get on. Doesn't my father say I'm like him? Wiry hair, flappy ears. And dark skin. Like his and my grandmother's.

Heavy leaden clouds were gathering in front of them. The wind pushing and pulling the clouds like a flock of black sheep had not yet reached ground level. It was the start of the stormy autumn. The seemingly endless days of summer were drawing to a close.

They went past the ruins of the Mello Freire ranch. Paulo

stopped to pee. He could remember how imposing the abandoned big house had looked on its thick wooden columns, until it had collapsed a few years earlier. Once a proud testimony to the wealth of the only family in the region that could compete in power and influence with the Marques Torres, the mansion suffered the same fate as the riches they had amassed during the golden age of coffee. The descendants of those early Mello Freires, who now worked as bank employees and modest civil servants, could not prevent it becoming a pile of ruined walls, rotten beams, smashed tiles, fragments of glass and rats' nests. Plump and dusty, one of the rats clambered up what had once been a doorway and stared defiantly at the urinating boy. It scuttled away when a stone Paulo threw bounced close to its pointed head.

Eduardo had continued on his way. Paulo soon caught him up. They were both so deeply engaged in their own concerns that neither of them noticed the silence that had grown up between them.

Eduardo's worries included a fear he had never known before: what if he had no future? The future that until that morning, in the headmaster's office, he had taken for granted. What if in Brazil, in this new Brazil where industries, high-ways, jobs, were springing up all the time, what if in this new Brazil, even though, as their teachers taught them, it was a democracy, where we, the people, have free elections and can choose who is to govern us, what if in this Brazil there were powers, forces he could not describe or explain, or point to where they were lurking, what if they existed, those forces, those powers that could decide his destiny without him being able to do anything about it? Decide to change everything irremediably? Just as on the day when they took Aparecida from the orphanage and married her to the dentist?

They reached the dirt track. They rode on for almost ten minutes before they saw the fence. They went even faster, anxious to reach the lake. All at once they had to stop and dismount. Fresh barbed wire had been put up in the open ground at the edge of the woods. On the wire, a hand-painted sign read: *Private Property: No Entry.*

Paulo took off his shirt, wrapped it round two of the barbs, and slipped through the space. Eduardo passed the bikes through. As soon as Paulo had taken them, he held the strands apart for Eduardo. Then they walked in the shade of the trees, the bike tyres and their feet thudding gently on dry leaves and rotten, greying mangoes. They still did not say a word to each other, until a slightly acrid smell hit Eduardo's nostrils.

'Can you smell that?'

'What?'

'That smell. Don't you notice anything?'

They entered the bamboo grove. Instead of the usual coolness of the green tunnel, an acrid odour filled the air. Flakes of ash floated round them. The further they advanced, the more of them there were. Throwing down their bikes, the two boys rushed to the end of the tunnel, where the bright blue gleam of water was no longer visible.

When they emerged into the clearing, they came to a shocked halt.

All round the lake, from the bamboo grove to the sugar cane plantation, from the undergrowth on the right to the mango trees stretching out to the left, what before had been a mixture of green grass, bushes, tree stumps and wild flowers had become a black, desolate, smoking circle. Someone had burned off all the vegetation.

The paradise they had known was destroyed.

The policeman loaded the heavy photographic enlarger into the back of the jeep, together with the developing trays, then went to sit in the driver's seat. Another policeman came out of the front door of the dentist's house, struggling to carry a trunk that was too big for his short arms. As he turned to thrust it into the vehicle, he lost his balance. The wooden chest slipped out of his grasp and fell, opening and spilling its contents out between pavement and road. The other policeman immediately jumped down and helped his colleague pick up papers, photographs and X-rays. One of them cursed. They closed the trunk again and put it on the floor of the car, wiped their hands on a piece of cloth, got into the jeep and drove off. It wasn't long before the neighbours left their windows and doorways to return to their empty afternoon routines.

It was only then that Ubiratan came over. He wanted to get into the house to start a new search. He had almost reached the gate when he saw that a third policeman had been left on guard inside. He walked on past. He would follow Sister Maria Rosa's suggestion and visit the cemetery. All he needed to know was where to look.

His attention was caught by a piece of paper emerging from a puddle. It rose to the surface. He bent down and picked up the rectangle, the size of a notebook. As the dirty water ran off it, he could see dozens of small images. It was a photo contact sheet. It showed shots of a young blonde woman, surrounded by several men. Her vagina and anus were penetrated by a variety of objects.

They pedalled as fast as they could along the middle of the asphalted road, avoiding the verges that the rain had turned muddy. They still said nothing.

Several times it occurred to Eduardo to ask Paulo if he felt anything similar to the weight he could feel in his chest, the impression that his guts were wrenching, that his blood was close to exploding from beating so hard at his temples. He wanted to say something, but it was more than his dry mouth that made it impossible. The words he was searching for rushed by too quickly for him to seize them, like balloons swept along by a furious wind.

Paulo could not understand his feelings either. Disconnected images and sounds crowded his memory: the pot of rice on the wooden stove, the headmaster's voice, monkey, just like your uncle, the chopped-off breast, the patter of rain on the roof, his father's hot hand slapping his face, the dust under the table, golliwog has no idea, good-for-nothing, blood, bread, grass, ashes, Chimène, *Le Cid*, Tarzan, I'm scared, no I'm not, I'm not . . .

Panting, unaware of how tired they were, sweating, they rode on. They wanted to reach the city as quickly as possible. They needed help to explain the flood of events that had engulfed them. Perhaps that was why they did not notice the car approaching. At least not until it was too late. Eduardo never knew if he first heard the noise of the engine or glimpsed the shiny gleam of black metal bearing down on them, whether it was him or Paulo who shouted to warn the other one, or how he managed to throw himself and his bike towards the muddy verge. What Eduardo did remember was flying over the handlebars into the mud as he heard to his horror how the car tyres crashed into metal on the asphalt and thinking: Oh no, Paulo, Paulo, no!

The cemetery stretched down the hill. It was divided into two areas of equal size, separated by a stone wall to the left of the entrance gate. On the arch over the gate stood an image of the Virgin Mary crushing a serpent beneath her feet, surrounded by bodiless cherubims. Black iron railings with gilded tips enclosed the entire burial ground.

To the right of the wall, beyond a stone cross littered with candle stubs and melted wax, stood rows of low tombs, rectangles covered with concrete plaques or lined with tiles. There were also several flat graves, with grass growing on the disturbed earth. What he was looking for would not be on this side, thought Ubiratan.

He turned towards the left-hand side of the wall. Beyond it, at the top of a burial monument, between two iron columns, a stone angel was brandishing a sword to the heavens in his right hand, while in his left he clutched the shaft of a tattered silk banner.

He went towards it.

The tombs in this part of the cemetery were larger, lined with marble, and decorated with busts, sculptures, metal inscriptions, photographs, vases, flowers. This was where the mortal remains of the region's leading families lay. Even in death they had no wish to mingle with the hoi polloi.

He made straight for the mausoleum with the angel, the largest in the entire cemetery. He was sure this was where he would find what he was searching for. He was surprised at the slime in the corners of the stained marble slabs, and the ferns growing in the cracks. This arrogant neo-Gothic monument had not been cleaned or visited for a very long time.

Ubiratan searched for some clue in the words engraved on the side wall. He read: *Gloria Virtutem Tamquam Umbra Sequitur.* And beneath it: *In Honoris Amarílio Rodrigues de Mello Freire.* He was wrong: this wasn't the one.

He looked all around. There was only one other tomb as big as the one with the armed angel. At the far end of the central aisle.

He soon reached it.

Compared to the Mello Freire family's pantheon, it was almost simple in its colonial chapel design: whitewashed, with no statues, images or plaques. At the front of the chamber, between two oval stained-glass windows, stood a gate with thick iron railings. In the centre was a hexagonal coat of arms with coffee-bush branches crossed over an open book with the letters M and T visible on it.

He pushed the gate. It didn't move. He pushed harder. It was padlocked.

Walking back to the right-hand side of the cemetery, he headed straight for the simple earth graves. Their numbers were fixed to the crosses with bits of wire. He chose the one that looked the easiest to unfasten.

Then he went back to the Marques Torres family mausoleum.

He got to his feet in a daze, covered in mud, anxious. When the black fog in front of his eyes finally lifted, the first thing he saw was his bicycle lying on the road. The raised back wheel was still spinning round. At the other side of the road, Paulo was flat out, motionless, his face in a puddle of muddy water.

Eduardo ran over to him, lifted his head. His eyes were closed. He turned him over, shook him. Called his name. There was no one coming along the road to whom he could shout for help.

Then Paulo coughed. He spat, first once and then a second time, his head still cradled in his friend's arms. He slowly started to get up, using both hands. He was on all fours. He coughed and spat again. Rising to his knees, he rubbed his face with his hands, in a useless attempt to wipe it clean. Eduardo felt in his back trouser pocket for the handkerchief he always carried, but what he pulled out was a filthy, dripping wet rag. He quickly put it away. Paulo was still rubbing his eyes, blinking constantly. He couldn't see anything. He tried to stand up, but lost his balance and fell on his backside again.

'Does it hurt? Is anything broken?'

Paulo shook his head, without much conviction. The whole of his right side, which had hit the road first, was aching. From his experience of having a broken arm and ankle, he thought it couldn't be too serious. Still bewildered, he could make out Eduardo's face. It was streaked with mud. He looked like a bushman from one of the tribes fighting Tarzan. He felt like laughing, but then groaned when he saw what lay beyond his friend.

'What's the matter, Paulo? Where does it hurt?'

Distraught, Paulo pointed to his mangled bike.

'Today's the day my father's finally going to kill me.'

A slight click told him the lock had given way. Slipping the piece of wire into his coat pocket, Ubiratan pushed the gate open and stepped inside the spacious Marques Torres family vault.

The slanting late-afternoon sun caught the stained-glass windows, casting multicoloured shapes on to drawers and niches, some of them open, and glinting off bronze letters set in the far wall, the only one lined with marble. In Gothic lettering at the top was an inscription: *In the arms of God the Saviour, awaiting the call of Resurrection, here lie Baron Olivério Santanna Marques Torres, his beloved spouse Maria*

Beatriz de Castro Marques Torres and all their descendants. Below it was a phrase in Latin: *Os ex ossibus meis et caro carne mea.* Bone of my bones and flesh of my flesh.

The names and dates that followed constituted a long list beginning in 1811, and were full of archaic Christian names and titles that had vanished with the Brazilian empire. He searched them until he came to Diógenes Marques Torres. Before his name was the title of senator, in capital letters; underneath, the dates 1882–1955. No other name was added after his. Above it, beyond a blank space, he saw two names written close to one another: Vicente Luiz Marques Torres – 1947, and André Luiz Marques Torres – 1947–1949. Contrary to his expectations, there was no woman's name since the 1940s.

He walked round the crypt, without knowing what he was looking for. The niches of the two little boys Vicente and André had the same phrase written on the front lid: *Forever in the thoughts of his parents, Adriano and Isabel.* So the twins were the sons of the mayor Marques Torres. One of them still-born, the other dead at the age of two. The family name was to die with them.

Beneath the twins' niche was an open rectangle. He bent down and peered inside. Another niche. It was empty, apart from a few fragments of marble and cement.

He straightened up, leaning his left hand on the lid of the bigger sepulchre. He felt a stabbing pain in his lower back. A sign that his rheumatism would soon return. He stretched. Raised his hands above his head. Sometimes this trick worked: his spine cracked, and the pain went away.

But not this time. He sighed. He was beginning to feel weary.

The sun had shifted and now threw a yellow stripe on the far wall. Indistinct at that distance, the lengthy names now looked like gleaming, harmonious metallic lists, with one dead person following another, then another, and another . . . All at once he noticed a gap in this regular list. A bigger space between the name of the senator and that of his grandson Vicente.

He went closer. The surface of the marble had been scratched, but faint shapes were still visible. They could be letters. A name might have been scratched out. And dates. He went right up to the wall. The vague shapes looked like the numbers 1, 9 and 5. Nineteen hundred and . . . ? The fourth number was hard to make out. It looked like a 7, or a 2. He remembered that 1952 was the year Aparecida was married.

He took the wire from his pocket, and started to dig at the marble above the numbers. Letters gradually emerged. First a C . . . then an L . . . then an E . . . and an A. Cléa? Who could Cléa be?

He saw the mistake he had made.

He began to scrape more firmly with the wire in the centre of the letter C, where it was almost completely obliterated, and soon also made out the original shape of the third letter, Z. So the nuns had been right: this was the past that the surviving members of the Marques Torres family wanted to remove all traces of from their tomb, their history, their lives. Elza. Aparecida's mother.

9

Mao, *Snow White* and Another Anita

THEY WALKED UP the street without a word, bathed in the golden evening sunlight that threw their long shadows on to the paving stones of the road. They didn't know what to say to each other. One of the boys was disconsolately pushing a twisted bike, imagining all the ruses he would have to come up with to prevent his brother and father seeing it before he had straightened it out even a little. The other boy walked beside him in sympathy, holding his own bike by the handlebars, experiencing the unknown, possibly liberating and yet uncomfortable feeling of being seen in public as filthy as a beggar. They both noticed the crowd outside the police station at the same time.

They pushed their way through the adults whispering outside the main entrance. At the top of the steps an elegantly dressed man was talking to the police chief. He was standing erect, without moving either his long arms or his hands, which held a sheaf of papers. It looked as if he were delegating tasks to a subordinate. His jutting jaw and pointed chin dominated his long, straw-coloured face. He was wearing a pair of round, gold-rimmed glasses.

Eduardo noted how white his starched shirt collar was, the way it was closed by the perfect knot of a plain dark tie, the elegance of his charcoal-grey pinstripe suit. He had seen material like that among his mother's fabrics. It was cashmere. He remembered how his hand slid easily along the soft, fine cloth. The opposite of the police chief's rough cotton suit. Boss's clothes versus those of an employee.

A nudge from Paulo jerked him out of these thoughts.

'Can you hear what they're saying?'

'No. He's talking in a low voice, and they're a long way off.'

'Who's talking low?'

'The factory owner. Over there, with the police chief.'

'No, Eduardo! I mean what these people' – he indicated the crowd around them – 'are saying.'

'Who?'

'Everyone. About what the dentist did.'

'What did he do?'

Before Paulo could reply, the voices around them went suddenly quiet. Everyone was gazing in the same direction: at the coffin emerging from the police station door, carried by several policemen. Geraldo Bastos and the police chief had to move out of the way to let them down the steps.

'He killed himself!' shouted Eduardo, from the entrance to the courtyard.

'He hanged himself!' added Paulo, starting to run over towards Ubiratan, who was seated under the only light the nuns had left on. He was shuffling through bits of paper of different sizes strewn over a small table, next to the notebook he always carried with him. Picking up one of the pieces of paper, he stuffed it in his pocket, without looking up at the approaching boys.

'He hanged himself with his tie!'

'He tied it round a bar in his cell window!'

'And jumped!'

'Just now!' As usual, Paulo was the one who arrived first. 'It only happened a few minutes ago!'

Ubiratan put down two small sheets of paper, placing two narrower strips on top of each of them. All the pieces had dates, names and notes written on them.

'The coffin was . . .' Eduardo came to a halt next to the table, trying to get his breath back, 'was being carried out of the police station just as we—'

Ubiratan interrupted him.

'Have you seen *Snow White*? Have either of you seen it?'

'. . . arrived on our bikes.'

'*Snow White*,' Ubiratan repeated.

'The people were saying that he had hanged himself, but Eduardo didn't realize—'

'I didn't realize they were talking about the dentist hanging himself, because—'

'Eduardo didn't hear a thing.'

'I was surprised to see the factory owner there. That was why—'

'It was then they came out with the coffin. Eduardo wasn't looking!'

'I was!'

Ubiratan was growing impatient.

'*Snow White and the Seven Dwarves*! Have you seen it?'

'It was then that they took the coffin out.'

'From the police station.'

'Sealed.'

'Yes, it was sealed. Nobody seed him.'

'Nobody *saw* him, Paulo.'

'Have you seen it or not?'

'We didn't see, Ubiratan! Nobody could see! It was sealed! Paulo told you, I told you: it was sealed!'

'*Snow White and the Seven Dwarves*! *Snow-White-and-the Se-ven Dwar-ves*,' the old man repeated slowly. 'Have you seen it or not?'

'Seen what?'

'The Walt Disney film,' said Ubiratan, pronouncing the 'W' like a 'V'. 'The cartoon. In colour. Well, have you seen it?'

Paulo spread his arms, palms upward, perplexed.

'Ubiratan, we're trying to tell you that the dentist—'

'Yes or no?' he insisted, shaking his pen in their faces.

'Ubiratan!' Eduardo tried to make him see sense. 'Ubiratan, the dentist killed himself!'

No reaction.

'We saw the coffin being taken out of the jail!' Paulo almost shouted.

'He hanged himself, Ubiratan! He hanged himself with a tie from a bar in his cell window!'

The old man waved his hands, to get them to speak more quietly. Then, without giving them time to respond, he added:

'It was made the year Aparecida was born.'

Paulo shook his head. Shifted his weight from one foot to the other.

'What?'

'*Snow White*. It was made in 1937. Do you think Aparecida saw it?'

'Ubiratan—' Eduardo tried again.

'The same year as *Guernica*!'

'Ubiratan, listen—'

'Do you know what *Guernica* was? What it signified? The carnage? The bombardment? The killing of children, old people, women? Do you know about all that? The rise of Fascism? Do you know about the Spanish Civil War? Picasso?'

Paulo felt like shouting, kicking, stamping his feet and covering his ears all at the same time. Instead, he thrust his hands into the pockets of his filthy trousers in disgust.

'Did you hear what Eduardo and me told you?'

Ubiratan bent over the bits of paper, picked one up, and shook it at the two boys.

'*Guernica*. Picasso. Picasso – *Guernica*. The same year: 1937. Could Aparecida have heard of Picasso?'

'Ah!' said Eduardo, suddenly remembering. 'And as well as the suicide, there was the lake.'

'Someone has burned everywhere around the lake!'

'Everything!'

'In the spot where we found her.'

'Her *body*.'

'And they said we could be expelled, and they've put a new barbed wire fence round the lake.'

'Expelled from school: the headmaster threatened us with expulsion,' Eduardo explained. 'And there's a fence round the lake now. They must have put it up overnight. With a sign saying *No Entry*.'

'And her grandmother died last night.'

'Aparecida's grandmother. Dona Madalena died.'

'After we'd been there.'

'She died yesterday.'

'And when we were coming back a car ran us down.'

'Today. On our way back from the lake. Not long ago.'

'My bike is all squashed.'

'Buckled.'

'When he see it, my father—'

'When he *sees* it.'

'It was in 1937 that the New State was founded in Brazil. The same year. Do you know what the New State was?'

Eduardo wouldn't give up: 'The dentist, Ubiratan.'

'Do you or don't you?'

'He killed himself in jail.'

'Paulo: do you know about it?'

Paulo sighed dispiritedly.

'More or less. The New State was Getúlio Vargas. But we're trying to tell you that the dentist—'

'Is that all you know? Is that trivial simplification all they teach you at school?'

'Of course not,' said Eduardo defiantly. 'It was Getúlio

Vargas's government after he shut down Congress and banned political parties. It was the period when the labour laws were created, when women got the vote, and everything else. It ended after the Second World War.'

'That year 1937 was the first time I was tortured. Vargas's police tore out all my fingernails. One by one. In the year Aparecida was born.'

'He committed suicide,' Paulo murmured, and Eduardo was unsure whether he was referring to the dentist or the creator of the New State.

'It was the year when Guimarães Rosa wrote *Sagarana*. Have you read Guimarães Rosa? Is he part of your school curriculum? Or are they still stuffing the minds of our young people with that nonsense by José de Alencar?'

'Never. Guimarães Rosa never.'

'Were you a Communist?' asked Paulo. 'Wasn't it the Communists that got beaten up by the police?'

'I don't have any more books. I got rid of them all when I moved here. If not, I would have lent you *Sagarana*. And *Memórias do cárcere*. Have either of you read that? Do they teach Graciliano Ramos in your school? It's a devastating account of the consequences of the 1937 coup. Of power in the hands of a caudillo. And yes, Paulo, I was.'

He fell silent, and went back to the papers scattered over the table. The boys were expecting him to make some comment about all the events they had described. After waiting for some time in vain, Eduardo took up the topic again:

'Did you hear what we told you?'

'I'm not deaf. Not yet.'

'So why didn't you respond to anything we—' Paulo began, only to be interrupted once more.

'You two were born in 1950, weren't you?'

'1949,' Eduardo corrected him.

'I was born on 11 January 1949. I'm older than Eduardo.'

'Only by a month! My birthday is 28 February.'

'I'm forty-eight days older than you!'

'You were little more than a year old when Vargas came back into power. Elected by direct voting. Just think: a dictator who had tortured, killed and persecuted, democratically elected! Aparecida was thirteen at the time. A year older than her mother, Elza, when she became pregnant with her. The year when Mao Tse-tung founded the People's Republic of China. Or . . .'

He began a frantic search among his papers, until he found what he was looking for. He read it and, waving the scrawled-on piece of paper, turned back to the two boys.

'I was wrong. Mao founded the People's Republic of China in October 1949. Only twelve years ago.'

Paulo grabbed the scrap of paper. On it was written: 'Mao – 49 – PRC'. He picked up another one: '*Casablanca* – 39 – Ingrid B'. He glanced at some others: 'Adhemar de Barros – 50 – GV'; 'GV – Aug 54 – Lacerada'; 'Franco – 37 – *Guernica*'; 'Eisenhower – 52 – USA'; 'Ary Barroso – 1939 – "Aquarela do Brasil"'. To him, it all seemed mysterious, impenetrable.

'What are you doing?' he asked.

'Equations,' Ubiratan replied.

'Equations?' Eduardo said in surprise.

'Equations. Situating Aparecida in the world she lived in. In

1952, the year she was married, a Second World War general was elected president of the United States, to command the American empire in the Western world. The mayor was forty-five years old, which means he was thirty when Aparecida was born, and Senator Marques Torres was ... hmm ... seventy. When he killed himself, the senator was seventy-three. Seventy-three minus fifteen leaves ...'

'Fifty-eight,' Eduardo said quickly. 'What general?'

'The senator killed himself?' asked Paulo.

'Yes, Paulo. General Eisenhower, Eduardo. The senator was fifty-eight years old when Aparecida was born. Take away twelve?'

'Forty-six,' Eduardo said, with a mixture of pride and annoyance.

'Forty-six! That's how old Senator Marques Torres was when Elza was born.'

Opening his notebook, he wrote something in it, muttering to himself:

'Fifty-eight when Elza gave birth to Aparecida ... Seventy when Aparecida got married ... And his son, the mayor ... was thirty when Aparecida was born. Thirty! A fine age for a healthy man.'

'It's all over, isn't it?' Paulo concluded, sighing.

'What's over?' Ubiratan wanted to know, finishing his notes and screwing the top back on his pen, which he placed on the cover of the small spiral notebook.

'The investigation. Our investigation. It's not going any-where, is it, now that he's dead?'

Ubiratan looked fixedly at both of them. He saw two mud-covered boys wearing the same crestfallen expression.

'What are you talking about?'

'You didn't hear a word of what we've been saying!' Eduardo exploded. 'Not a word! Nothing, nothing, nothing!'

'Of course I did. The dentist died, the car knocked you down, Madalena died, the land round the lake was burned, the fence was put up . . . What else?'

Paulo was indignant at what he saw as a lack of concern for his own private drama:

'My bike is completely twisted! Wrecked! And you sit here doing sums! When my father sees it—'

'Equations,' Ubiratan corrected him, picking up the sheets of paper and separating them into two piles, before putting one bundle into each of his side pockets.

'Now that the dentist is dead, there's no point trying to discover the real killer,' Eduardo said disconsolately.

'Why not?'

'Well . . . Anita was murdered and—'

'Aparecida,' Ubiratan corrected him.

'Aparecida. She was murdered, and the murderer killed himself.'

'The sham murderer!' Paulo was quick to point out.

'There's nothing more to investigate because there's no longer an innocent man we can get out of jail,' Eduardo concluded.

Ubiratan took off his glasses, folded them shut, then put them in the inside pocket of his jacket.

'Who says the dentist was innocent?' he asked, folding his arms.

'But . . . you yourself said that . . .'

'I never said the dentist was innocent,' he stressed, standing up.

'But he . . . he . . .' stammered Eduardo.

'The struggle, the stab wounds, the . . .' Paulo protested.

'There are many ways to kill someone. Aparecida was destroyed long before she was murdered.'

Passing between the two of them, he headed towards the refectory door. Eduardo and Paulo followed him. An everyday sound of plates, voices, cutlery came from within. The smell of hot food filled Paulo's nostrils, made his mouth water, and reminded him he had not eaten a thing since breakfast.

'The dentist isn't the murderer,' Eduardo said to himself, desperately trying to follow Ubiratan's reasoning. 'But he's not innocent either . . .'

Ubiratan halted. Either because they reflected the light from inside the home, or because they were gleaming with the intensity of their first steps from the certainties of childhood to the tortuous complexities of the adult world, the boys' eyes filled the old man with an immense (and as he well knew, impotent) desire to protect them.

'Things aren't always what they seem,' he said, with a warmth that took even him by surprise. 'Eduardo. Paulo. That's a cliché. But it's true. I'm hungry.'

'Me too,' said Paulo, already starting to think of the magic he would have to weave in order to get home, scrape off the layer of mud and hide the damaged bike, without being seen or punished.

'Let's go. My mother gets worried if I'm late.'

'Why are you two so dirty?'

'Ubiratan, you didn't hear—'

'I'm ravenous and tired. I've been busy the whole day. I even went to the cemetery. Do you like opera?'

'Opera?' said Paulo in astonishment.

'I heard some once in my *nonno*'s house. He used to like it.'

'I want to take you to hear *Tosca*. By Giacomo Puccini. It's wonderful. But not today. Today I've got other plans for us.'

They didn't understand, but were not upset. *Sagarana*, Mao, Guernica, Graciliano, there were already so many names for them to digest that one more made no difference. Ubiratan was plunging far beyond their reach. Time to go home.

'All right then. 'Bye.' Paulo said goodbye unenthusiastically.

'See you tomorrow, Ubiratan.'

They left him and headed for the corridor on the other side of the kitchen. Paulo was in the lead, spurred on by his hunger and the anxiety at having yet again to get into the house by climbing through the bathroom window slats. The last few times, he had realized it was getting harder and harder for him to squeeze through. Perhaps he was growing. Getting stronger. Could it be? He wanted to think it was. He also wanted to think that his father had not yet come home. That he was in no hurry to get there, and was drinking another beer in some bar or other. He wanted to think that he was having another beer because he was in no hurry to get home because he was going to spend the night at the brothel with Antonio. He wanted to think that—

'Paulo and Eduardo!' they heard Ubiratan call out.

He was still standing where they had left him, although by now he was nothing more than a silhouette they could barely distinguish among the shadows of the yard and the walls of the home.

'No one wears a suit and tie in a prison cell,' he said softly. 'Nor a belt. Nor shoelaces. It's forbidden.'

Eduardo looked from Ubiratan to Paulo, then back at the old man. He wanted to ask something like So how did he kill himself? but in order for his doubt to become a proper question he would have needed to be aware of a perversity he was not yet familiar with. So he said nothing. He heard Paulo ask:

'Never?'

'Never. In no circumstances. Do you like the cinema?'

Another twist. This time it didn't take them by surprise. Shoelaces, belts, ties, jacket, cinema: why not? They were getting used to the extraordinary links made by the man in the shadows. They both nodded.

'Good. I stopped going to the cinema some time ago. But today there's a film I want to see. Tonight, the three of us can go to the movies.'

'No, we can't!' Eduardo said regretfully. 'It's a film banned for under-fourteens.'

'Find a way,' Ubiratan said, shrugging his shoulders, then turning and entering the refectory.

The moment Anita Ekberg went spinning through the air in the arms of a broad-shouldered man to the sound of rock 'n' roll, Paulo felt his body grow hot. He was sitting, his eyes glued to the screen, in the balcony of the Cine Theatro Universo. He was burning as if he had a fever, yet it was below his waist. Anita was dancing, smiling, shaking her thick blonde hair and revealing her quivering milky-white breasts as she circulated barefoot among the guests at some incomprehensible party, until she climbed on to a dais and was lifted high into the air by the man with the blond satyr's beard. The longer the display of acrobatic dancing and teasing went on, the greater the uncomfortable, prickling sensation became, and the greater Paulo's confusion. Because it was a pleasant sensation, it made his heart beat faster, brought him a feeling of ... almost ... almost a feeling of happiness. He felt a great desire to reach out and touch the exuberant flesh of the woman being whirled through the air. He wished it were his hands clutching the ankles of this immense blonde. He wanted to plunge his face between the ample breasts squeezed into the neckline of her dark dress, to breathe in the sweet-smelling perfume. Without realizing what he was doing, he raised his left hand to his trouser front. He sensed that his body was no longer responding to this unknown maelstrom with a boy's physical anxiety, but with the hard evidence of his entry into the world of desire. He smiled silently in the darkness. With a shiver of pride, he clasped his penis in his first-ever erection.

Oblivious to the courting couples seeking refuge in the darkness of the balcony to exchange caresses forbidden outside by the moral conventions of a city still rooted in the nineteenth century, Ubiratan was moved and disturbed by what he was seeing of an Italy he no longer recognized. He had always felt an affectionate link to a country he had never visited but had glimpsed in numerous films shot in the streets and alleyways of Rome, Milan, Genoa and Naples, devastated by the war and inhabited by a population trying to survive with dignity and to renew their interrupted futures. One of his last visits to the cinema had been to see an Italian film: *Umberto D*. D for Domenico, if he wasn't mistaken. A retired pensioner, wandering through the dilapidated post-war Rome with a dog, thrown out of his home, with no future or hope. One more – of many – workers who discovered the system did not need them. It had been barely nine years earlier that he had gone into the cinema in Recife to see it. It seemed such a short while ago. But to the two boys sitting beside him, nine years was almost their entire life. In nine years of tedium and the Marshall Plan, Italy had been transformed into this cynical circus now displayed on screen. Ubiratan felt as though he had emerged from a time capsule and found himself in a world where frivolity, meaninglessness and indifference reigned supreme. Could it be that everything humanity had achieved, at the start of this second half of the twentieth century, had become nothing more than a vehicle for sterile passions? Did progress lead only to lives stripped of meaning; did freedom and even the freedom of the press end up in these senseless Edens?

When the wife of the sceptical intellectual, unaware of his suicide, is surrounded by paparazzi desperate to capture her reaction to the sight of her husband's dead body, Ubiratan felt like closing his eyes the way children do in horror films, to avoid being engulfed by the sensation that the world that so horrified him now was the same as the one for which, two decades earlier, millions of men and women had sacrificed their lives in the name of a freer, more dignified and more equal future.

Sitting on his right, quiet and almost without moving, Eduardo was watching the film as if it were a dream taking place outside his mind. As with dreams, what he saw projected on to the screen did not have a logical narrative, and yet, just as when he saw himself in his own dreams without knowing what he was dreaming about, everything seemed intensely real. He couldn't tell whether he was enjoying it or not. He had no way of understanding a universe inhabited by indolent nobles wandering like blind men through ruined castles, ordinary people seeking redemption in miraculous visions, statuesque women bathing in public fountains, fathers whose sons casually offer them their lovers, a crazy sequence of images where each event might have a meaning, but not one he could grasp. He could only perceive, with instinctive certainty, that the good and the bad, heroes and villains, cops and robbers, dancers, parents, actresses, the religious faithful, photographers: none was any different. They were all part of the same ... the same ... he didn't know the word. He remembered another one, although not where he had heard it: sordidness. As so often happened, he felt sad without knowing why. And when, after a night on the tiles, the journalist tries to respond to the little girl's gesture next to the fish that looked like some sea monster, Eduardo could not understand why his eyes brimmed with tears so that he could hardly see the final scene.

∼

When they left the cinema they were hit by the cold night air that had emptied the streets. Ubiratan paused for a few minutes in front of the billboard of *La Dolce Vita*, while an excited Paulo went on ahead with Eduardo.

'. . . And those breasts! Did you see what huge breasts she had, Eduardo? Did you see what tits that blonde had? Well, Eduardo? Did you see the size of them? That time she went to . . . ?'

Eduardo said nothing; he was still sniffling in secret. Paulo was talking so much he didn't notice. Ubiratan caught up with them. The two boys began walking slowly the way the old man did, under a bright, starry sky. Paulo continued with his excited account of the film.

'. . . What about that party? Do you remember that dark-haired woman riding on the back of the guy on all fours? She was a bit old, but she was still gorgeous. Not as gorgeous as the blonde one. She was the best of all of them, the most gorgeous of all the women the journalist picked up. Much better than his wife, the one with light-blue eyes, wasn't she, Eduardo? Don't you think so?'

Eduardo couldn't remember ever having seen his friend so talkative. And the things he was saying! The two of them had talked about women, had shared their doubts about what they would do when they were grown up and went with one, had discussed whether a girl's thing was just under her belly button or hidden further down, but . . . Never like this. Never so confidently.

'. . . And when the guy with the blond beard picked her up, that time when she was whirling through the air, just like in a circus, don't you think she was the most absolutely gorgeous, the most beautiful woman you have ever seen, Eduardo? Don't you?'

'I . . . I liked . . . I thought that scene with the fish was nice. When the little girl says farewell to him, waving to him from the far river bank.'

'It was a beach.'

'Wasn't it a river? I don't think I saw it properly. But she, the young girl, was very nice.'

'She was only a kid. Not a real woman.'

Without noticing, they had taken up position on either side of the old man, who was still walking along in silence. Paulo's voice grew louder and louder.

'. . . that blonde woman going into the fountain with all her clothes on, and calling to him: I liked that scene too, that big fountain, and him jumping in to meet her in the middle of the water. And her dressed as a priest, walking up those steps, what about that? What did you think of that? Ah, and there was that scene where I thought, you know, I liked it, the one where Christ flies through the air suspended from a helicopter! I think it was really funny, with those women in bikinis waving and blowing kisses to the statue of Jesus, I thought that was really funny! Did you like it?'

'Yes . . . I did. But I don't think they were blowing kisses to the Christ.'

'Yes, they were. And they were shouting things I couldn't understand to the journalist in the helicopter. And do you remember when he was running up the steps inside the church after the blonde woman dressed as a priest? What did you think of that scene when the journalist tried to get hold of her inside the church, when she was dressed as a priest and everything, eh, Eduardo? He wanted to kiss her, didn't he? Did you like that?'

'Yes, I did. But there were some boring bits as well.'

'Yes, there were. The scene with the white kitten on her head and her walking around the streets was pretty boring. Nothing happens, she simply walks around, from one side of the street to the other. And that strange Japanese dance in the nightclub, near the beginning, do you remember that, before the skinny dark-haired woman appears, the one in dark glasses? I thought that was boring too.'

'The journalist wears dark glasses as well.'

'And the scene with that guy who plays the organ and talks and talks, while he's in the church? That was the most boring of all.'

'I couldn't work out why that man killed himself.'

He looked over towards Ubiratan, who said nothing.

'He had a pretty wife . . .' said Eduardo, trying to fit the character into models he understood. 'He had children, and friends . . . There was nothing wrong with his life. Or was there?'

He looked at Ubiratan once more, but there was no response.

'He had no reason to kill himself, did he?'

His question was aimed at neither of them in particular. Paulo ignored it, still enthralled by the intoxicating images of

219

Anita Ekberg and the euphoria of his first erection. Realizing that the idea of a chosen death was a threatening concept for a boy inclined to melancholy, Ubiratan simply said, in all sincerity:

'It's important not to believe, ever, that you can't go on. Always, Eduardo, you must always go on.'

They reached the end of the slope, opposite the Maria Beatriz Marques Torres School.

'I liked the look of being a journalist,' said Paulo, still enchanted by the film. 'A convertible, lots of girlfriends and parties, work only when he felt like it, trips all over the place . . . I think I'm going to be a journalist.'

'What about medicine?' Eduardo interrupted him. 'Are you going to give up medicine just like that? Have you forgotten all those incurable diseases?'

'Medicine!' said Paulo, his eyes opening wide. 'Oh, my God!'

'What's the matter?'

'The science test, Eduardo! It's tomorrow!'

'Yes, I know.'

'I haven't studied at all!'

Eduardo went up to Paulo and, imitating Ubiratan, shrugged his shoulders and said:

'You'll have to find a way.'

All three of them laughed. Eduardo was pleasantly surprised at the pleasure he got from a sense of humour he did not know he possessed. When they had finished laughing, he said goodbye and went off towards his home. Ubiratan and Paulo walked on a few more streets, until they reached the city jail.

'OK, here's where I leave you.'

'Hmm, hmm,' Ubiratan concurred.

'Will we see you tomorrow?'

'Hmm. Hmm.'

'What about our investigation? Are we going on with it?'

'Hmm. Hmm.'

'He didn't kill himself, did he?'

'We'll talk tomorrow about everything that's happened today. Go home now, Paulo. It's late.'

'Before now you never thought this time of night was late.'

'Today wasn't a day like the others.'

'Why do you never talk like other people?'

'Hmm?'

'Why don't you ever answer questions the way others do?'

'And how do they answer them?'

'Why do you never say yes or no, like everybody else?'

'Not every question can be answered with a yes or no, Paulo.'

'Every time I talk about something with you, you make me think of something else, beyond it.'

'That's good.'

'Why good? All it does is fill my head with questions.'

'That's better than having it filled with answers. Good night, Paulo.'

'Good night,' he replied, watching the white-haired man amble into the distance. He gave a last glance at the run-down police station building, and started on his way home, at first muttering about the impenetrable adult world, and then, as the voluptuous images from the film flooded back into his mind, he felt overwhelmed by an inexplicable sense of joy.

'What a pair of tits!' he sighed into the darkness.

10

Josef and Svetlana

PAULO STOOD UP, the science test in one hand, his dog-eared books and textbooks in the other, as two other pupils got up to leave the chemistry classroom. He walked up with them, left his test on the teacher's desk, turned and went out of the room.

Exactly as we agreed, thought Eduardo.

Now came his part.

One by one, he checked the answers he had given on each page of the two sets of foolscap paper on his desk. Almost all of them correct. Then he scribbled on one set, rubbing things out and dirtying parts of it, before carefully signing it. He placed the paper under the other impeccably composed and written set of answers, and signed these nonchalantly, without thinking. He waited, pretending to be rereading it.

When two girls stood up, Eduardo did the same. He reached the teacher's desk in time to place the two tests on it, one signed with his name and the other with Paulo's, just before the girls covered them with their own. No one, least of all the teacher, Ronaldo Abreu, had noticed that Paulo had merely pretended to hand his in earlier.

This was Eduardo's greatest feat so far: to write a whole exam in someone else's handwriting. He considered, jokingly but with a slight twinge of genuine pride, whether perhaps he should abandon his plans of studying to be an engineer and become the world's greatest forger instead.

The priest in the threadbare cassock finished the prayer, closed the black-backed book, blessed the coffin. He cast a swift glance at the police sergeant beside him, and made the sign of the cross before withdrawing, passing close to the gravediggers who were already shovelling earth on the casket. The policeman waited a few minutes longer, then he also left, stepping over the edge of the grave to reach the avenue.

The gravediggers went on working unhurriedly, taking little care and showing no interest in what they were doing. It didn't take long for them to fill the grave dug the previous day. One of them banged a wooden cross into the mound of red earth; the other picked up their spades, and they walked away together.

The woman dressed in black stayed on for a while. In her old-fashioned dress, with short kid gloves, her face shaded by the veil draped from her hat, she looked like a character from an old silent film. She didn't seem to be praying, and was certainly not crying, yet she didn't appear to want to leave either. Finally, risking her suede shoes in the soil scattered round the hole, she began to walk away.

When she reached the stone cross, she stopped. She opened the bag on her arm, took out a silver cigarette case and a mother-of-pearl holder, and placed a cigarette in it. She lifted the veil up to her eyes, then put the holder between her crimson lips. Sliding the case back in the bag, she took out a gold-plated lighter. She lit the cigarette, and inhaled so deeply that the tip soon glowed brightly. She kept the smoke in her lungs for a while, then blew it out. Clasping the holder in her gloved hands, she headed for the arch where the Virgin Mary stood, surrounded by disembodied cherubs and with the evil serpent beneath her feet. It was there she came face to face with Ubiratan.

Hanna Wizorek slowed down, and for a brief instant it seemed she was going to come to a stop. But she merely glanced at him blankly before taking another puff on her cigarette and continuing on her way. She was soon outside the cemetery, walking past the black iron railings.

Ubiratan caught up with her.

They walked side by side down the empty street, without exchanging a word. Anyone seeing them would have thought they were out for a stroll together.

'Sad, isn't it?' said Ubiratan finally.

She gave another pull on her cigarette, openly ignoring him, her head turned in the opposite direction.

'Very sad that such a generous person should take his own life. A dentist, a man from the best circles, buried in an unmarked grave like a pauper. Don't you think that's a shame?'

She blew the smoke high into the air, without replying. The hot morning sun revealed a mass of fine lines at the corners of her painted lips. The lipstick started to ooze down them.

'No friends came, no relatives. As far as I could tell, not even the poor people he treated for nothing came to pay their last respects. Nobody came to the dentist's funeral. Doesn't that seem sad to you?'

There was no reply this time either. Ubiratan's nostrils detected a strong aroma of rice powder, sickly-sweet perfume and camphor exuding from her and her clothes.

'That is, no one except the priest, the policeman and you.'

Hanna continued on her silent walk. Her high-heeled, old-fashioned shoes clacked rhythmically along the pavement.

'Strange. Very strange.'

She raised the holder to her mouth, inhaled deeply again, and still refused to look at him.

'Of course, deep down I can understand perfectly well why nobody came to the funeral. After all, the dentist wasn't the understanding, charitable man he appeared to be. In all truth, he was a crook. A murderer. He killed his own wife. A man like that doesn't deserve to have his old friends turn up at his burial. The lack of colleagues from the past is perfectly natural, isn't it?'

She blew out the smoke, still without a word.

'Strange that a priest did come though . . .'

She inhaled again, more quickly this time.

'I noticed that you didn't pray, which means you can't be a Catholic. Nor am I. I don't know if you have another religion. I don't; I'm an atheist. But I worked in a Catholic school so I know some of the taboos – or more exactly, some of the precepts of the Church. I know, for example, that it forbids any religious ceremony for suicides.'

Hanna came to a halt, the cigarette smoke seeping out of her nostrils. With a dramatic gesture, she tore the cigarette out of the holder and threw it to the ground. She crushed it with the tip of her shoe.

'But the priest prayed at the graveside and blessed the coffin. He can't have done that on his own initiative. All I can imagine is that the monsignor gave special permission. That's the only explanation that occurs to me. What do you think, Madame Wizorek?'

She opened her handbag, tossed in the mother-of-pearl cigarette holder and set off again. Ubiratan followed her.

'A final gesture of friendship from Dom Tadeu to his old seminary colleague. I imagine you know they were at a seminary together, don't you?'

Still not looking in his direction, she brought the veil down over her face.

'Friendships formed in our youth are the most solid. They create long-lasting affection. The bonds remain throughout a lifetime, don't they say?'

The silence between each of Ubiratan's outbursts was broken only by the tick-tack of the woman in black's heels on the pavement. The old man took a box of matches out of his coat pocket, and extracted one of his rolled-up cigarettes.

'Do you have a light?'

Yet again Hanna Wizorek gave no reply; nor did she stop.

Ubiratan held the cigarette in his hand for a moment, then put it back in the box.

'The dentist was a man of great religious faith. I don't know if you're aware of it, but his house is full of images of male and female saints. I know he went to mass every morning. Seven times a week. He confessed and took communion each time. It's hard to believe that a man of such faith could go against one of the most fundamental Catholic precepts and commit suicide. To repent of the crime he committed, yes. To have a crisis of conscience, yes. But to commit suicide . . . To hang yourself with a tie, in a prison cell . . . Possibly the bishop doesn't believe either that he committed suicide.'

Hanna came to a halt.

'Are you going to go on pursuing me?' she asked, rolling the 'r's in the middle and end of her words. To Ubiratan's un-practised ear, the accent sounded more French than Polish.

'I only want to chat for a while,' he replied, almost jovially.

'Why don't you go and chat with the other old men in your home?' she suggested sarcastically. She walked on once more.

'If you know I live in the St Simon home,' he said, catching up with her again, 'then you'll know that the old men in there aren't interested in talking about crimes or crises of conscience.'

Still striding along, Hanna opened her handbag, took out the cigarette case and holder, and repeated the same careful procedure, slightly more rapidly this time. In order to light the cigarette, she was obliged to come to a stop again. Ubiratan did the same.

'It's also hard to understand why a man of such profound

religious faith, someone as devout as the dentist, didn't stay in the seminary, don't you think?'

As soon as she had lit her cigarette, she set off again. Ubiratan pursued her.

'Doesn't it seem curious that such a pious man didn't follow his religious vocation? Or do you think something happened in the seminary, something so irreparable it made him change his mind? That altered the course of his life, against his wishes and his vocation? Something that prevented him going on? Or perhaps abandoning the seminary was not his decision? Who knows whether an episode took place which led the seminary to advise him to give up the idea of becoming a priest? What could have led such an apparently mystical young man to abandon a religious calling? He definitely was not opposed to celibacy. Even outside the seminary, the dentist was never seen in female company. He never patronized the girls in the hotel you run. A bachelor. Until he was almost fifty. Then all of a sudden, he got married. To a fifteen-year-old girl. Young enough to be his granddaughter. An orphan.'

'Has it occurred to you,' said Hanna, without stopping or looking in his direction, 'that the marriage might have been a charitable act?'

'Yes, it did occur to me,' Ubiratan admitted.

'You yourself live on charity in the old people's home.'

'But I changed my mind after I saw a photo.'

She inhaled and exhaled the smoke hastily.

'It appears the dentist liked taking photographs,' Ubiratan said casually.

Hanna cast him a sidelong glance.

'He even had a darkroom in his house. He liked to develop the photos he had taken on the spot.'

He could see Hanna was quickening her step. He did the same.

'Photos of those who came to visit.'

'I don't want to know.'

'The visits he liked to see Anita have.'

'I'm not interested.'

'Did you know he and his wife slept in separate rooms? Each in their own bedroom. A very odd couple.'

They were walking more and more rapidly now.

'They received visitors late at night. The couple received male visitors. He liked to watch.'

Hanna snatched the cigarette from the holder and threw it into the street.

'To watch and take photographs.'

The holder was stuffed back into her bag. She strode out even more forcefully. Ubiratan started to fall back.

'The dentist liked to watch and photograph the visitors and what they did with his own wife, to watch and photograph everything they forced his wife to do with them, with the friends who visited, to photograph what they did to her, inside her, and which gave him pleasure, as if it was being done to him, as if they were inside him.'

By now she was almost running. Both of them were out of breath.

'I've got one of those photographs, Madame Wizorek.'

'I don't want to know.'

'What the photo shows is disgusting.'

'I don't want to know!'

'Why? Are you scared?'

'I've got nothing to do with that. Nothing!'

'Scared of what? Of whom?'

'You're a crazy old man!' Hanna exclaimed, breaking into a run.

He wasn't willing to let this opportunity escape. He started to run as well. He was panting, speaking in short gasps.

'You're scared. Because those meetings happened in your hotel too. Isn't that right? With several men. Many men. Together. Isn't that so? And also with objects. The dentist was there. Taking photographs. The girl he took out of the orphanage. In that supposedly charitable act. That you spoke of. The girl. Changed into that. Into that plaything. Of all of them. Where every hole had to be . . . penetrated. With flesh. With rubber tubes. Bottles! Who was there? Who took part? Who were the others? Why did they have to kill her? Why? What for? Why did they kill her? Why did they have to do it? Why? Why?'

Hanna ran across the street to the far pavement, her body shaking in her mourning clothes.

Ubiratan couldn't keep up any more. Fighting for breath, sweating, he leaned against the cemetery railings, befuddled with weariness and rage.

Geraldo Bastos strode angrily into the glassed-in office where

Ubiratan was standing waiting for him, his hand outstretched in a greeting the other man ignored. He was still carrying the clipboard where he had been noting observations about the performance of his new Belgian looms before he was interrupted with the news of this unannounced visit.

Ubiratan let his hand drop, untroubled.

'May I sit down?'

The industrialist made a vague, unfriendly gesture in the direction of a chair opposite his desk.

'I've been walking the whole morning,' said Ubiratan, still on his feet. 'I went to the cemetery. I was at the burial of Dona Anita's husband. Then I went for a stroll with that Madame Wizorek, that Polish lady who runs the brothel. You know her, don't you?'

No reply. Ubiratan said nothing for a while, waiting for some reaction from Bastos. Then he sat down.

'Before I came here, I passed by the bishop's residence. Unfortunately, I was unable to talk to him. I was received by the good-looking young man who acts as his secretary and chauffeur. Do you know him perhaps?'

Geraldo Bastos closed the door. The rhythmic clacking of the looms disappeared. The soundproofed office, built up on this mezzanine only two years earlier, became a silent glass cage hanging over the vast floor of the Union & Progress textile factory.

'It seems the monsignor has a very full agenda. He couldn't see me today, or tomorrow, or any time next week. Not even next month. That is what I was told by that boy, that young man . . . what's he called, that friend of this city's bishop?'

232

The factory owner stared at him without a word. Ubiratan slowly lifted his hand to his coat pocket, reached for the box of matches, and then took out one of his rolled-up cigarettes. He waited again. Bastos did not move.

'Do you have a light?'

'I don't smoke.'

Ubiratan waved the unlit cigarette.

'Do you mind if I do?'

Bastos put the clipboard on the desk and stuffed his hands in the pockets of his starched coat. Ubiratan lit his cigarette.

Without a word, Bastos went over to a fan on a stand, pointed it in Ubiratan's direction and switched it on. Walking over to the other side of the room, he did the same with a second identical fan.

The noisy draughts of air enveloped the old man. He lifted the lapels of his coat to protect his neck. He felt slightly ridiculous.

Geraldo Bastos went back to the desk, picked up the clipboard again and rested it on his arm.

'You know I have no time to waste, that I'm a very busy man.'

'No doubt. I just thought I ought to come and see you, because—'

'I have to check how the new machinery I imported is performing. They're extremely expensive looms, paid for in dollars. I can't leave that responsibility to anyone else. I don't wish to. Therefore—'

'Since it was not possible for me to meet the bishop, I thought that—'

'What you've been doing during the day is not of the slightest interest to me. And how Dom Tadeu conducts his private life is none of my business. I interrupted my work because I was told that the lawyer of Dona Anita's family wanted . . .' he corrected himself, 'needed to talk to me. About some photographs.'

'Precisely.'

'You are not the lawyer of Dona Anita's family. You are a retired cook, who used to work at a school in Recife. You're on the police files as a Communist agitator.'

'Yes, I did come here to talk about photographs. I've just left one with the monsignor. A contact sheet with lots of images. To remind him of the happy days in the seminary, where he and the dentist met and became such good friends. They were very close, so devoted to one another.'

'That doesn't interest me.'

'But photography does. The photographs do. There are several images on this contact sheet. And there are lots more sheets. A trunk full of photos and negatives. I think they will interest you. Although it was of recent photos and contained new members of the group, the sheet I left for the monsignor shows the continuity of that intense—'

'We're wasting time,' Bastos interrupted him.

'Perhaps not. Do you know what photographs I'm referring to?'

'Yes, I think so.'

'The ones the dentist used to like to take. Of his wife with—'

'I know the photos you mean.'

'What you possibly don't know is that the police took them from the dentist's house and that they've now vanished.'

'No, they didn't vanish.'

'I saw with my own eyes when the jeep—'

'I have them.'

Ubiratan's self-confidence evaporated.

'The negatives as well,' Bastos added.

'So then . . .'

'I've got everything.'

Not knowing where to go from here, Ubiratan tried to play for time. Taking the cigarette from his mouth, he glanced over to the desk looking for an ashtray to stub it out in. When he saw there wasn't one, he crushed it on the sole of his shoe. Some of the ash fell to the floor and the air from the fan blew it all over the office.

'Those photos . . .' he began, not knowing how to continue. 'They . . .'

Geraldo Bastos walked over to the door and opened it.

'Is that all you had to say to me?'

Ubiratan put one hand on the glass desktop, and stood up, unconsciously obeying this order to leave.

'I didn't think that you took part in those . . .'

The memory of the muddy photograph flashed through his mind. Like hyenas devouring their inert prey. A pack of animals, tearing at an open belly.

'Was that all?' Bastos insisted.

The old man felt stupid. Yet again a feeling of nausea rose from the pit of his stomach, making him shiver.

'I never thought you would be in those photos.'

'I'm not.'

'So why then . . . ?'

'I'm not an exhibitionist, and I don't like being photographed.'

'Why then?' he said, straightening up with difficulty. 'Why then . . . ?'

'As you yourself said, some . . . acquaintances of mine . . . possibly led on by their lack of shame and Dona Anita's erotic arts, allowed Dr Andrade to take photographs of their moments of lust with his own wife. They were less careful than me. That's why I thought it best to keep the photos. In the hands of an unscrupulous person they could damage the private lives and the careers of people I appreciate. I could never permit that.'

Ubiratan took a deep breath. He looked for any sign of cynicism in Geraldo Bastos's face, but could not detect any. All he could see were the bland, impersonal features of a man who had been well fed for generations. There was no hint of irony either. He was dealing with someone who sincerely and honestly believed he was morally superior.

'So you're going to destroy them,' said Ubiratan, heading for the door.

'Yes, I ought to.'

They were standing next to each other. Geraldo Bastos smiled slightly.

'But I think it will be better if I keep them.'

His level voice did not alter, but Ubiratan thought he saw a fresh glint in his eyes.

'Our mayor is an impulsive man, but he has a valuable

legacy: the name of Marques Torres and the memory it evokes of his closeness to Getúlio Vargas. A partnership that was responsible for so much progress in this region. So many industries. So many jobs. So many votes for his party. With proper support, in the next elections Adriano Marques Torres could be the congressional deputy who wins most votes. He could become a party leader, the head of commissions, even the minister for industry. After that, who knows: perhaps even state governor. Or a national senator, like his father and grandfather before him. Dr Marques Torres's potential is limitless. With proper guidance, our city mayor can be very useful to our country.'

'You're going to use the photos to keep him under control.'

'Don't jump to hasty conclusions. I'm not going to use anything. It won't be necessary. In this new Brazil of ours, new industry and new politics will go hand in hand. We're going to establish links that are increasingly fertile and long-lasting. Which will not be undermined by a few dozen or hundreds of poor-quality photographs.'

'But very clear ones.'

'Yes, really very clear. It would be a shame to destroy them. They contain a considerable part of the history of our city over the past eight years. The next time you dare trespass on my workplace, I'll have you kicked out immediately.'

Ubiratan left the office. He had taken only a couple of steps when he turned to face the textile factory owner once more. He still had the slight smile on his thin lips.

'Do you know the photo of Josef Stalin with his daughter on his lap?'

'No.'

'Stalin is holding the girl, with his face next to hers as if he is about to kiss her. Svetlana Alliluyeva is smiling, arms round his chest. He's smiling too. It's a happy photo, a domestic scene with a loving father. It was taken at the same time as Stalin was ordering one of the most obscene campaigns of mass extermination humanity has ever seen.'

Ubiratan turned on his heel and left.

'So finally I'm going to get a hundred per cent in science!' crowed Paulo, at the end of lessons that Wednesday as they walked to the wall where they had left their bikes propped up.

'No you're not,' Eduardo warned him.

'What do you mean? You were the one who answered all the questions for me.'

'I gave some wrong answers.'

'Wrong answers?'

'On purpose.'

'Why did you do that? Aren't you my friend?'

'Precisely because I am.'

'I don't get it.'

'The person copying can't get everything right, Paulo. It looks suspicious. To look real, it has to have mistakes in it.'

Paulo didn't have time to reply, because he was surprised to see the old man waiting for them.

'We have to go and check something straight away,' said Ubiratan, getting hold of Paulo's bike. 'Come with me!'

'Where? To check what?' Eduardo wanted to know.

'Which of you can take me on the handlebars?'

'Take you where, Ubiratan?'

'Is your bike the one that got smashed?'

'No, that's Paulo's.'

'Is it strong enough to ride on?'

'I rode it here from my house, but it's a bit wobbly. I don't know if it will take two people.'

'Where do you want to go? What for?'

Ubiratan was still talking to Paulo.

'Do you think it can take us far?'

'That depends. How far?'

'Where to?'

Ubiratan turned to Eduardo.

'Your bike's not damaged. You take me. Come on!'

'Where to? It's lunchtime and my mother—'

'On second thoughts, it's better if I pedal and you ride on the crossbar.'

'Do you know how to ride a bike?'

'Get on!' the old man ordered him, climbing on the bike and leaning on his left leg with an agility that took the boys by surprise. But Eduardo was reluctant for other reasons:

'My mother will be worried if—'

'Let's go! Get on!'

'But—'

'Come on, Eduardo. We're wasting time.'

'You've discovered something!' Paulo exclaimed, beaming.

'Not yet. I'm not sure. It's just a feeling. Come on, Eduardo!'

After a moment's hesitation, Eduardo put his school bag in the bike basket and clambered on to the crossbar.

'How am I going to explain this to my mother?' he grumbled to himself.

～

There were no reflections in the muddy water. The banks and all the surrounding area were burned, ash grey, stripped of vegetation. He took a few steps away from the bamboo grove. The smell of scorched earth was stronger with each step. Mosquitoes buzzed past his face. So this was the paradise they talked so much about, he thought sadly. A banal lake in the midst of a not particularly beautiful landscape. The unremarkable scene of the end of an orphaned girl who had never been in charge of her own destiny.

A distant bird call, the shrill cry of an ani bird, broke the silence. Ubiratan saw that Eduardo was staring at him intently.

'Where did it happen?' he asked the boy.

'Over there, more or less,' said Eduardo, pointing. 'Over towards the mango trees. That was where we found the body.'

Paulo tugged at his coat sleeve.

'Come and I'll show you.'

They went in the direction he indicated, with Paulo in the lead. Eduardo was still sulking over having to abandon the routine that meant so much to him.

'Why have we come here? Everything's been burned. I'm hungry. My mother's going to be really angry. She'll have made lunch for me, and I haven't been home. You can see how it's all been destroyed. I don't think we'll find anything here.'

'Who said we needed to find something?'

'Oh, Ubiratan,' sighed Paulo. 'There you go again with your mania for answering questions with more questions!'

'Why did you want to come here? What lead are you looking for?'

'I'll only know if I find it.'

'So you don't know what you're looking for?'

'Is it the knife we're trying to find, Ubiratan?'

'I don't think so,' said Eduardo, drawing out every syllable. 'Unless the murderer was stupid enough to leave the weapon exactly where the police were bound to look for it. And besides, with the way they set fire to everything here, it's obvious there's nothing left to give us a lead.'

Paulo thought the opposite.

'I think he could have dropped it. When he ran away from us. When he saw we were getting close.'

'But we weren't at the lake yet, Paulo! The crime took place an hour or two, roughly, before we arrived. We must still have been in the classroom, looking at that magazine, when she was killed.'

'How can we be sure?'

'Wasn't the blood all congealed?'

'More or less.'

'Well then, that's a sign that—'

Ubiratan came to a sudden stop. Eduardo almost bumped into him.

'It's further on,' said Paulo, tugging at him again. 'It was further down there that . . .'

Ubiratan was looking at an opening hidden by the mango trees and beyond the undergrowth, that was only visible from the angle they were at now.

'What's that?'

'It's the other path down to the lake.'

'The entrance is further on than the one we took,' Eduardo added. 'But the track to reach it is very bumpy.'

'You can only use it if you have a car,' Paulo said.

'You mean it's possible to get down here in a vehicle?'

'Yes, it's possible,' Eduardo agreed. 'But it's better to come the way we did.'

'It's quicker to leave the car up by the road and cut down through the bamboos. That's what everyone with a car does in the summertime.'

'Except for someone who doesn't want to be seen,' Ubiratan mused out loud.

'Who?' asked Paulo.

'Is that the lead you were looking for?'

'The person who brought Anita?'

'Aparecida. No, a hidden car isn't a lead. But it shows she and he came here in secret.'

'Who is "he"?'

'Did they come here to make love?'

'I don't know, Eduardo. Show me where you found the body.'

Paulo ran to the spot where, a week earlier, he had stumbled over the body of a blonde young woman, covered in blood, before she even had a name, before she became Anita de Andrade Gomes and then Aparecida dos Santos.

'Here! Right here!'

Ubiratan did not move. He was busy calculating the distance between the opening in the mango trees and the point where the two boys were standing, observing him closely.

'Was there blood around the body?'

'Lots of it!' said Eduardo.

'On her clothes, on the grass, the mud, all round here, it was covered in blood!'

It was as he thought. Aparecida was not killed somewhere else and then brought here.

'Then close by, over here,' Eduardo pointed, 'there was one of her red shoes, with the heel snapped off.'

'I don't remember that.'

'I remember it well,' said Eduardo, taking three steps and showing the spot. 'Right here.'

Ubiratan went up to him.

'Are you sure?'

'Yes, I am.'

'And the body was on the ground over where Paulo is standing?'

'Yes, there.'

'That's a fair distance. Was one foot without a shoe?'

'Yes. And the shoe with the broken heel was over here. It was a high heel, much higher than the ones my mother wears. Tall and narrow. In the middle of the grass, stuck in the mud. Because there had been a downpour the night before. Do you remember, Paulo?'

'I remember the rain. And I remember the foot without a shoe.'

She must have stumbled, thought Ubiratan. The heel snapped off and she fell. But why come out here, in the midst of the clearing, if she was making love with someone in the car? And fully dressed. What kind of encounter could it have been?

'Her blouse was torn off.'

Paulo was talking to himself. He must have been thinking out loud without realizing it.

'And her bra was cut in the middle,' Eduardo added.

'And her breast . . . you know.'

'OK,' Ubiratan muttered, kneeling down to examine the ground around them. 'She could have stumbled because she was running. Trying to escape from the man who brought her to the mango plantation.'

But escaping from what? If she came out here, she must have trusted him. She must have known him well. She preferred to meet him here rather than in the sessions her husband organized with other men. Was he someone special to her? A secret lover for a woman everybody thought was public property? What happened between the two of them? A crisis of jealousy?

'Could he have started to stab Aparecida inside the car?' wondered Eduardo.

Absorbed in his search among the cindered trees, Ubiratan did not reply. Eduardo and Paulo glanced at each other. They fell silent for a few moments.

'Why didn't he use a revolver?' Paulo suddenly asked, intrigued.

'A knife makes less noise,' Eduardo argued.

'Who was going to hear? Nobody ever comes out here at this time of year. And we hadn't arrived yet. It was only him and her.'

'Unless, that is . . .' A possibility had struck Eduardo.

'Unless what?'

'No, nothing, forget it. I was just thinking he might have used a knife because he didn't have a revolver. But all the men here have got one. Even my father. Do you remember I told you, it's in the same drawer where he keeps the condoms. It's locked. But I discovered where he keeps the key, so I opened it and saw. It's a black Colt . . .'

Ubiratan straightened up.

'That's it!' he shouted. 'That's it!'

'That's what?'

'What have you found, Ubiratan?'

'You found it! The pair of you!'

'We . . .'

'What did we find?'

'The lead! You found the lead!'

'We didn't find anything.'

'Yes, you did! That's the lead. All the men in this city have guns! It's as clear as daylight!'

'But Aparecida was stabbed to death!' Eduardo reminded him.

'Exactly.'

'Exactly, what?' asked Paulo.

Ubiratan turned and started walking off hurriedly towards the bamboo grove where they had first come from.

'We have to get back to the city at once!'

Eduardo was astonished. Paulo didn't move.

'I'm not leaving here until you tell me: how, exactly?'

'Where are you going, Ubiratan? Why the sudden hurry?'

The old man continued striding out in front of them. Eduardo ran to catch him up.

'What lead did we find? What lead are you talking about?'

Paulo had no choice but to follow them.

'Wait for me, Ubiratan. Why are you in such a hurry?'

'Didn't you say that all the men in this city have got a revolver?' he replied, without looking back.

'Eduardo said that.'

'I did. I said that even my father . . .'

'Aparecida was stabbed to death.'

'That's right.'

'More than fifteen times,' Paulo recalled.

'Seventeen,' said Ubiratan. 'If she was stabbed to death, and if all the men in this city have got guns, what can we conclude?'

'That she was killed by a woman?' Paulo's voice was a high-pitched squeal.

'This was a crime full of hate, of an almost biblical anger. Any man who hated her so much would have emptied his revolver at her face. Or strangled her, if it was a crime of passion. Instead . . . the stab wounds were made by a woman who envied her, who was jealous of her beauty and her youth. And the most obvious proof of that was what you two call the trophy: the one the other woman cut off Aparecida's body. The mutilation. The scalped breast. Not both of them, just one. A savage proof of one woman's triumph over a rival.'

They reached the bikes.

Without fully understanding what Ubiratan had told them, Eduardo and Paulo's minds were flooded with previously unimagined possibilities. A woman, that almost abstract being composed of images of their mothers, statues of the Virgin Mary, seductive smiles from movie actresses and the imprecise lines of drawings in erotic comics, was capable of crimes as repugnant as those committed by men.

11

A Corpse of No Importance

THE TENOR'S THUNDEROUS vow of revenge on the gramophone echoed round the red-lined room.

> *Ah, Tosca, pagherai*
> *Ben cara la tua vita!*

The blonde Polish woman rose from the sofa. She was in tears.
The salon of this brothel in a city hidden among the
mountains where she had been brought twenty-six years
earlier by the then parliamentary deputy Diógenes Marques
Torres, had been transformed. She was in Rome, in the after-
math of Napoleon's victory, and once more she was Floria
Tosca, torn apart by the death of the man she loved, arrested
after stabbing the police chief who had tried to rape her and
send her beloved to the firing squad. One of Baron Scarpia's
men tells her she will pay for the murder with her life. Tosca
pushes him aside. Hanna pushes him. She struggles free, but
is cornered on the roof of the Castel Sant'Angelo. Every exit is

blocked: there is no way she can escape. She resolves that she will not give these traitors the final victory. She goes over to the battlements. If she is to lose her life, it will be by her own hand.

Colla mia!

Before plunging to her death, she heaps one last curse on the aristocrat who has committed so many despicable acts. Scarpia, you will be judged before God!

O Scarpia, Avanti a Dio!

Slowly, Hanna Wizorek lifted her head, closing her eyes and raising her clenched right hand to her heaving breast, as the voices of Scarpia's followers and soldiers confirm the tragic end of Puccini's heroine.

At that moment Hanna heard a noise behind her. She turned round.

Through the tears rolling down her heavily made-up cheeks she could make out a shape slightly smaller than her, and two even smaller ones. Startled at this invasion of her sanctuary, where no one was allowed to enter when she was listening to opera, she quickly wiped her eyes, hearing as she did so a rasping voice in Portuguese saying something that sounded like 'More and more like Tosca' or 'A murderer like Tosca'. She immediately recognized the thin, white-haired man standing in front of her.

'Ah . . . the lunatic from the cemetery.'

Two boys in school uniform flanked the old man. The shorter of the two was dark-skinned, with flap ears, broad shoulders and a narrow waist, and built like an adult in miniature. The other, taller one had a melancholy look in his eyes that reminded her of the consumptive poets who had been in love with her in her youth.

'Who are these children?'

A crackling sound warned her that the needle had reached the end of the record. She went over to the gramophone, lifted the arm and replaced it on its cradle. She switched it off. The old man came over, picked up the record and waved it in her face.

'When Tosca stabbed Scarpia, she was defending her honour and her love for Mario Cavaradossi. Neither of those excuses applies in your case, Madame Wizorek.'

'Be careful, *vieux dingue!*' she warned him, in the language she had learned enough of to pass herself off as French to the naïve clients and impress the bumpkins who frequented her hotel. 'That's a rare recording, which can't be found in Brazil! *Il m'a pris plus d'un an pour l'obtenir!* It took me a year and a half to get someone to bring it here for me!'

Disdainfully, Ubiratan tossed the record on to the pile scattered on the table next to the ancient phonograph.

'We've been out to the lake.'

Checking the disc had not been damaged, Hanna put it in its box together with the other three that made up the set, and closed it.

'It wasn't hard to figure out what had happened there.'

Hanna saw that the trio had left a trail of mud from the

250

window they had climbed through over to the rug near her. Their trousers were splashed with dirt. The dark-skinned boy's clothes looked badly crumpled.

'This is no place for children,' she said imperiously, pointing to the dirtier boy.

'But you've had girls their age in here!' said the old man.

'Look at the mess you've made of my rugs!' said Hanna, hands on hips. 'You can clear out, and take those kids with you. You have no right to invade my salon. I want to listen to my music in peace.'

'Adolf Hitler liked opera too.'

'Nonsense. *Il aimait Wagner, il n'aimait pas la vraie opéra.* Get out! And take those boys with you!'

Seeing they did not move, she threatened:

'Are you going to leave, or am I going to have to have you thrown out?'

'We're going to leave here and go straight to the prison, Madame Wizorek.'

'That's right, *vieux dingue*! That's exactly where I'm going to send you.'

'We'll go together. But first I want to hear you confess to your crime.'

She walked over towards the door.

'Humberto! Humberto, come in here!'

Paulo and Eduardo stepped in front of her, preventing her from going any further.

'What is this? Are you mad? Humberto!' she shouted. 'Humberto, can't you hear me?' She turned to Ubiratan: 'Tell those brats to get out of my way.'

Ubiratan ignored this order, spoken in an accent full of rolled 'r's.

'Aparecida was killed by a woman. A woman who could only have committed the crime if she was as tall, big and strong as she was.'

'Humberto! Humberto! Come here!'

'A woman she knew well. And who called her to say they needed to have an important conversation far from anyone else's prying eyes. Outside the city.'

'Humberto! I'm calling you!'

'A woman she didn't fear.'

'Humberto! Humberto!' she shouted, trying to push her way past the boys.

Paulo leaned back against the door. Eduardo locked it, took the key from the keyhole and slipped it into his pocket.

'What are your kids doing now?'

'Aparecida was killed by a woman she trusted.'

'Get those boys out of my way! Tell them to open this door!'

'You fooled Aparecida. You tricked her. You betrayed Aparecida.'

'Humberto!'

'You met somewhere where nobody could see you, then you took Aparecida down to the lake. You parked in among the mango trees, where the car couldn't be spotted. Aparecida had no inkling of your murderous intentions. Until you—'

The door burst open, flinging the two boys away from it. Eduardo fell next to the high-backed armchair. Paulo rolled as far as Ubiratan's feet, almost knocking over the table bearing the gramophone and records.

'Humberto!' sighed Hanna, relieved to see her watchdog finally arrive. 'Throw these intruders out!'

The hulking brute made straight for Ubiratan.

'You knew about everything,' he shouted, as he was gripped round the waist and lifted effortlessly into the air.

'Throw that old lunatic into the street.'

Carried like a light parcel, Ubiratan struggled to free himself.

'You knew about the humiliation they forced Aparecida to suffer! You knew it and agreed to it! You allowed the orgies, the photographs, you allowed her to be penetrated by all those objects!'

'Let go of him,' shouted Paulo. No one paid him any attention.

'You allied yourself with them! You betrayed Aparecida!' roared Ubiratan, flailing arms and legs. 'You allowed Aparecida to be used like a sewer! When you, you yourself had suffered the same abuses as her! When you had been humiliated and penetrated just like she was! By anyone who wanted to! Anyone who paid!'

'Get him out of here quickly, Humberto!'

'Why did you kill Aparecida? Did they tell you to do it?'

Paulo was trying to make himself heard above all this shouting. He was holding a record aloft in one hand.

'Let go of him. Let go of Ubiratan!'

'Did they want to get rid of Aparecida? Why? What had she done? What did she know? Did she know too much? Or did you kill her out of jealousy?'

The brothel strongman was finding it difficult to carry his struggling captive, who was now clinging on to the side of the sofa, pulling it with them. He stopped when it became entangled with one of the rugs.

'Even if they gave the order to kill her, you stabbed her out of jealousy! You were jealous because she was young! And beautiful! You killed her out of jealousy. The chopped-off breast is the clearest proof of that! You mutilated her out of spite, jealousy, envy!'

'Let go of Ubiratan or I'll break it!'

'Go on, Humberto! Throw him out of here!'

'Aparecida was young, she still had hopes! You're old! You have shut your life away in this brothel, and this city is your burial mound! Was Aparecida going to leave? Might she have revealed secrets that would ruin people's careers? Was that what signed her death warrant?'

'Let go of Ubiratan! Let go of him, or I'll smash the record!'

Paulo finally managed to make himself heard above all the commotion. Hanna turned towards him and stared at him in horror. She leapt towards him, trying to snatch the record he was waving in the air.

'Stop!' Paulo ordered. 'Stop where you are!'

Hanna came to a halt.

Eduardo picked up the whole set of *Tosca* records.

'I'll smash them all if you go any further!'

The brothel-owner turned to her bouncer, uncertain what to tell him to do. He shook Ubiratan so hard that the old man let go of the sofa.

'Nobody move!' shouted Eduardo.

Hanna Wizorek took a step closer to the boys, her arms outstretched.

'We'll break all of them!' Paulo threatened, getting ready to throw the record he was holding to the floor.

'No!' shrieked Hanna, aghast. She came to a halt again. 'Don't do that to my records! Don't do it!'

'Tell your man to let him go, then.'

Hanna Wizorek hesitated. She realized that these little monkeys had no idea of the value of the records they were clutching. If they had, the dark-skinned idiot and the pale-faced lanky one would never use *Tosca*, and especially that version of *Tosca*, to threaten her with. It was *Tosca* conducted by Victor de Sabata and the orchestra and chorus of La Scala, Milan. A masterpiece that had cost her a small fortune, not to mention all her enquiries, frustrated requests, letters to shops in Rio and São Paulo, appeals to salesmen, a disappointing series of orders, reams of carbon copies, interminable import bureaucracy, a long and apparently endless wait for inter-national airmail, all of which added up to nineteen months of seemingly useless efforts, until the four black records reached her in this far-flung corner of the earth. And this, her only consolation in her everlasting exile, could be smashed to bits in the blink of an eye by these two savages. The exquisite 1953 recording of the opera made in London with Giuseppe di Stefano, Tito Gobbi and Maria Callas, that she had heard many years before on this same radiogram, transmitted directly from the Theatro Municipal in Rio de Janeiro, could be destroyed. By a skinny little boy and that wild half-breed, who even now was demanding:

'I want him freed now. Right now!'

She glanced towards Humberto, who had almost reached

the door. Ubiratan grabbed hold of the doorknob. He was still shouting his defiant questions.

'What story did you invent to entice Aparecida? That you were going to present her to the same organization that protected you when you got to Brazil? The Jewish pimps who turned you into a high-class prostitute? Or the Jewish Communists who tried to save you from that fate?'

Taking Hanna's silence to mean she refused to accept the threats from the boy clutching the records, Humberto tugged at Ubiratan so hard that his hands slipped off the doorknob. He was about to leave the room with his wriggling burden when Paulo swung the record violently towards the table corner. Hanna shrieked at him:

'No!'

Humberto stopped in his tracks. Hanna lifted her hand to her mouth.

'Please, my boy . . . don't do that.'

It was only at that moment, still dangling from the bouncer's waist, that Ubiratan clearly saw the situation: queen threatened by pawn.

Nobody moved.

The impasse lasted only a few seconds. Hanna admitted defeat.

'You can let the old man go,' she accepted finally.

Humberto dropped Ubiratan to the floor.

'Now tell him to leave,' ordered Paulo.

Hanna was confused about which of them the boy meant. Paulo realized this, and made it clear:

'The big brute. Tell him to leave.'

Yet again, she was in two minds. Just in case, Ubiratan scuttled away from the bouncer, who was still standing there, waiting for the order to attack.

'Now!' demanded Paulo, waving the record in his right hand.

Hanna took a deep breath. She nodded her head, and Humberto understood. He left the room, and she stretched out her hands towards Paulo.

'Give me that *Tosca*.'

Paulo still had his hand in the air.

'Give me the record.'

Glancing over at Ubiratan, who was closing the door, Paulo did not move.

'Make sure it's locked, Ubiratan!'

'That's not necessary,' replied Hanna. 'The record,' she said, pointing to it: 'Give it me.'

Paulo grudgingly handed it to her. Hanna took it carefully by the edges, wiped it clean with the hem of her peignoir, and slipped it into its sleeve. She took the box set from Eduardo, opened it, put the record with the other three, then closed the lid.

'Aren't you going to interrogate her?' asked Eduardo, turning towards Ubiratan.

'*Comment ça?* What are you talking about?'

'I'll keep the door shut,' Eduardo said hastily, jamming a chair under the doorknob exactly as he had seen it done in so many gangster films.

'I've already told you, that's not necessary!' Hanna protested. She turned to Ubiratan. 'What is it you want?'

'To clear up some obscure points, Madame Wizorek.'

'*Cette situation est ridicule.* Everything you were bleating about, everything you accused me of – it's all nonsense.'

'You were the one who killed Aparecida.'

'Ah! . . .' sighed Hanna disconsolately. 'He really is off his head. *Alors!* So you're the old man who likes boys that I was warned about.'

'Being offensive,' replied Ubiratan calmly, 'will get you nowhere. The crime you committed might have been covered up for ever as a crime of passion or an insane attack by some anonymous maniac. But your jealousy meant you left your signature on the killing. A savage signature, one that only a woman could do to another: cutting the breast off. To get rid of the greatest proof of femininity.'

'That's right!' Eduardo backed him up. 'We know everything!'

Hanna picked up the cigarette box from the table beside the high-backed armchair, took out an unfiltered American cigarette and inserted it in her mother-of-pearl holder. With the gold lighter in her other hand, she faced all three of them.

'A paedophile old man and two almost pretty boys . . .'

'All we have to do is find the knife you used to kill her with,' said Paulo.

'Or the dagger,' Eduardo cut in.

Hanna sat down. She inhaled deeply, lowering her head to her chest and waving the cigarette holder with all the exaggerated drama of a silent movie vamp.

'Three little lunatics,' she said, puffing out the smoke and smiling, '. . . playing at detectives.'

She was recovering her composure. She was in charge once more.

'You have no idea what you've got involved with. Who you've got involved with.'

Hanna's self-assurance disconcerted Ubiratan.

'But you . . . you killed . . .'

'I killed . . . ?'

'You killed Aparecida.'

'Her name was Anita. She stopped being Aparecida a long, long time ago. Are you going to stay standing up? Why don't you sit down?'

She pointed to the sofa opposite her, letting the cigarette smoke trickle from her nostrils. Ubiratan sat down. Paulo and Eduardo went to stand on either side of him, as if mounting guard.

'Do you really think this is the sort of conversation that children should hear?'

'There are no children here,' protested Paulo.

'We're helping with the investigation.'

She ignored them.

'Would you like a cigarette?' she said, offering him the box. 'They're imported. *Tabac blond*, from Virginia.'

Ubiratan took a butt out of the matchbox in his coat pocket. Hanna leaned forward and lit it. She placed a glass ashtray close to them both.

'If we're going to talk about Anita, if you want me to tell you what Anita's life was like, I don't think it's a good idea to do so with these two children in my salon.'

'I already told you, there are no children here!' Paulo repeated, even more annoyed this time.

'Don't you think you should ask them to leave?'

'I'm not leaving here!' Eduardo said indignantly.

'No way!' added Paulo.

'What I can tell you about Anita's life, Mr . . . what is your name, by the way?'

'Ubiratan.'

'What I can tell you about Anita's life, Mr Ubiratan, if you're at all concerned about the upbringing of these two almost good-looking children, is not the kind of thing that impressionable minds should hear. I imagine you realize that. From the photos that I know you saw, you must have some idea of what our conversation will entail.'

'What photos is she talking about?' Paulo wanted to know.

'You never told us about any photos.'

'What's in those photos that we're not supposed to know about?'

'Don't you think, Mr Ubiratan, that it's rather too soon to initiate *ces deux enfants* into these kinds of special tastes?'

'What is she talking about, Ubiratan?'

'Whatever it is, I'm not leaving here,' said Eduardo.

'We started this investigation together, and we've reached this point together. If one stays, we all stay. If one leaves, we all leave.'

'You're the one who has to choose,' she said, before inhaling again, falling silent and waiting for his decision.

In the silence that came over the salon, the strains of a bolero could be heard from somewhere within the brothel.

Precious little woman
In the calm of night
No one owns your body,
Your lips are full of venom,
I know you want me to suffer . . .

Ubiratan lowered his head. When he raised it again, he turned towards the boys behind him. He gave an awkward smile that was at the same time a polite request and a demand they could not refuse.

'Oh, Ubiratan!' moaned Eduardo dejectedly.

'No, not that!' Paulo exclaimed, punching the sofa.

'Please, Paulo. Please, Eduardo. It's necessary.'

They trudged out slowly, in angry silence. Paulo gave Ubiratan one last infuriated look before slamming the door.

'Good . . .' Hanna inhaled, then blew out the smoke from her cigarette. 'Let's continue our game. The detective and the murderer.'

'A murder isn't a game.'

'No, it isn't. Depending on who dies. Anita, poor thing, is nothing more than a corpse of no importance.'

Stubbing out the cigarette, she removed it from the holder and tossed it into the ashtray. She crossed her legs with their thick ankles. She was wearing dark nylon stockings to hide the countless varicose veins.

'*Qu'est-ce que vous voulez de moi?*'

'Don't you feel any remorse for what you did to Aparecida?'

'Monsieur, what Anita lived through in eight years happened to me in little more than three months. From the

261

night when I left my village in Poland, to the evening when I set sail for Brazil from the port of Marseilles, I went with more men than most women do in their entire lives. Slovaks, Lithuanians, Poles. Hungarians, Germans, Turks, Australians, Congolese, Tunisians, Greeks, French, Canadians, Americans, English, Irish, Russians, Moroccans, Spaniards, Senegalese, Italians, Yugoslavs, Ethiopians, Egyptians, Palestinians, and even an Oriental whose nationality I never knew. I wanted to eat, and I wanted a passport for America. Anywhere in the Americas. That was why it didn't matter to me what I did with my body. What they did with it. I was certain that when I reached America I would be clean again, and would go back to being the young girl I had been in Jedwabne.'

'In Jeb—?'

'Jedwabne. My village.'

Taking another cigarette, she placed it in the holder, lit it and inhaled deeply once more.

'But when you reached Brazil you found compassion and support. Aparecida was surrounded by indifference.'

'When I arrived at the docks in Rio de Janeiro, that protection society you spoke of took me straight to a brothel in a street behind Praça Onze. The square no longer exists. It was demolished. So was the brothel. In it there were other girls like me. Europeans as well. Girls who had fled the hunger of war, like me. Pure melodrama, monsieur. But why am I telling you all this boring soap opera?'

'You were going to tell me why you killed Anita.'

She gave a long, high-pitched, theatrical guffaw.

'*Vous êtes vraiment fou.* To think, *quelle folie*, that Anita was

262

going to run away from here, to try to start another life far from here. How naïve! How simple-minded you are! Anita starting again from nothing! And taking with her secrets that couldn't be revealed! What a farce. Do you really think it makes any difference to women like Anita or me if we go somewhere else?'

'She was young. She could have started over.'

'Started over what?'

'Everything. Life. A new life.'

'A new life? With what skills? Washing clothes, ironing, embroidering, sewing and opening her legs?'

'Everything is possible when you're twenty-four.'

'Only an old man could believe that. I can assure you that there was no way that Anita could start over at the age of twenty-four. Just as there wasn't for me at seventeen, when I embarked in Marseilles. The difference was I didn't know it.'

She fell silent. Crushed out her cigarette.

'So why did you kill her?'

'Don't be ridiculous. It's obvious I didn't kill her. Why would I?'

'Jealousy.'

'Jealousy of what? Of the anguish of pretending to be a colour I wasn't? Of being handed over to an effeminate old man? Of not being allowed to talk to any neighbours, to meet my relatives, to leave the house on my own? Jealous of being the female of all the men my husband would have liked to have, if his sense of sin had not prevented him?'

'Jealousy of . . . of . . .' Ubiratan did not know how to finish his sentence.

'Jealousy of having my vagina, my mouth, my thighs regularly offered to my husband's former colleagues from the seminary? Of being photographed with all kinds of objects stuck in my orifices? Of being pissed on, shat on, ejaculated on, of being tied up, gagged? Jealousy of that? Jealous of watching my husband masturbate while two men, sometimes four, five or six men took turns to penetrate me? Including my own brother?'

Ubiratan turned pale. His reaction appeared to take Hanna by surprise.

'You knew that Anita and the mayor were brother and sister, didn't you?'

'I . . .' He stuttered. 'I suspected there might be some family connection between them. But . . .'

'In fact, she was his half-sister. They had the same father.'

'Senator . . .'

'Diógenes. Senator Diógenes got a housemaid from the estate pregnant. I don't know what she was called . . .'

'Madalena . . .'

'He liked young girls. To be the first man for the girls on the estate. *Le droit du seigneur*, if you follow me.'

'Madalena was raped by the old man.'

'In those days he wasn't an old man. Or violent. Rough, yes. But he didn't hit them or mistreat them. He had a great appetite for women, as we used to say at the time I met him. It was soon after I arrived in Brazil. He was a very attractive man. Thick lips, like an Indian. Big green eyes. Broad shoulders. Heavy. A bit brutal, yes. But extremely virile. A wild animal. Especially with young girls. You've gone very pale: don't you feel well?'

'It will pass.'

'Would you like a cigarette?'

'No, no. No, thanks.'

'When Adriano took Anita out of the orphanage . . .'

'Adriano?'

'The mayor. Adriano Marques Torres. When Adriano took Anita out of the orphanage and handed her over to Dr Andrade, the dentist, he thought she was nothing more than another unwanted child from their estate. Like others who were sent to that orphanage. He had no idea Anita was his niece.'

'But you said she was his sister.'

'Diógenes, Senator Diógenes . . . Do you know all that the senator has done for this city? Do you know it was him, or his family, who founded the orphanage, the health clinic, the—'

'Yes,' he said, interrupting her, 'in this city there's no way of not being aware of the Marques Torres family. But a short while ago, you told me that Aparecida and the mayor were brother and sister.'

'Her half-brother. Anita was the daughter of a mixed-race woman.'

'Elza. Who had her when she was twelve, I know.'

'That girl Elza was the daughter of Senator Marques Torres with a maid who worked in the big estate house.'

'Madalena.'

'I don't know her name. But she was the blood link between Anita and the mayor.'

'So Aparecida was the mayor's niece rather than his sister.'

'According to what the senator told me, he was fifty-eight when he fell for a pretty mulatto girl on the estate. He had no idea who she was. She resisted him, and he raped her.'

Ubiratan could feel drops of cold sweat running down his scalp.

'Nine months later, when that mulatto, that mixed-race girl, Elza, gave birth to a light-skinned baby, with green eyes like the senator, they took the child and placed her in the orphanage. Are you sure you wouldn't like a cigarette? A glass of water?'

'A cigarette? Yes, I'll take one.'

Hanna took two out of the box, put them in her mouth, and lit them both, with the feigned intimacy of a lover. She held out one, smeared with lipstick, to the old man. Ubiratan took it, but held it between his fingers, without smoking it.

'Anita was the mayor's sister and niece. The daughter and granddaughter of Senator Marques Torres. Wouldn't you like a glass of water? *Un cognac? Un petit liqueur?*'

He waved his hand briefly to refuse her offer.

'You seem to be growing paler by the minute.'

'It's nothing. Nothing. It'll pass. So Elza's children . . . so Anita . . . or rather, Aparecida. So Aparecida and Renato are the mayor's brother and sister?'

'No. Anita is the mayor's sister. The boy isn't his brother.'

'Renato isn't . . .'

'That's him. Renato. No, he isn't.'

'He isn't the mayor's brother?'

'He's his son.'

The memory of water dripping in an empty corridor flashed through Ubiratan's mind. Lights switched off. The greenish stain of a leak above his head. A changing room. The changing room at the sports ground where the five-a-side football game was taking place. The echoing sound of the bucket he knocked over. The whispers from one of the cubicles. The young man who leapt out of one of them and seized him by the wrists. His face with the high cheekbones. His fine nostrils.

'Renato . . . the mayor's son . . .'

'Yes.'

The smell from his body. The mixture of sharp sweat and sweet perfume. The cubicle door opening. The girl emerging from the shadows. The fragrance she gave off.

'Anita's brother is the mayor's son, but he doesn't look like him. He's much more like his grandfather.'

Lavender. When she left the cubicle where she had been with Renato, adjusting her bra, she had the fragrance of lavender. She had fair hair, tied up in a ponytail. She couldn't have been more than fifteen.

'Renato looks like the senator. Tall, broad-shouldered, thick lips *comme un indien*. A womanizer. Brutish. Just like his grandfather. *Il ressemble beaucoup à son grand-père.* More Indian than Negro. Renato comes here from time to time. One of my girls is crazy for him, she gives him money; I pretend not to notice. I can understand. Men like Renato know how to drive a woman wild.'

'Renato is the mayor's son . . . with Elza . . .'

'Yes. He doesn't know it. But Anita did.'

'She knew . . .'

'Of course.'

'Elza . . .' Ubiratan sighed, almost inaudibly. 'Poor Elza . . .'

Hanna went on. Her voice remained neutral, as if she were telling a commonplace, everyday story.

'What Anita only recently discovered was that Renato had become Isabel's lover.'

A door opening on to the veranda of the mayor's house. The fragrance reaching his nostrils even before he saw her. Lavender. The young girl with fair hair. Tall. With plump, arched lips like the wings of a bird in flight. Her small, dark eyes, constantly flicking back inside the house.

'So Renato became the lover of the mayor's daughter . . .'

'Of Cecilia? No. Cecilia is only fourteen. Renato isn't her lover. He's Isabel's lover. The mayor's wife.'

The veranda suddenly flooded with light. The tall, slender woman wearing no make-up, behind the fair-haired young girl. The long eyelashes shading her almond-shaped eyes. Her condescending smile. The tone of authority in her voice.

'She and Renato used to meet regularly in a house in a village outside the city. She bought the house for him. In his name. She also gives Renato money, just like the girl here. A man like him . . . I can understand it. He can drive a woman to madness. Any woman. His grandfather was the same. I can understand. Your cigarette ash is going to fall on the rug,' she warned, holding the cut-glass ashtray out to him.

Ubiratan tapped the ash off, then nipped out the cigarette without even trying it once. He still held it between his fingers.

'I'm sorry. I'm . . .'

'Obviously, the mayor has no idea that his wife and his son,' she paused to take another drag on her cigarette, 'are lovers.'

'What about Renato? Does he know that . . .'

'That the mayor is his father? No, he doesn't. And Anita decided—'

'To put a stop to it,' Ubiratan concluded.

'No. Anita decided to make money out of it.'

12

The Snake Comes Out of Its Nest

'DO YOU THINK you could turn the music down?' Eduardo asked the prostitute sitting beside the radio painting her toenails. 'I can't hear what they're saying in there.'

The red-haired woman paid no attention to him, but went on applying the varnish, nodding her head and singing along quietly to the tune of the bolero.

> *No one belongs to anyone,*
> *In life everything passes.*
> *No one belongs to anyone,*
> *Even those embracing us . . .*

Eduardo decided he didn't like the music. He didn't like any music: it only muddled your thoughts. Irritated, he turned to Paulo.

'What about you? Can you hear anything they're saying in there?'

'Nothing,' said Paulo, who was closer to the door guarded by the bouncer. 'Nothing at all.'

Ubiratan had been shut in the red-lined room with the brothel-keeper for a long time. Neither of the boys understood why they had been kept out of the conversation. And on top of that, they had to put up with this loud music:

> *I once lived in hope*
> *Of having a great love.*
> *Perhaps someone thought*
> *Of the love of my dreams*
> *That I also lost.*

Two stocky women in gaudy frocks were dancing cheek to cheek next to the wooden staircase that led up to the second floor. In a nearby armchair, a thin, dark-complexioned woman was leafing through a weeks-old *O Cruzeiro* magazine. The cover picture was of a man dressed up as Harlequin at the feet of a woman with long, tanned legs. One of the headlines read: *Adolf Eichmann trial begins in Jerusalem.*

'Who is Adolf Eichmann?' asked Paulo.

'But are they still talking?' insisted Eduardo, ignoring Paulo's question because he didn't know the answer.

'Yes, they are. I can hear that much, but not what they're saying.'

'It must be about those photographs.'

'But we didn't see any photos. Not anywhere.'

'That must be the secret we're not allowed to know. That's what they must be talking about.'

'But they've been in there for ages!'

> *. . . So I saw that in life*
> *No one belongs to anyone.*

The music came to an end. Eduardo breathed a sigh of relief. Then a jingle began to broadcast the benefits of Dr Ross's Life Pills . . . Health and Happiness for Everyone, and how they cured liver problems. The red-haired prostitute began to varnish the nails on her other foot. Paulo tried again to put his ear to the door, but retreated at the threat of the bouncer's raised fist. He looked round. The paint was flaking off the walls. The furniture was old, with the stuffing coming out. There were no naked women strolling around, sitting on men's laps, drinking rum and giggling. None of them was pretty. The brothel was not the merry sort of place he had imagined.

'What photo are they talking about?'

'I don't think it's only one. I think he said photos in the plural. I'm sure he did. He ought to have told us. We were the ones who discovered the clue!'

'You were the one who found it, Eduardo.'

'We all did. It's our investigation. All three of us. It's not right to leave us out. I want to know!'

Another tear-jerking song came on the radio. The woman painting her toenails knew this one as well, and started singing along passionately:

Stay with me tonight
You won't be sorry by my side,
It's cold out in the moonlight
But so warm here inside.
You'll have my loving kisses,
Stay with me tonight . . .

The door to the salon burst open. Ubiratan emerged, breathless. He glanced from side to side, apparently unsure of where he was. He was holding a stubbed-out cigarette between his fingers. Eduardo and Paulo ran over to him.

'What's going on?'

'What did she tell you?'

'Did she confess to killing Aparecida?'

'Did she hand over the knife? Was it a knife or a dagger?'

Let me lie in your arms
To fall asleep and dream,
Forget we said goodbye
Without ever knowing why.
You will listen to me . . .

Ubiratan saw the boys over near the radio, and a redhead who was drying the varnish on her toenails with a paper fan as she sang along to the music. Further off, two women were dancing without much enthusiasm. Eduardo and Paulo were waiting for his answers.

'What are you doing here? Why didn't you go home?'

'We're waiting for you, of course!'

'Why weren't we allowed to listen to your conversation?'

'Why did you throw us out?'

'What did you talk about?'

'Did she confess?'

'What do those photos you hid from us show?'

'Are you going to have her arrested or not?'

Ubiratan took them by the shoulders.

'There's somewhere I have to go.'

'Let's go then!'

'Yes, let's go!'

'No. I have to go on my own.'

'What are you talking about?'

'Where are you going?'

'I can't take you two.'

'Who are you going to see?'

'If you go, we're coming along.'

'Where are we going?'

'You can't go.'

His stern voice brooked no argument.

'You can't!'

'Why?' Eduardo insisted.

'I have to go alone. You two stay here!'

Looking round again, Ubiratan finally realized where he was. The tenor voice on the radio was promising shelter and redemption. The red-haired prostitute stood up and started to dance on her own, echoing the music's promise in her own high, out-of-tune voice:

I will listen to you
And we'll be happy too . . .

'No! Don't stay here! Go home!'

'What happened? Why are you so nervous?'

'What went on in there with that old woman? What did she tell you that's made you so nervous?'

'Go home! Go home!'

'You've found out something you don't want to tell us!'

'On your own in there, after you threw us out.'

'Wherever you go, we'll follow you.'

'Promise you won't follow me!'

'Why?'

'Promise!'

'Where are you going?'

'Eduardo, promise you won't follow me. You too, Paulo! Come on, promise!'

'I'm going wherever you go.'

'We're going with you!'

'Together!'

'No, Paulo.'

'The three of us!'

'Not this time, Eduardo.'

'Yes, let's go!'

'It's my bike, I can go wherever I want.'

'No you can't, Eduardo. Not this time!'

'Eduardo's going with you, and so am I.'

'Both of us are going with you!'

'Not where I'm going, Paulo. You can't!'

'You've no chance of stopping us. We're going with you. Now!'

Ubiratan saw that he wasn't going to get them to change their minds. He turned towards the bouncer still guarding the door to his mistress's sanctuary.

'Humberto!'

By the time the two boys realized what was happening, the bouncer had seized them by the arms and was dragging them off to the back of the room. He shut them in a narrow store cupboard. Paulo immediately ran to the only window. A mixture of steam and mist from the mountains clouded the glass pane. The streets were closing in as darkness fell. He caught a glimpse of Ubiratan disappearing round a corner on Eduardo's bike.

He had no idea how long he had been pedalling, or even if he was going in the right direction. He was following the Polish madam's directions, but this was the first time he had travelled outside the city. His legs were aching. Every so often, he stopped to get his breath back. He had seen tiny circles of light that could be from the village, but he could not always manage to head directly towards them: the contours of the dirt track appeared and then disappeared as lightning bolts flashed from the clouds. Thunder was rumbling ever closer, like a line of trucks from an approaching army.

There's a snake about to leave its nest, he thought.

Sudden gusts of wind blew the dust in his face. A fine rain

that was barely more than a thin drizzle began to fall. He was utterly weary, but could not stop. He had to find Renato as quickly as possible. He had to try to break the vicious circle that had begun with the rape of a girl called Madalena. He had to tell Renato that the girl he was fooling with in the changing room was his sister. His other sister. He had to tell him that his lover's husband was his own father. He didn't know how he was going to do it. But he had to try. Several lives depended on it.

Far off to his left, two parallel lights sped through the countryside. They looked like car headlights. Ubiratan tried to use them to guide him, but they soon vanished.

The bike skidded on a thin film of mud produced by the rain. He lost his balance, almost fell off, steadied himself, then skidded again. Wiping the raindrops from his eyes, he thought the village must be close by, and decided to continue on foot, pushing the bike. It didn't take long for him to realize his mistake. He was losing time. He grew even more anxious. He climbed back on the bike, then struggled to pedal on towards the lights.

The rain came down more insistently. His clothes were sticking to him. He felt cold. He heard his own voice, and realized he was talking to himself.

Now that he knew the details of the origins and the life that the blonde woman stabbed to death by the lake had led, he understood the strategy she had adopted without her masters even suspecting it: Aparecida stayed alive because she refused to accept her existence as Anita. She survived by being absent from herself, locked into silence, resolute in the negation of all desire. She was powerful thanks to the passive way she accepted everything she was made to endure, free in her in-difference to her own fate. What he would never know, Ubiratan concluded, was why those who owned her had decided to kill her, or to have her killed: this blonde doll they could use without any sense of guilt to satisfy the desires their respectable wives could not fulfil.

A bigger pothole than usual jolted him in the saddle. He was finally getting close to the string of lights. Windows, verandas, porches, walls, roofs, began to emerge from the darkness.

With the cold rain still beating down, he reached some-thing resembling a village. Not even that: an untidy row of squat houses. A housing development for people on low incomes, built around an open space that the rain had turned into a mudbath.

There was no one in sight to ask where Renato lived. Ubiratan rode on to the nearest house, thinking he would knock on the door and ask.

Before he reached it, he heard a shot. The loud, clear sound rent the night and made him shudder.

He turned the bike towards where he thought the sound had come from. In front of him he saw several identical tiny dwellings, most of them unplastered, with the bricks exposed.

He heard another shot.

Then a third.

All of them came from somewhere behind him.

He turned round.

More identical houses, with the same roofs, walls, doors and muddy yards in front of them.

Trusting to instinct, he dropped the bike and ran, feeling awkward and old, towards a shack where the only light came from the veranda. As he drew close, he saw a car parked at the back: a green American car with a white top. A second car was parked just opposite it. He halted. He recognized the sleek lines, the raised tail fins and the big lights: the mayor's car.

The snake has struck, he thought, hastening on towards the house.

A fourth loud report stopped him in his tracks. Then another one, followed by a cry. Short, high-pitched, almost a sigh. Or a child wailing. And then silence.

He reached the building. He climbed the step up to the veranda. Saw that the door was ajar. He pushed it open slowly. The light from a single bulb flooded the interior. It lit up a bed, and on it Renato's naked body. There were two bullet holes in his chest, one in his throat and a fourth in his hand. The blood that poured from these wounds was staining red the white sheet Isabel was clutching to her, unsuccessfully trying to hide her small breasts. She was moaning. She was wounded in an arm as well.

'Where is he?' Ubiratan asked desperately. 'Where is the mayor?'

Isabel did not seem to understand. He insisted.

'Where did the mayor go? Where did your husband go?'

She began to tremble, staring at the far side of the room. She tried to say something, but failed. Ubiratan followed her gaze.

A figure that until now had been hidden in the shadows

slowly emerged, revolver in hand. The fragrance of lavender reached Ubiratan's nostrils before he saw her contorted face and small, dark eyes, swollen with tears.

'Cecilia!' he shouted, making to move towards her.

She pointed the revolver at him.

'Don't move!'

Ubiratan obeyed.

'Don't come near me!'

'Stay calm, Cecilia.'

'Keep away from me.'

'I wasn't going to—'

'I still have one bullet left!'

'Listen, don't—'

'Be quiet! Be quiet!'

Isabel stretched out a blood-soaked hand.

'Daughter—'

'You be quiet too,' she shouted, swinging the gun round towards her mother.

'Little daughter—'

'Quiet!'

'Listen—'

'I don't want to hear you, old man. Keep your mouth shut.'

'Cecilia, my little girl—'

'You whore!'

'My little Cecilia—'

'You whore, whore, whore! I didn't believe it. I couldn't believe it. I didn't want to believe it. Whore!'

'Cecilia, please, give me the—'

'Stay away from me, old man! Well away! I didn't believe that it was all true! Absolutely everything!'

'Cecilia, calm down . . .'

'I'll shoot! I'll kill you!'

'For the love of God, my little girl . . .'

'You're a whore. More of a whore than the filthiest of whores!'

'Daughter . . .'

'You used to talk about Anita, but it was you who behaved like a tramp! You! She told me everything. Anita told me everything!'

'She wanted money, my little one . . .'

'You and Renato! She even told me about this place! That you two met here every week! Every week, at least once. Sometimes more often. And that you gave him money.'

Ubiratan couldn't believe what he was hearing.

'Aparecida couldn't have done that. She didn't—'

'Anita was blackmailing me, Cecilia. Me and Renato.'

'Don't do it . . .'

'My mother and my boyfriend! You were his lover!'

'My little girl . . .'

'Cecilia, give me that . . .'

'Get away from me! Get away. Back over there! Go on!'

He took a step back.

'Daughter, she wanted to destroy our family . . .'

'Anita told me everything. I didn't believe her! I hit her. I slapped her face. She began to cry.'

'She was a tramp, sweetheart. She deserved to die as she did.'

'You're the tramp! You killed Anita! I know you did!'

'It wasn't me, daughter. It wasn't me.'

'I heard you talking about it to Papa.'

'I lied. I had to lie when he found traces of blood on the car seat. I couldn't tell him the truth, that I was with Renato. And that it was Renato who killed her.'

On the bed, the dead man's eyes were staring emptily. The hand with the bullet hole in it was lying across Isabel's stomach. She caught hold of it, trying to pull the body towards her. Renato's top half slid off the mattress. The blood oozing from his wounds trickled across the cement floor.

'I took Anita to the lake. Renato was in hiding, waiting for us.'

The mother was speaking gently to her daughter, oblivious to the old man looking on incredulously and to the naked, lifeless body beside her.

'Anita wanted money. She said it was to leave here. Money wasn't a problem. I could easily get that. But she was obsessed with another idea. She wanted to separate you and Renato.'

'That's a lie!'

'She said that you two couldn't stay together. She demanded I forbid you to meet. She demanded I separate you.'

'It's all lies!'

'I swear it, my love. I swear it! But I couldn't do it. How could I? You would suspect something: it would only confirm the suspicions she had put in your head. It was too much to ask of me. I told her it was impossible. I offered her more money. As much as she wished! She didn't accept. Instead, she threatened me. She took a knife from her bag.'

'Lies, lies, all lies! You killed her with one of Daddy's daggers. I know it was one of his!'

'It was a kitchen knife. A knife that belonged to her, not me. I didn't take any knife with me, daughter. Renato saw Anita getting the knife from her bag and threatening me. He came up behind her and hit her on the side of the head. I was frightened. I opened the car door to escape. She grabbed me by the skirt. Renato took her by the hair. She pointed the knife at him, shouting something I didn't understand. Your sister, your sister, or something like that. Renato dragged Anita out of the car, punching and kicking her. She was yelling at him, trying to get away. He caught hold of her by the blouse. It ripped. Renato punched her again. She fell, but soon got back to her feet. I think she was sobbing. After that, I can only remember her running away. She ran towards the lake, with Renato behind her. I started running as well. She stumbled and fell.'

'It was by the lake that you killed Anita! I heard you telling my father that. And between you, you forced Dr Andrade to confess to the crime!'

'We brought Anita to the ground. I held her down. Immobilized her arms. Renato got hold of the knife. I didn't see how often he stabbed her. We had to do it, daughter. We would have had no peace if that woman had lived. Renato did what was necessary.'

The pool of dark liquid seeping from Renato's body grew and grew until it reached Ubiratan's shoes. He begged again:

'Cecilia: give me that gun.'

'Be quiet, old man!'

'Too many people have already died, Cecilia. There's been too much pain. Give me the gun.'

'Don't come near me!' she shouted, pointing the revolver at his head.

'For the love of God, little one.'

'Shut your mouth, or I'll kill you too! I killed him, and I'll kill you!'

'Cecilia . . .'

'Don't come any closer! I warn you!'

'Stay calm, daughter. Calm. Give him the gun. Don't worry about what happened here. We can explain it as self-defence. We can say that Renato tried to rape you, that he was violent towards you. That's what we'll say. Renato tried to force you, and you took out the gun and fired. To defend your honour. That's what it was. That's how we'll explain it. Or we can say I was the one who fired. I discovered what was going on, and came here with your father's revolver. It makes no difference. We can see what line of defence the lawyers prefer.'

'I loved Renato!'

'We don't even need lawyers! We don't have to use them. Your father can sort this out, daughter. He'll get rid of Renato's body. Renato has no family. Nobody will report his disappearance, daughter, absolutely nobody!'

'I loved Renato!'

'Give me the gun, Cecilia,' said Ubiratan softly, edging towards her.

'Put the revolver down, daughter. Let your father sort—'

'You're the guilty one! I was aiming at you, not him! He pushed himself in front of you! He protected you!'

'Please, little Cecilia, my little daughter, put that gun down.'

'There's still one bullet in it! I can kill one of you!'

'Give me the weapon, Cecilia.'

'My little daughter . . .'

'The gun, Cecilia. Give it me.'

'Be quiet! Just be quiet!'

'Please, give—'

'Don't talk to me, either of you. Get away from me, old man!'

'Give me—'

'Don't come any closer, or I'll kill that whore!'

Isabel broke down in tears.

'No, my little girl, please,' she begged, terrified. 'Please don't shoot, don't kill me, Cecilia, my little girl . . .'

'Give me the weapon, please.'

'I'm going to kill her!'

Isabel began to weep disconsolately.

'No, little daughter, no!'

Her sobs grew more and more desperate.

Cecilia pointed the gun at her.

'I'm going to kill that whore!'

'Cecilia, hand me that revolver.'

'No, daughter, please, I beg you!' Isabel moaned, raising her hands to cover her face.

'Give me . . .' said Ubiratan yet again, so close to her by now he could reach out and seize the weapon.

Cecilia drew back, and fired the last bullet.

13

São Paulo, 28 February 2002

THE TELEPHONE RANG twice, three, eight, fifteen times, before he gave up and put it back on its cradle. He was still sitting on the bed. He calculated quickly what he still had to pack: not much. A change of clothes, the report from the Brazilian supplier, the laptop, a few diskettes and CDs. His shaving kit. His toilet bag. He could carry his overcoat. He could stuff the scarf in the sleeves, and put the gloves in the pockets. It was cold in Paris, where he had his first stopover, even colder in Geneva, where he would catch the train to his final destination, Lausanne. He had no intention of working during the flight. He was tired after four days of meetings and visits in a city where the traffic was always chaotic. He wanted to sleep: as soon as the plane took off, he would take a pill, and ask not to be roused for either dinner or breakfast. But he would keep the diskettes with him anyway, with all the information he still needed to study and analyse before he wrote his final report. The turbulence in the mid-Atlantic at this time of year was so bad it sometimes woke him whether or not he had taken a Lexotan.

He dialled the front desk, and asked them to call him a taxi in forty-five minutes. It was still early for his flight, and he would probably arrive at Guarulhos airport far too soon, but he didn't want to run the risk of getting stuck in a traffic jam, and perhaps this way he might even avoid the queues for passport control. If he had to wait a long time, he would buy a book or magazine: with any luck he would find the day before's edition of *El País* or a recent copy of the *Financial Times*.

He got up, went into the tiny bathroom, picked up his shaving kit, then went into the cramped shower and turned on the tap. The jet of cold water brought him a sense of relief that no air-conditioning could equal, in the heat and humidity of a Brazilian summer that he had become unaccustomed to. It was worse in Dili: air-conditioning was a rare luxury in East Timor.

He dressed, and put the remaining things in his hand luggage. He glanced at his watch: there was still half an hour before the taxi was due to arrive. He switched on the TV, and tuned in to CNN International. In front of a map of Afghanistan, an expert in military strategy was explaining the objectives of a US troop operation near Kandahar. The blonde, serious-looking presenter behind an acrylic and Formica desk asked a supposedly intelligent question about a recent bomb attack in Baghdad and the challenge the British troops stationed in Basra could face from an apparently pro-Saddam Shi'ite resistance group. Before the expert could begin his reply, he switched off the TV. He picked up the phone, and once more dialled the number he had underlined in the directory.

It rang once, then a brief pause, then another ring. Another pause. After the sixth ring he gave up, and was about to put the phone down when somebody answered.

'Hello?' said a voice. 'Hello!'

It was a woman's voice. She sounded out of breath.

'Hello! Who's there?'

A young woman.

'Yes, hello,' he replied, his own voice thick with an emotion that took him unawares. 'Hello there.'

'Who is this?'

'I'm sorry to call you like this, out of the blue. You don't know me . . .'

He was speaking slowly, without an accent, but like a foreigner who is trying to find the exact terms in a language he's no longer familiar with.

'Who's there?'

'I looked in the phone directory for—'

'What is it you want?'

'I'm sorry, I haven't introduced myself . . .'

'Who do you wish to speak to?'

'I've been ringing throughout the four days that I've been in São Paulo . . .'

'Who's speaking?'

'The phone kept ringing, but nobody picked up. There was no answering machine for me to leave a message.'

'Who is this?'

'I don't live here. It's a long time since I've been here. It was on an impulse that I looked for his name in the directory.'

'Yes, but who is "he"? Who do you want to talk to?'

'I did the same when I was in Rio, ten years ago. I also tried in Porto Alegre. And in Recife. In Brasilia, Manaus and Belo Horizonte. Wherever I go in Brazil, I look for his name. I never thought of it until recently. I'd given up . . .'

'But who are you?'

'. . . Until, four days ago, when I saw the phone directory here in my hotel room, I opened it and looked. And found the name. I think it must be him. I hope it is.'

'What is it you want?'

'The name's the same. I thought it might be him.'

'Who's speaking?'

'I'm sorry, I didn't say who I am. I'm a bit . . . emotional. Forgive me: I didn't think I was ever going to find him. It's been such a long time since we . . . since we saw each other. I never lost hope of meeting him again some day. But, living abroad as I do . . . and coming here for only short periods of time . . . only a few days . . . meetings, talks . . . and yet deep down, I always believed that one day . . . I'm sorry. I'm not someone who finds it hard to express himself, but when you answered the phone, so many things went through my mind. It's been so many years . . .'

'Are you trying to sell me something, is that it?'

'No! No! As I told you, I simply want to talk to him. I don't even know what I'll say to him, after such a long time. We were friends in our childhood. Our adolescence. Well, when we were almost adolescents. Circumstances drove us apart. Ever since then . . .'

'Were you friends in Taubaté?'

'No. We were classmates in the interior of Rio de Janeiro state.'

'My husband has never lived in Rio. He's lived in many places throughout Brazil, but I'm sure he was never in Rio. You've got through to the wrong person.'

'He never lived in the interior of Rio de Janeiro state? In a city called—'

'Never.'

'No?'

'Never.'

'Ah . . . well then, I'm sorry. It's just that I saw his name in the directory, the same name as my friend, so I thought . . . I thought it could be him. I thought it was him.'

'Which directory?'

'This one. The directory for São Paulo.'

'I thought you'd looked in Yellow Pages. My husband's name isn't in the general directory.'

'It isn't? But this phone number . . .'

'Have you called to speak to Fábio?'

'Fábio?'

'My husband.'

'No, not Fábio. I didn't call to speak to anyone called Fábio. I'm sorry. I made a mistake. But the name's here in the directory. I even underlined it . . .'

'It must be an old book.'

He looked at the front cover.

'It's from 1996.'

'Ah, that's why. The number was still in my father-in-law's name then.'

'Your father-in-law? This is his number? Could I speak to him? It's been many years since we saw each other, but he must remember me.'

The woman's voice did not reply.

'May I speak to your father-in-law?'

'What is it you want?'

'Forgive me insisting, but I'm in a hurry. My taxi will be here any minute. I tried to get through earlier. As I said, I rang several times, but no one answered.'

'We were away, with the kids. School holidays.'

'Yes of course, I understand. Your father-in-law . . .'

'Who exactly are you?'

'A friend. From way back. We each went our own way, and . . .'

'Wait a moment. I'll call my husband.'

He heard the sound of the phone being put down on a hard surface. Then there was silence for a while. The noise of children in the background. The woman's voice, then a man's. Her voice once again. More silence. Her voice. The sound of footsteps. The telephone being picked up, then a man's voice at the other end of the line.

'How can I help you?'

'Good day. You don't know me . . .' His voice dried up. He was so moved he couldn't go on. He was talking to his friend's son! After all these years!

'Good afternoon.'

'Yes, of course, good afternoon. Good afternoon. You don't know me, but I'm a friend of your father's.'

'I know all my father's friends. There weren't very many of them. Which one are you?'

'From a long way back. When we lived in the interior of Rio de Janeiro state.'

'Papa left there when he was twelve.'

'I know. I left at the same age. Both his parents and my father were forced to—'

'Did you study with him at the Faculty of Engineering?'

'We never saw each other again.'

'Why are you trying to get in touch now?'

'I'd like to talk to him. I've been trying for years. I lost contact with him. We split up. Life split us up.'

'What is it you want?'

'Nothing. I can understand you being so cautious. I'm a stranger to you. But not to your father. As I said: I don't want anything. I don't live in Brazil. A taxi is about to come to pick me up. I'm flying out quite soon, so I don't have much time. I'd like to talk to your father, if only for a few minutes. Now that I've found him, we could arrange to meet in the future. Is he there? Can I talk to him?'

'How long is it since . . . you heard from him?'

'Forty years. It'll be forty-one years in April.'

'So you really knew my father?'

'Yes, yes, I knew him. He was my best friend. I was his best friend.'

'What were the names of his parents?'

'I can't remember.'

'You can't remember my grandfather's name? Or my grandmother's?'

'No, quite simply, I can't.'

'Didn't you say you were friends?'

'Yes, we were. But I never thought about his parents' names. I don't know if I even knew them.'

'You never knew? The name of your best friend's father? Or of his mother?'

'It's been forty . . . forty-one years since we last spoke, since I last saw him, since I had any news of him. His father and mine had to leave the city where we were living. A crime took place there. Did he never mention that?'

'Never.'

'Did he never talk about the murder of a woman called Anita?'

'No.'

'Aparecida?'

'No. Aparecida or Anita?'

'I've remembered!'

'What?'

'His father's name: Ronaldo.'

'My grandfather wasn't called Ronaldo.'

'He wasn't?'

'No. Are you sure you didn't dial the wrong number?'

'Adolfo. Was that his name?'

'No. Who do you actually want to speak to?'

'Your father had lost his mother. I remember that.'

'My grandmother is still alive.'

'He hadn't lost his mother?'

'It was my grandfather who died young. At forty-something. He had a heart attack. The same problem that killed my father.'

Silence.

'Your father . . .' he began, but couldn't finish the sentence.

'Papa died six years ago. Of a heart attack too.'

'Your father . . .' he began again, his voice trembling. He saw his face in the wardrobe mirror. He had gone pale. He took a deep breath and tried again:

'Your father's name was . . .'

'Eduardo.'

'Eduardo . . .' he said, with a sigh. 'Eduardo José Massaranni.'

'That's right. Eduardo José Massaranni. So you knew him?'

Silence.

'Hello?'

No sound at the other end of the line.

'Hello?'

Still no reply.

'Hello? Are you there?'

Nothing.

'Hello? Hello?'

Nothing.

The sound of breathing into the mouthpiece. But he didn't say a word.

'Can you hear me? Hello, hello!'

More breathing. But not a word.

'Hello? Are you still there? Hello?'

'I'm here,' said the voice, faintly. Then, in a louder tone: 'I'm here.'

'Forgive me for giving you the news so abruptly. I didn't think that you . . . I can tell it came as a shock.'

'Yes. I never imagined that. I never imagined he . . . I've

been searching for Eduardo for so long, and just when I thought I'd found him . . . How long ago did he die?'

'Six years ago. In 1996.'

'He must have been forty-seven.'

'Yes, that's right.'

'We're the same age. We were. I'm slightly older. Forty-eight days older. I was born on 11 January. His birthday is 28 February. Was. It was his birthday today.'

'Yes. I'm sorry to break the news to you like that. I never thought . . .'

'Did you say he studied engineering?'

'Yes, he was a civil engineer. He helped build lots of hydro-electric dams in Brazil. Including the one at Itaipú. We lived in Paraguay when he was working on that. My father took his family with him wherever he went.'

'Always?'

'Always. We lived in places no one has ever heard of: Itumbiara, in the state of Goiás; Icém, in Minas; Três Lagoas, in Mato Grosso do Sul; Candeias do Jamari, in Rondônia, close to the border with Bolivia; and even somewhere that had no name, a tiny village in Pará, in the midst of the Amazon jungle. Four hundred kilometres from Belém, when they were building the hydro-electric plant at Tucuruí. Have you been there?'

'To Belém? Yes.'

'There was one place, in Rio Grande do Sul, that had the most incredible name you can imagine: Passo do Inferno, the gates of hell. In the mountains there. It was unbelievably cold. I hate the cold. We lived in loads of places. My brother liked it, but I didn't.'

'You have a brother?'

'And a sister. There are three of us. I'm the youngest. Julia is the middle one. She's in Brasilia. She works as a dentist. And Paulo—'

'Paulo?'

'Paulo Roberto.'

'Paulo Roberto? Eduardo called one of his sons Paulo Roberto?'

'My elder brother. He's a doctor. He lives in the United States. In Cleveland. He's a cardiologist. He wasn't here when our father had a heart attack.'

'Does he look like Eduardo?'

'I resemble him more. Paulo is more like his mother. He's darker-skinned. He looks almost like an Indian. His mother is from Rio Grande do Sul.'

'You and your sister . . .'

'We're from his second marriage. Paulo used to spend his holidays with us. He only came to live with us when he was about fourteen. That was in Uruguaiana, down near the frontier with Uruguay. Our father was working on some hydro-electrical project or other on the border. I can't remember which exactly.'

'What was he like? Your father, I mean. What was Eduardo like as an adult?'

'Thin. Lanky. Always well dressed.'

'What was he like as a person? You can understand why I'm curious, can't you? We got to know each other as kids, and . . .'

'He was very quiet. He didn't laugh much. He went to bed early. He used to go out to buy bread, milk, the newspaper. He read a lot. Newspapers, books, magazines. He wrote. He listened to music at night, when he thought we were asleep. He liked opera.'

'*Tosca*? Did he listen to *Tosca* a lot?'

'I don't know. All opera sounds the same to a young boy, doesn't it? He tried to get us interested in opera and classical music. But I never got hooked. Nor did Julia. Paulo did though. He also likes to read. Comics, newspapers, books, he always read everything that fell into his lap. Just like our father. He must still do the same, in the States.'

'Don't you see each other?'

'I've never been there. My daughter is still small, and you know how complicated it is to travel with children. And now since 9/11 everything is even more difficult, what with the American paranoia over terrorism, the restriction on visas and all the rest. Besides, it seems Cleveland is a very cold city. I can't bear the cold. The winter here in São Paulo is bad enough. And Paulo and I were never very close. Are you an engineer as well?'

'A sociologist.'

'Great. And what do you do, as a sociologist?'

'My most recent work has been in East Timor. We're building schools there. I work for an agency linked to the UN. Some Brazilian contractors have put in bids for the construction work. That's why I came to São Paulo.'

'If you work for the UN, you must live in New York.'

'No, the headquarters of the agency I work for is in Lausanne. I have an apartment there, a base. But I don't live in Switzerland. I don't live anywhere, really. I live where I work.

At the moment that's East Timor. Before, I've been in Mozambique, Algeria, Bosnia. Sri Lanka . . . Some months here, some months there . . .'

'Do you have children?'

'Two. One lives with his mother in Sweden. Joseph. The younger one. He doesn't know whether to study architecture or biology. He's only seventeen. The other boy is in India. He's a web designer. Neither of them looks like me. Thankfully for them. Their mother is very pretty. She's Swedish.'

'What's his name?'

'His name?'

'Your eldest son.'

A pause.

'Edward,' he said eventually.

'Eduardo? Like my father?'

'Yes. Like your father.'

A silence fell at both ends of the line. Neither of the two strangers knew how to continue with a conversation that was distant and yet intimate. Still sitting on the bed, Paulo looked at his watch. The taxi must already be waiting for him down-stairs. Outside the double-glazed window that let in no noise, from the twenty-eighth floor of the Alameda Santos Hotel he could make out the milky summer sky of São Paulo, above and beyond the mass of tall buildings that made up the city centre. Then the landscape became blurred, and he realized he was seeing it through a mist of tears.

'It's been so long . . .' he murmured.

'What's that? What did you say?' Eduardo's son asked.

'Forty-one years,' he said softly, wiping away the tears.

'I didn't hear what you said.'

'I would have liked to have met your father again. I really would. It's a shame I only found out where he lived when it was too late.'

'I'm really sorry.'

'Tell your brother . . . and your sister . . . Tell Paulo and . . .'

'Julia.'

'Tell Paulo and Julia that a friend of your father's called, and sends them a big hug.'

'I'll tell them.'

'He was the best friend I ever had. I learned a lot from him. Above all, about solidarity. Eduardo even corrected the mistakes I made in Portuguese. Whenever I wanted to know the meaning of a word, he would look it up in his dictionary and write it on a bit of paper for me. Eduardo was the only boy I knew who had a dictionary. I hid the bits of paper in my wardrobe so my father and brother wouldn't find them and destroy them. I took them all with me when we left there.'

'I understand.'

'He was my best friend at a time when I didn't have anyone. He lent me my first Tarzan book. He also lent me the first Charles Dickens book I ever read. *David Copperfield*.'

'I remember my father reading and re-reading that book many times. It was an old edition. I think it had a blue cover.'

'No, it was yellow. Yellow with black letters, and the title in red.'

'That's right. That's how it was.'

'Do you still have it?'

'Paulo took it. It was one of the few possessions of my

father's that he took to the States. That and some photos, some old records and, if I'm not mistaken, my grandfather's social security card. He worked on the Brazilian Central Railway.'

'I know. His name was Rodolfo.'

'That's right. You remembered.'

'And your grandmother was called Rosangela.'

'She still is. She lives in Rio with a sister-in-law who's also a widow. They live in Tijuca. They're getting on in years now. She was hit very hard by my father's death. We all were. Paulo most of all. Perhaps it was because he didn't live with him much, and spent less time with him. The two of them used to talk a lot. They could spend the whole night talking. Paulo was the only person my father wasn't reserved with.'

A fresh silence fell between them.

There was a knock on the hotel door, a voice saying that the taxi had arrived, and asking if there was any luggage to take down.

'Just a minute!' he shouted. Then he said to Fábio: 'I'll be right back.'

He opened the door, pointed to the biggest case, gave the bellboy a tip and thanked him. The youngster left, dragging the case behind him.

Paulo sat down again on the bed. He hesitated. He didn't want to say goodbye. He knew this meant the end of the link with the warmest memories he had of his past. But he picked up the phone, raised it to his ear and said, his eyes again moist with tears:

'I have to go. A big hug for you, and for your brother and

sister. If you talk to your grandmother, tell her I called, looking for Eduardo. Perhaps she'll remember me.'

'Who shall I say called?'

'I'm sorry, I forgot to introduce myself. My name is Paulo.'.

'Paulo and what else?'

'Paulo Roberto. The same as your brother.'

'Paulo Roberto what?'

'Antunes.'

'Paulo Roberto Antunes?'

'Yes. Thanks, and goodbye.'

'Wait!' he heard Eduardo's son gasp, just as he was putting
the phone down.

'Your name is Paulo Roberto Antunes?'

'Yes.'

'Wait a moment, will you please?'

'My taxi's waiting. I have to go.'

'Just a second! Don't put the phone down!'

The sound of the telephone being laid rapidly on a hard
surface. Muffled noises in the distance. Car horns, even
further off. The wail of an ambulance siren. One minute. A
minute and a half. Two minutes. Two minutes ten seconds.
Fifteen. Twenty seconds. Two and a half minutes. He couldn't
wait any longer. Two minutes forty-five seconds. Two minutes
fifty. Two minutes and . . .

'Sorry!' he heard Fábio say on the other end of the line. 'I
went to look for this envelope. I wanted to be sure.'

'Sure of what?'

'Your name is . . .'

'Paulo Antunes.'

'Paulo Roberto Antunes?'

'Yes, Paulo Roberto Antunes.'

'Then I need your address.'

'Why's that?'

'To send you this envelope.'

'What envelope?'

'The one we found among my father's things.'

'And why do you want to send it to me?'

'Because on the envelope it's written, at the top, *For Paulo Roberto Antunes*, and underneath, *From Eduardo José Massaranni*. It's a brown A4-size envelope.'

'What's in it?'

'A lot of typed sheets. The envelope was sealed when my mother found it. You'll have to forgive us for opening it, but we had never heard anything about you, and we had to do the inventory of Papa's possessions. There might have been an important document inside. There's also a letter, attached by a paper clip.'

'Have you read it?'

'I'll post everything to you.'

'Send it by express mail. Please, write down my address.'

'I've got paper and a pencil ready. Go ahead.'

14

Lausanne

THE LETTER WAS not dated. It was handwritten in blue ink, on a sheet of lined paper. It was in the same neat, careful handwriting that Paulo knew so well. The paper clip holding the letter to the typed pages had gone rusty and left its mark. It looked like the outline of a labyrinth.

Dear Paulo

My son was twelve yesterday. My eldest son. From my first marriage. He doesn't look anything like me. He's dark like his mother. Almost as dark-skinned as you. I named him after you.

The two of us were twelve when we last saw each other. Perhaps that's why I remembered you. Even more than I always do. Because I remember a lot. Not always for good reason. It's often when she astounds me. She still does so today. It was twenty-four years ago that we found her by the lake, and she still astounds me. It's twenty-four years since I last saw you. Since we saw each other.

I sometimes dream of her. I wake up exhausted. Does that happen to you too? Do you remember her? Does she astound

*you the way she does me? Do you remember those days in
April?*

*I read somewhere that you were a political prisoner during the
military dictatorship. That you fled to Chile, or possibly to Mexico.
Or that you had gone to Sweden. I lost the newspaper clipping in
one of my many moves. I don't like moving, but my job makes it
necessary. I'm a civil engineer. I work for a state company. I wonder
where you work? What profession did you choose? I never learned
anything more about you. I would have liked you to be Paulo
Roberto's godfather, but I couldn't discover your whereabouts.
Letters were censored. People in our embassies were linked to the
dictatorship's security services.*

*Following the amnesty, I thought you would return to Brazil.
Many other exiles came back. But it appears you stayed where you
are. Wherever that may be.*

*I would have liked to talk to you about her. About the nightmares
I have. I thought I could free myself from them by writing about
her. About what happened to her. What happened to us because of
her. To me, you, Ubiratan.*

*But there are lots of things I don't remember properly. And others
I never knew about at first hand. There are situations I imagined in
one way or another. Perhaps I imagined them as they really were,
perhaps not. I'm not sure of anything. I wrote down what I thought
had happened and what I could remember, as more and more came
back to me. I tried to make a whole out of the fragments. But there
are a lot of gaps in my memory. Perhaps you can recall things more
clearly. Perhaps you can complete what's missing. Fill in the gaps.
I'd like you to do that.*

I'll keep these sheets until I find out where you are and can send

*them to you. Possibly we'll meet, and I can give them to you? Then
we can write it together.*

*Feel free to correct, eliminate or add whatever you like. My
address and phone number are given below.*

A fraternal hug from your friend

Eduardo

Paulo kept the letter in his hands for a long time. He re-read
it. He did the calculation: Eduardo must have written it in
1985. The year when Tancredo Neves was elected the first
civilian president of Brazil after twenty-one years of military
dictatorship. The year of the death of Tancredo Neves, only
three months later, which destroyed all hopes of radical
change in the country. The same year that Mikhail Gorbachev
was elected secretary-general of the Communist party in the
Soviet Union. The beginning of the break-up of the Soviet
Union and of the utopias it had represented. History lessons.
Ubiratan would have been pleased he had learned them.

He put the letter on his cluttered desk, on top of the
scanner next to his computer. The envelope from Brazil that
he had torn open lay between the printer and a pile of
documents that never seemed to grow any smaller.

He took out the typed sheets. They were numbered 1 to 76.

They were carbon copies on thin paper, typed in a small
font. The type had faded, and several parts had been written
over with thick black pen. There were lots of notes in the
margin, written in pencil or ball-point pen, some of them
erased.

On the last page, on a sheet of plain white paper, was just

one sentence, typed in a different font. Underneath was a handwritten note in brackets:

'The dead don't stay where we bury them.'
(Find out where I read that)

Paulo went over to the armchair beside the window, sat down, and began to read.

15

20 April 1961 and the Following Months

Paulo was still angry, and stayed angry through all his classes. He had been angry when they were set free by the bouncer, a long time after Ubiratan had left, and he had been uselessly kicking at the door of the tiny storeroom. He came out cursing. The prostitutes laughed. The Polish madam laughed. The bouncer laughed. Eduardo flushed. Paulo cursed even more. Still swearing, he walked back in the teeming rain to his house, not bothered about what time it was, or how his father would react when he saw him arriving so late and soaked to the skin.

But there was no reaction. His father was sitting at the dining-room table talking to Antonio. They looked up at him, then resumed their conversation.

Paulo was annoyed when he fell asleep, annoyed when he woke up. His brother's bed had not been slept in, and his father had not made any coffee: they had spent the night at the Hotel Wizorek. They must have found out he had been there with Eduardo and the old man. Let them find out. What did it matter? If they asked what he and the others had been doing in the brothel, he wouldn't say a thing. Let them ask.

The old man: that was how he thought of Ubiratan now. The old man. Shameless. A traitor.

When he reached school, he hardly exchanged a word with Eduardo, who was as gloomy and silent as he was. Paulo didn't want to talk to anyone. He felt betrayed and humiliated. And that made him angrier still. If any teacher dared ask him a question, he wouldn't reply, even if he knew the answer. If the teacher scolded him, he would swear at him. In front of the entire class. Then if he was sent to the headmaster, he would tell him to expel him there and then.

At the end of classes, he stormed out of school, but did not head for home. He had no idea where he was going. He simply wanted to get away from there, from everywhere.

Eduardo ran to catch him up.

'Where are you going in such a hurry?'

'To shit!'

'Calm down, Paulo!'

'I'm going to shit because I am shit. Everybody laughs at me! Everybody mocks me! Nobody respects me! My father doesn't respect me, none of the teachers respect me, none of my classmates respect me, nobody at school does. Nobody. Anywhere. Not even the old man respects me!'

'Calm down, Paulo, calm down!'

'The old man left us locked up in that brothel! He went off who knows where and left us behind! Locked up with the whores. Did you see how they laughed at us? I bet they don't laugh at Antonio like that. Or at my father. I'm nothing but shit. And I don't like it! I don't want to be a shit in life.'

'You're not. And I respect you. I'm your friend.'

'What does that get me?'

'Lots of things.'

'What things?'

'Things a friend can give you.'

'What things? What, eh? What things, Eduardo?'

'Things. Like now.'

'Now what?'

'Now I can tell you you're not shit.'

'What?'

'You're not shit.'

'Why not?'

'Because you're my friend.'

'So what?'

'If I had a brother, I'd want him to be you.'

Paulo said nothing. He dropped his head, and felt ashamed. He wanted to apologize and to hug Eduardo, but didn't do either.

'I'd also want . . .' he said, but couldn't finish the sentence.

They both lapsed into an awkward silence.

'Are you hungry?' Eduardo asked finally. 'I've got two cruzeiros, I can buy two pasties.'

'No,' lied Paulo. 'I'm not hungry.'

'Well then . . .'

'What?'

'Well then . . .' Eduardo searched for a neutral topic they could talk about freely. 'My bike.'

'Your bike. The old man didn't give it back.'

'No.'

'Does your father know? Does your mother know you have no bike?'

'I told them I lent it to you.'

'Do you want to go to the old people's home to look for it?'

'Let's go. The old man has to explain why he did what he did.'

Ubiratan was not sitting at the table under the tree that spread over the walls. Nor anywhere else in the courtyard. Nor in the refectory. He wasn't in the bathroom, or in the dormitory. Nor in the corridor or in the garden at the back of the property. Nor in the kitchen, the chapel, nor in the visitors' room. They scoured the home from end to end, but there was no sign of him. Or of the bike. The other inmates – those who could still understand what they were talking about – knew nothing of Ubiratan. They hadn't seen him since the day before. They were certain he hadn't slept there. Paulo didn't believe any of it. He suspected that the old man was trying to avoid a face-to-face argument because he was ashamed of his lack of loyalty. Before the boys left, they tried in vain to get some information from the nuns.

They left the home. Eduardo was more worried than Paulo: he was concerned about the fate of the black Phillips. Ubiratan might have forgotten it somewhere. What if he couldn't remember where? If the bike was damaged, would they be able to repair it? Repairs cost money, and Ubiratan didn't have any. Nor did Eduardo. What if it had been stolen? How was he to explain to his parents that the precious English bike, which looked as good as new even though it was second-hand, the bike he had been given as a reward for the good marks he had received in the entrance exam for the Colegio Municipal Beatriz Maria Marques Torres, the bike they had paid for with such difficulty, had simply vanished into thin air? Just like that? If he told them he had lent it to an old man from the home, it would be worse. If he told them he had lent it so that the old man could go Eduardo had no idea where, to do he had no idea what, and on top of this, that the old man, he himself and Paulo were investigating a crime that had already been solved thanks to the murderer's confession, then he was well and truly done for.

Paulo suggested he tell them that he needed the bike to do errands for his father the butcher, and that he had promised to return it before nightfall. It was a convincing lie. But sooner or later, Ubiratan would have to come out of hiding, face them, and give the bike back. The lie would get Eduardo off the hook for a few hours, and yet he felt increasingly anxious. He wasn't so much worried about the bike, how much it was worth or the money he might have to spend to get it repaired, or even his parents' anger or disappointment. It was none of that. It was . . . that. Once again. Yet again that same strange and distressing, nameless sensation that sometimes took hold of his body. What could it be?

They agreed to return to the old people's home after lunch. They said goodbye. Paulo went off without knowing where to go. He felt hungrier and hungrier, but did not want to go home. He continued wandering aimlessly. He didn't realize that he was whistling one of the tunes he had heard in the Hotel Wizorek.

A green American car with a white top passed by. The mayor was driving. Next to him sat a thin woman. Her left arm was swathed in bandages. On the back seat was a blonde girl, with narrow eyes. The car sped on towards the asphalted road leading to the capital.

The weight would not leave his chest. Pressing and squeezing him. An odd pain. As if someone were burying a sharp spear in his guts, splitting and twisting everything inside him. He couldn't understand it. He couldn't get rid of this . . . thing. Whatever it was.

What was this burden? Why? Where did it come from? What caused it? What was this . . . this thing that made it so hard for him to breathe, that brought a cold wave of fear that was not quite fear, stabbed at his heart beating in his chest and . . . what could it be called? It must have a name. Why did he feel it? Why did it leave him so empty? Why couldn't he get rid of it?

When Eduardo pushed open the door at home, sweaty and breathless, he immediately felt a great sense of relief. His breathing returned slowly to normal. He felt sheltered. Protected. In front of him were the same pieces of furniture, smelling of peroba oil, the same few reproductions of famous paintings, the same china ornaments, the same crochet squares, the same maidenhair ferns, bromeliads, violets and begonias in the same pots and in the same places they were in the week before and the week before that, where they were the day before yesterday, yesterday, and where they would be tomorrow.

He went in, closing the door quietly. He leaned back against it. He could hear the intermittent sound of the sewing machine, indicating that his mother was working, as she did from morning to evening six days a week until his father came home from the station of the Brazilian Central Railway. Familiar sounds, so habitual he no longer even noticed them, but which now brought him an overwhelming sense of relief and gratitude.

He was about to announce his arrival when the sound of the sewing machine stopped. His mother must have heard him come in. Now she was calling out to him. To Eduardo her voice sounded different, more nasal, as if she had been crying. He went to her room. She was sitting behind the Singer sewing machine; her eyes were red and swollen. His father was standing beside her, looking grim, and still wearing his work overalls. He was holding a telegram in his hand.

Paulo never discovered who bought the butcher's shop, or how his father came to be appointed head of store-keeping at a ministry in Rio de Janeiro. Antonio had no idea either, but he didn't care. To live in Rio, even if it was in a suburb far away from Copacabana beach, was beyond his wildest dreams. He was going to the city with the most brazen, most beautiful, most tanned women in all Brazil: what difference did it make who was responsible?

They had the next day, a holiday, to sort out the move. It wasn't much work: their furniture and household goods fitted on to one truck. On the Saturday they boarded a bus to take them away from the city where Paulo was born and grew up, never to return. His single suitcase contained the few clothes he possessed and dozens of bits of paper. Written on them were words he had once not known the meaning of, together with their definitions. Before leaving, he gave back the copy of *David Copperfield* that he hadn't finished reading. Eduardo insisted he take it as a leaving present, but Paulo wouldn't hear of it.

On Sunday, Eduardo went by train with his father to Barra do Piraí, where they caught the connection to São Paulo. There they took another train to Taubaté, the city where the telegram stated that Rodolfo Massaranni was to be transferred with immediate effect. Rosangela Massaranni stayed on in the city long enough to take care of the practical side of their move.

Over the first weeks and months, Eduardo and Paulo wrote each other many letters. Eduardo's were long and sad, going into great detail about how cold his new classmates were, how the teachers showed no interest in him, about the tiny squares and almost treeless streets, the ugliness of the modern buildings in the city they had moved to. He wrote how much he missed their bike rides and the squawking of the macaws in the bamboo groves round the lake. Paulo's letters spoke in short sentences of his weekend trips to the neighbourhoods of Méier and Cascadura, and how lively they were, and of how much he enjoyed the cries of the vendors on the trains he took to go from Bento Ribeiro, where he lived, to Marechal Hermes, where his new school was.

Eduardo also wrote occasionally to the old people's home, but never received a reply from Ubiratan. Finally, in September, all his letters were returned to him in a bundle, together with a note informing him that nobody of that name lived there.

A few months later, in a letter sprinkled with exclamation marks, Paulo wrote that he had been with a woman, and that it was great. Eduardo wrote back that he had also had sex with a woman, and that he had also enjoyed it a lot. He soon regretted his lie, but had already posted the letter. In his next one, he wanted to tell the truth. He ended up writing vague sentences in response to Paulo's questions about this first, non-existent conquest. Once again he was embarrassed at lying to his friend about an experience he would only really have five years later, in São Paulo, with a female colleague on his pre-university course who was also a virgin and just as clumsy as he was about finding pleasure.

Perhaps it was as a result of this first breach of confidence between them, or perhaps it happened some time later: in the years to come, neither of them could tell when or why their letters became shorter and shorter, and increasingly less frequent. Until one day, without them noticing, they stopped altogether.

16

Brazil, 12 April 1961

THE SKINNY, PALE-FACED boy lying on the grass that bordered the blue lake like an undulating green frame opened his eyes and saw his dark, flap-eared friend standing over him. He was dripping wet.

'Did you believe the story about the Russian?'

'The one this morning? About the first man in space?'

'Yes. Do you really think he went round the world in a hundred and eight minutes?'

'I think I do.'

'Would you like to do that?'

'Yes. Both of us. In ten years from now, space travel is going to be much more common.'

'So we can are astronauts.'

'We can *be*,' the thin boy corrected him.

'Even though we're Brazilian.'

'Everybody is going to be able to be an astronaut. But I think I would prefer to be an engineer.'

'I want to be a scientist. To discover remedies for incurable diseases.'

'For all incurable diseases!' the pale-complexioned boy added.

'All of them!' his friend agreed enthusiastically. 'Every single one!'

They laughed. It was a fine, warm day.

Edney Silvestre is a Brazilian writer and well-known TV presenter and journalist. He lives in Rio de Janeiro. His first novel, *If I Close My Eyes Now*, has won several prestigious prizes in Brazil and has been published in eight territories to date. His second novel, *Happiness is Easy*, has just been published to great acclaim in Brazil and is available in translation as a Doubleday hardback and ebook.

Happiness is Easy

Edney Silvestre

Olavo Bettencourt is an important man, a man of spin. With Brazil adjusting to the new idea of democracy, his PR firm holds the balance of power in its hands. Which has also made Olavo very rich, if not very popular.

Loathed by his trophy wife and mired in a web of political corruption that spreads from Sao Paolo to Switzerland, Israel and New York, Olavo is an obvious target for extortion. And what better leverage can there be but the kidnapping of his only son?

A gang closes in on the child who is on his way home from school in Olavo's armour-plated car, absorbed in his colouring book . . .

But he is not Olavo's son.